How did you get from investigating my father's murder to diving in my panties? She was mildly attracted but the timing couldn't be worse. "We don't even have a relationship and you're thinking about sleeping with me."

"I'm a guy. You're a girl. Of course, I'm thinking about sleeping with you. You smell good. You make me laugh. You're pretty."

He just laid it all out there and frankly she had to admit she appreciated his honesty. Not that she was going to sleep with him. "Are you saying that all you want is nothing more than to have sex with me?" To be honest, that was all she needed—to jump into bed with a guy. Sex, for her, was just another form of exercise. Not that she was going to drop that bit of information; she had way too many other things to think about.

"You know what's so cool about you Ripley? You're a beautiful woman who thinks like a guy. That's sexy."

Odessa didn't know whether to be flattered or not. "Are you saying you have a man crush on me?"

He shook his head. "No."

She liked that she couldn't fluster him. He was cool under pressure. A good skill to have when hanging around her. "So that was a compliment?"

"Yes."

Wow! That was a curious admission from him. She'd always been a love and leave 'em kind of girl by her own choice. She couldn't help being taken aback by the fact that Wyatt was like her.

"Silence from Odessa Ripley," Wyatt said. "That is a new side of you. I kind of like it."

Odessa backhanded him on the arm. "Shut-up, dumb-ass."

"There's my Odessa aback. So how about it? Are we gonna sleep together or what?"

"No."

"Don't play hard to get, Ripley. I'm not about the chase. I want to catch it, stuff it and mount it."

Did this guy ever get a clue? "That was a huge sexual innuendo if I ever heard one."

A DANGEROUS WOMAN

J.M. JEFFRIES

Genesis Press, Inc.

Indigo Love Spectrum

An imprint of Genesis Press, Inc.
Publishing Company

Genesis Press, Inc.
P.O. Box 101
Columbus, MS 39703

ISBN: 1-58571-195-0
Manufactured in the United States of America

First Edition

Visit us at www.genesis-press.com
or call at 1-888-Indigo-1

DEDICATION

Jackie: For Karen Semore because you always know where your balls are.

Miriam: For my hubby, what can I say, you put up with me. There is a Nobel Prize in your future.

ACKNOWLEDGMENTS

To Sidney: because you're right most of the time.

PROLOGUE

Toronto, Canada

Late September

Odessa Ripley hated waiting around to kill someone. If this guy didn't turn up soon, she would miss the last plane back to D.C. and the ballet. The American Ballet Theater was performing *Sleeping Beauty*, her favorite. Four hundred bucks a ticket. Damn, she was gonna kill this guy slow.

She glanced once more at her watch. Five P.M. and dark already. Hurry up, she mentally urged him, shivering despite her black leather coat and leather gloves. The room had a chill that no heater could remove. A born and bred Arizona girl, she liked hot weather, hot men, and big guns.

She tapped the barrel of the homemade silencer against her knee, unhappy with the feel of the Glock .28. She preferred the maximum fire power of the .45 auto. But when a person needed a throwaway gun, what did it matter?

The stench of the seedy motel room in Toronto made her want to hold her nose. The room smelled of poverty and despair. She'd killed a Portuguese terrorist in a back alley of Paris, a Columbian drug dealer in a dank jungle, and once she'd chased a double agent into the sewers of Manhattan, and the smells hadn't bothered her then. So why now? Was she getting soft?

This kill should be a piece of cake, if the guy would just get his ass here. Her stomach growled. Damn! She was hungry, too. She should have taken the time for pizza.

The door suddenly swung open and Allan Putnam entered carrying a fast food bag. The aroma of french fries made Odessa's mouth water.

From his brown hair, mild brown eyes and pasty skin to his cheap shoes, Allan didn't look like much of a troublemaker. Nothing special about him. He just blended in like the bland bastard he was. Which was probably why he was such a good double agent. "Hey, Allan. How's it hanging?"

Allan started at the sight of her sitting on the chair, her Glock in her lap. "Do I know you?"

She raised her Glock, letting the gun do the talking for her. He eyed the gun nervously, understanding filling his eyes. He knew why she was here. And what was going to happen to him.

"I'm a dead man." He gave her a tight, brittle smile as he set the fast food bag down on a rickety table.

Odessa shrugged. "It's a dirty job, but someone's got to volunteer to do it." Maybe. She was still annoyed that he'd been so late.

"I knew they'd send somebody," he said in a resigned tone, "but didn't know who."

"That's because I'm the first string."

"I'm flattered the 'powers that be' sent the best."

"You made a lot of people unhappy, Allan. Three CIA agents and their families are dead because of the information you 'shared' with those Ukranian terrorists." She pointed the gun at him. "I'm here to even the score."

He flinched and gave her a strained half smile. "I had to."

Had to! What he should have done was keep his pants zipped. If he had he wouldn't have ended up in this predicament. "Elena Talbot was a former beauty queen, and seven weeks pregnant. Do you know what the bastards did to her during that staged home invasion robbery? Do you even care?" She was surprised by her anger.

He lowered his head. "I didn't—"

"Shut up. I'm not done." Odessa narrowed her gaze at the sweating man. Her emotions were getting out of control. "Five kids, you bastard. The Coast Guard couldn't find enough of Barton Finch's twins to get a positive ID. They were going to be six on September 30th." Odessa couldn't keep her contempt for Putnam out of her voice. Although she wanted him to die painfully, to suffer as those children had suffered, she didn't have the time. Her need for expediency would save him a whole lot of pain.

Allan stared at his feet. "I'm sorry." He didn't sound particularly sincere, just desperate.

"Maybe you should have thought of that when you unzipped your pants with a sixteen year old. Anybody could have picked up that information to use against you, asshole." She pointed at his McDonald's bag. "Is there a burger in there?"

He held the bag toward her as though the food were a peace offering or a bribe. "Yeah. Fries, too."

She didn't take her eyes off his free hand, just in case he had a surprise for her. "Sweet." She wondered why he wanted to give the food to her. Once he was dead, she'd just take it anyway. "Pickles?"

"Yeah."

"I can take them off." She hated pickles. "Now put your free hand on top of your head."

He complied. "You're going to off me and then eat my hamburger. That's cold."

Was he trying to hurt her feelings? "That's the kind of girl I am."

"I have money." He inclined his head toward a black leather bag. A hopeful glint appeared in his brown eyes. "U.S. dollars. Take all of it."

"I don't think so." She fired the Glock three times center mass—three pops and the deed was done. Putnam, looking surprised, as though he really hadn't expected her to kill him, sank to the floor. Blood streamed from the fatal wounds in his chest. As the light dimmed in his eyes, his expression of total disbelief changed to blankness.

She would have preferred a little torture with the kill, but torture was noisy. Allan was a slug. He was supposed to keep people safe. He had not only betrayed the public trust, but his fellow agents. Finch, Talbot, and Merrick and their families were all gone. Hell, they'd even killed Talbot's cocker spaniel. Her throat tightened and she squeezed her eyes closed. *Focus on the job. Leave no trace. Don't let emotions get in the way.*

Odessa picked up her small duffel bag, unzipped it, and dropped the gun into it, along with the burger bag. She didn't want the cops to trace his movements back to the fast food place. A lot of those places had camera surveillance. If he showed up on the tape, the cops would be able to pinpoint his activities more accurately and easily arrive at a time of death.

She searched Putnam's body, careful not to disturb the blood evidence, and removed his money and U.S. driver's license from his wallet, replacing the driver's license with a Canadian one in a fictitious name. She had A.J. to thank for hacking into Canada's computers and creating a new Canadian identity for Putnam. He had no credit cards. Putnam had dealt in cash during his run from retribution.

Then she tossed the room to make it look like a robbery, turned off the heat, and cracked the window open an inch. Icy winter wind swirled into the room. The cold would further obscure the time of death.

Putnam had paid for a month and this wasn't the kind of place where the proprietor paid much attention as long as the bill was paid. She doubted anyone would worry about Allan until he started stinking up the place, but that didn't mean she could be sloppy in her cleanup.

She picked up the bag of money that Putnam had offered. The bag was heavy and she wondered how much money was inside. Then picking up her own duffel bag, she opened the door and checked out the dilapidated hallway. Loud French music blasted from the room across the hall, and the sounds of a heated argument came from another. But the hallway was empty. No one had heard anything.

She eased out of the room and headed toward the back stairway and the exit to the alley.

The cold, dark streets were deserted already. To anyone passing her on the street, she'd look like a young boy holding two duffel bags, one with a sports logo on the side, the other solid black. She caught a bus ten blocks from the hotel and when she got off, walked to her rental car another mile and a half away.

Safe inside the car, she dialed her boss in D.C. When the phone was picked up, Odessa said, "Code Name: Nemesis."

"Is the situation handled?"

Odessa patted Allan's duffle bag. "No problem and I recovered a hefty amount of change."

"Good." Carlyle paused for a second. "Your mother called."

Odessa felt a shiver of apprehension move down her spine. Her mother never called her. If Odessa talked to anyone, it was her father. "What's wrong?"

Her boss hesitated and than said, "Your father's dead."

Odessa stared at the street. She didn't believe it. Her father was the best cop in Phoenix. He couldn't be dead. "Did my mother say how?" She was surprised at how calm her voice sounded. Not even a waver, not the smallest trickle of concern, even though inside she was falling apart.

"He walked in on a burglary taking place at a convenience store. That's all she knew."

The Friday night beer run. Getting ready for poker with the boys. He loved those his weekly date with the fellows. Had they been notified?

Carlyle's voice interrupted her thoughts. "I arranged for you to catch a flight to Phoenix tonight, at midnight. United has a ticket for you under the name Cynthia St. Croix. And I'll have an agent meet you at the airport to take charge of the money."

Cynthia St. Croix was one of Odessa's several different aliases. "Thanks," she managed even though she felt dead inside. Oh God, her dad was dead. Her hero. Her best friend. It couldn't be true. Memories of her father tried to crowd into her mind but she pushed them away.

"Take all the time you need," Carlyle said.

But what about her next target? "Igor Strova and I have a date." Actually, he had a date—with death. His death.

"He's not going anywhere. Call me if you need more time."

"Yeah." Odessa disconnected. A hot tear ran down her cheek.

CHAPTER ONE

Phoenix

Early December

Odessa stopped at the gatehouse to be passed through into the gated community where her mother lived. This was the first time Odessa had been back since the whirlwind three-day trip for her father's funeral.

The guard rifled through a stack of papers attached to a clipboard and handed her a temporary pass which she tossed on the dashboard. As she waited for the gate to open, she considered all the ways she could have avoided the guard and gained entry. For all the money her parents had paid for the security of the development, Odessa knew that any determined criminal could get in. Most people thought criminals somehow got in through the front gate, but the reality was that they were sneaky bastards and tended to find the big holes that security never thought of.

As she accelerated past the gate, her cell phone rang. "Hello, Mom."

"You're five minutes late," Celeste Ripley said in a scolding tone, the faint accent of her childhood on Martinique still in her voice.

"If I'd driven over the little old lady in the walker at the airport, I would have been on time, but those pesky good manners you beat into me got the better of me."

Her mother sighed. "Did I raise you to have such disrespect for your mother?"

Odessa almost groaned. She was thirty-four years old and still her mother treated her as if she were five. "Did you know it's not safe to talk on a cell phone and drive at the same time? In five minutes you can scold me in person."

"How long are you staying this time? A week? Two weeks, or three days like you did for your father's funeral?"

"That's low, Mom." As much as she mourned her father, if she had stayed longer, she never would have caught Igor and the surface-to-air missiles he was bringing across the border from Canada.

Her father would have understood. He was the only one who'd known what she did for the CIA.

Which made his letter to her all the more puzzling. The letter, a single sheet of paper with a typed note, "You are the key," and a computer CD, had been in her mailbox when she'd returned from the assignment in Canada. The envelope had been post-marked the same day he'd died. Grief and a crazy schedule had prevented her from pursuing the matter until now. She assumed she'd find the answer to the puzzle on his computer.

She maneuvered the rented BMW Roadster down the curving streets. Most of the custom houses were dripping with Christmas lights and elaborate lawn decorations. She passed a brightly-colored Santa sitting in his sleigh with two reindeer attached by rope reins. Another home sported a gingerbread house with blinking multicolored lights. A third had fake snow strewn across the lawn with spotlights trained on three snowmen with carrot noses and top hats.

The pain of loss swept through her and tears gathered in her eyes. Christmas had been her father's favorite time of year, and now he wouldn't be here for Christmas ever again. Not that she'd spent much time with her family at Christmas since she'd joined the CIA. Being the top bag girl didn't allow for many holidays. She'd usually flown in the day before and the left the day after.

But this year was different. This year was time for penance.

She pulled into the driveway of the hacienda-style custom house. A nativity scene decorated the lawn and lights lit every line of the house and bushes. When Celeste married Odessa's father, she had brought along not only the customs of her country, but had also embraced the customs of her new one. Christmas was a joyous time in Martinique and that joy manifested itself with her mother's festive decorating.

By the time Odessa put the car in park and turned off the motor, her mother had opened the front door and was standing on the veranda waiting. She was a slender, petite woman with a flawless aristocratic face. Kinky black hair, threaded with strands of silver grey, framed her tired face. She wore a designer-label black suit with a black fringed shawl pulled over her shoulders to shield her from the night chill.

Odessa paused on the walkway for a moment to study her mom, aware of her own scuffed leather jacket, jeans, tomboy haircut and the rows of graduated earrings in each ear. Hardly the outfit her mother approved of.

"You look like a boy." Celeste's critical gaze swept Odessa from head to toe, pausing briefly on the row of silver earrings before she broke into a strained smile.

Here I am, a trained assassin able to operate in any situation, in any country, with no fear, and yet five seconds in my mother's presence, and I feel like a naughty child caught with her fingers in the cookie jar. "Hi, Mom. Nice to see you." Her best defense, hell, her only defense, was to ignore her mother's criticism. Odessa was well aware of her mother's disappointment in how she had turned out. Celeste had expected Odessa to enter into marriage with a pre-approved husband and give birth to several well behaved grandchildren. But Odessa wasn't made of the same stuff as her brother, who had done exactly what had been expected of him all his life.

Celeste offered a smooth, unlined cheek for Odessa to kiss. Though Celeste was nearly sixty, she looked in her mid-forties. Hardly a wrinkle marred her dusky face or the corners of her dark brown eyes. Odessa smelled the faint musky perfume her mother favored.

"Is that your automobile?" Celeste gestured at the BMW Roadster. "It doesn't look safe."

"It's a rental, but I bought myself one just like it for my last birthday." A defiant gesture on Odessa's part, knowing how her mother would disapprove of her choice. Celeste was a Mercedes sedan kind of girl.

"Why a deathtrap?"

"Sometimes, when a woman gets older, she doesn't want to be safe." She rattled a silent curse on her boss's head. Carlyle had ordered Odessa to go home and not worry about the job. Nothing critical was on the shelf at the moment. Nobody needed killing and Raven, Odessa's best friend and fellow agent, was safely married and playing honeymoon at her father's house in Florida. Odessa should have argued more. Maybe if she had she wouldn't be here under her mother's eagle-eyed scrutiny being criticized for her choice in wheels, clothes and hairstyle.

"Why can't you find a nice man to settle down and have children with? You are running around the globe, scolding spoiled adults who act like children who don't want to take responsibility for their indolent lifestyles."

Odessa bit the inside of her lip. If only her mother knew how unglamorous her life was. "But I get to torture celebrities who have too many cheeseburgers and cocktails. Where they go I have to go." Her cover story was that she was a high-priced personal trainer. Who would think a personal trainer would also be a CIA assassin?

Her mother opened the front door and led the way inside out of the cold. Odessa trooped in behind her preparing for day one of her four weeks in Purgatory. Make that Hell, she'd passed up Purgatory at the airport.

"Has Andrew arrived yet?" Odessa asked, trying not to let thoughts of her brother send her screaming back to her car and then back to D.C. Andrew was the perfect son, a Yale-educated lawyer who'd married his homecoming-queen sweetheart and had three perfectly behaved children. He'd never done anything wrong or unexpected in his whole life.

Celeste shook her head. "He could not get away early this year. He will be here next week."

Odessa followed her mother through the huge house decorated with formal furniture shipped from Martinique, expensive artwork on the walls, and statues of the Virgin Mary and various saints residing in a dozen different niches.

Their footsteps echoed on the rusty brown tile floor. Odessa tried not to shudder. Her mother lived in a museum, not a house. Not that

Odessa's apartment in D.C. was anything to rave about. She had a futon in the living room, a TV on milk crates and an oven that still had the packing material and plastic-wrapped instruction booklet inside. She'd always intended to decorate, but was seldom there. So why bother, she reasoned.

"Jacques," her mother called in an imperious manner. "See to my daughter's luggage."

Jacques, an old family retainer who was her mother's butler-cook-chauffeur-sort of housekeeper, appeared in the doorway to the kitchen wiping his hands on a towel. Odessa smiled at him and he smiled back, the deep laugh wrinkles around his mouth and eyes deepening, a testament to his perennial good nature. Jacques had been a fixture in her childhood. Co-conspirator, confidante and mentor to Odessa while her mother was away at charity functions, spas and fashion shows, Jacques had always been there for her. She blew him a kiss and he pretended to catch it and touch his palm to his cheek.

Odessa entered the living room to find her mother already seated on a gold upholstered sofa in she had found in Spain, an imperious look on her slender aristocratic face. The living room was huge with three conversation areas and thick rugs strewn across the tile floor. A fire crackled merrily in the fireplace. Jacques's grizzled old tomcat was stretched out on the hearth, one torn ear tilted toward Odessa and the other twisted toward her mother. Her mother didn't like animals, but Jacques's cat was as much a fixture as he was and if Celeste wanted to keep Jacques, she had to accept his cat.

Christmas decorations were everywhere, from a heavily decorated pine tree in front of the bay window and already surrounded with elegantly wrapped presents, to an intricately carved nativity scene her mother had found on a trip to Germany. A pine garland had been draped over the fireplace mantle and little lights twinkled against the greenery.

Odessa could never figure out what had drawn her mother to her father. Though he'd graduated from law school, he found the task of law deadly boring and had taken a job with the Phoenix Police Department, eventually ending up in the Homicide Division. He'd been a regular guy who'd liked baseball, ribs and beer. And her wealthy mother, the daughter of a diplomat who also had owned several hotels, liked cocktail parties, polo and caviar. Though her mother had loved her father passionately, they were definitely the original odd couple. How they'd managed to make their marriage work without killing each other was the eighth wonder of the world.

"Mom," Odessa said, hoping to delay the inevitable, "why don't I head upstairs, take a shower, put on a dress, and take you out to dinner."

Her mother looked astonished. "You would wear a dress for me?"

Odessa couldn't resist a little teasing. "Just to hide the tattoo."

"You have a tattoo?" her mother cried, one hand placed over her heart, her face stricken with shock.

Odessa chuckled. Celeste was so easy to bait. "Just kidding, Mom."

Celeste frowned. "That was not funny."

Oh yes it was. From which parent she had picked up her sadistic streak was beyond her. The scowl on Celeste's face was hilarious, but dutifully, Odessa said, "Sorry." Without her father around to run interference, Odessa could feel the weight of her four weeks in Hell pulling her down.

"Thank you for the invitation," Celeste said gravely, "but Jacques has already prepared dinner and he would be hurt if you took us to a restaurant after all his hard work."

Odessa preferred Jacques's cooking to restaurant food anyway. She didn't argue. Instead, she headed upstairs to her bedroom to take a shower and put on a dress anyway. That would thrill her mother.

Her luggage was already on the bed. She felt guilty that Jacques had gotten it for her when she could have managed on her own. Coming home was like a retreat back into childhood dependency. The only difference between now and then was that her father was dead.

After dinner had ended and Odessa had spent the required time in after-dinner chit chat, her mother went to bed. Odessa helped Jacques clean up and then she, too, went up to bed. Not to sleep, but to wait until both Jacques and Celeste were fast asleep and wouldn't disturb her. Then Odessa crept down to her father's office.

The moment she entered a feeling of loss invaded her. The feeling was so strong she stood rooted in the middle of the room, waiting for her father to enter and sit in his favorite recliner and ask Odessa to sit and visit with him awhile. He'd ask for a drink and she'd pour him a shot of his favorite brand of bourbon and then she would curl up in the opposite chair and talk to him about her life.

Some of her favorite memories included this room, especially the one when she'd been sent in for punishment and her father had whacked the desk with his shoe and Odessa had wailed like a banshee so Celeste would be satisfied that the punishment had been carried out. Odessa and her father had combined forces against Celeste in a conspiracy that would always remain.

The office was a shrine to American masculinity, the one place in the whole house her mother seldom entered. Odessa was surrounded by all the things that had belonged to her father. His baseball cards, his police memorabilia, the stuffed carcass of a tiger shark he'd caught ten years ago off the coast of Alabama, and the family pictures tracing the Lanois and Ripley families back nearly a hundred years. Odessa loved this room, because he had loved this room.

A computer was nestled inside an armoire designed to hide the fact that it held a computer. A large walnut desk faced the door. Two high-backed chairs flanked it. The room smelled faintly of his aftershave—a clean and masculine scent with just a hint of citrus and spice.

On his desk, in a place of honor, sat the humidor she had given him for his birthday some years ago. Her father had loved a good cigar even though Celeste did not permit smoking in the house. Odessa remembered all the times she and her father had stood in the backyard smoking cigars.

The windows were dark, the house silent around her. She could be alone with the memories of the father she deeply loved. The first person who had accepted her for who she was—faults and all.

Odessa opened the humidor and breathed in the scent of her father's favorite cigars. She took one out as she waited for the computer to boot. She sniffed it and rolled it between her fingers, then glanced guiltily at the door, wondering what would happen if she lit it. But for all her vices, Odessa wasn't really a smoker. She had smoked with her father because he liked to smoke. Now that he was gone, she doubted she would ever light up again. The memory brought tears to her eyes. She hastily wiped them away. She wasn't much of a crier either.

She put the cigar back in the humidor and stared reflectively at the monitor. What had her dad been into? She fingered the jump drive in her pocket. What did he mean by saying, "You are the key?"

When the computer finally booted, Odessa sat down in front of it. Her father had loved technology and he had the latest of everything, from the best digital camera to the most advanced computer with all the bells and whistles possible. She searched through the different directories with no idea of what she was hunting for.

She found a file containing photos of her and her brother as children. Her father had scanned every photo he'd ever taken. Odessa smiled when she found one of herself at three and still sucking her thumb despite her mother's efforts to stop her. She found a photo of her parents' wedding. Phil had gone to Martinique after his graduation from law school, a gift from his family, had met Celeste, and after a whirlwind romance had married her. In the photo they both looked impossibly young and incredibly vulnerable. She wondered what her mother had felt, marrying a lawyer who turned into a cop. Lawyers were acceptable in her family. Cops were not. And yet they had stayed married.

Odessa closed the directory when tears threatened yet again. Would the grief ever go away?

She sat back in the desk chair to think. If her father had hidden a file for her, she would have to search more carefully than the random way she'd been going about it. She tried to think how he would label the file so that it looked innocent, but would contain what he wanted her to find. He'd known sneaky was her stock and trade.

When she finally found the file, she almost passed it up because it was simply labeled "Odessa's birthday." Photos? Something else? Finally, curiosity brought her back to the innocently labeled file. What did her father have to say about her birthday?

She clicked the cursor on the file. A window opened, demanding the password. For a moment, she studied the screen. 'You are the key' played over and over again in her thoughts. Was the password Odessa? She typed in her name. Denied. Daughter. Denied. She thought for a few moments, then typed in the code word the CIA had given her—Nemesis.

The file opened, but gibberish appeared on the screen and Odessa sighed. Her father was not making this easy. Obviously the file was encrypted. She remembered the little jump drive in her pocket.

She inserted the CD. A window opened and a file folder appeared on the screen. Odessa clicked on the icon that appeared after that and after a few moments, the gibberish started to reassemble itself into a readable format.

Odessa smiled as she waited, knowing that finally she would know her father's secrets. When the gibberish was finally readable, she discovered that she had nothing more than a list of five names.

Rabbi Jacob Tannenbaum, community activist—dead.

Juan de Cordova, illegal alien legal counsel—dead.

Martin Borland, gay activist—dead.

Donald Lambert, civil rights attorney—dead.

Joanne Summersby, women's rights activist—dead.

There was a trend going on here. A lot of dead people. Including her father, even though his name was not on the list.

A yellow window, looking a like sticky note, popped up—a reminder to call Detective Wyatt Whitaker in the Cold Case Crime Unit. Was the note to speak to Whitaker a reminder for her father, or a note aimed directly at her? At the bottom of the note was a web site address. Her father's DSL was still active; her mother hadn't cancelled the service yet. Odessa signed in and was again confronted with a password screen. Nemesis, she typed. Denied. Great, another guessing game. She typed in Odessa. Denied. Daughter. Denied. Finally, she typed in her mother's name and was allowed to continue.

She clicked on the URL address and was immediately taken to the site, which turned out to be a white supremacist group hit list of over a thousand prominent people from all over the country who were active in some way that did not conform to the white supremacist group's ideology.

What was she looking at? Why was she looking at it? She glanced at the names on her father's list and starting scrolling through the site list. Eventually, she found that each name on her father's list was crossed out on the web site—as though they had been targets.

She sat back and studied the list, a cold chill running through her. What had her father been investigating?

She heard a sound in the hall and turned around but saw nothing. When she turned back to the computer she noticed an odd, blinking icon in the system tray. She frowned. That icon hadn't been blinking earlier. She put the cursor over it, but no window popped up to explain it.

She reached for her cell phone and dialed A.J.

A.J.'s sleepy voice answered. "Hello."

Odessa answered, "Code Name: Nemesis."

"Code Name: Athena." A.J.'s voice was sharp, the sleepiness gone. "Do you know what time it is, Odessa?"

Odessa had forgotten the time difference between Washington, D.C. and Phoenix. The clock on her father's desk said one A.M. which made it three A.M. for A.J. But she knew exactly how to catch A.J.'s attention. "I have a little computer issue here."

"Talk to me," A.J. commanded.

"I'm using my father's computer to do an Internet search and at the bottom of the screen I have this blinking icon in the system tray that wasn't there a few minutes ago. I haven't done anything that I know of that would cause it. Is this thing going to explode?"

"Describe the icon to me."

"Looks like a little window with a grinning cat."

"Power off the computer now," A.J. ordered in a stern voice.

"What?"

"Just turn it off."

Odessa reached behind the computer tower and flipped the switch to the off position, and then switched off the monitor as well. "Tell me, have I just been hacked?"

A.J. sighed. "You've been bitch slapped. Didn't I tell you never to turn on a strange computer unless I'm in the same room."

"It's my dad's computer."

"Well, that little icon indicates someone is spying on you, and everything you're doing on the computer is being recorded on some remote computer someplace else."

This wasn't regular cop shit, she thought, but the dark, shadowy world she inhabited where people did all sorts of nasty things. How had her father become involved in that?

"What are you doing?" A.J. asked. "I thought you were visiting your mom."

"I am. But something came up and I was checking it out."

"Looks like someone was checking you out instead."

Odessa stared at the computer. "Explain to me what just happened."

"Someone planted a piece of software on your dad's computer that signals someone else down the line that the computer is in use. That unknown someone else activated the program which keeps track of what you were doing. So everything you did, the other person knows. But whoever your unknown spy is, they probably didn't realize that the icon would start blinking in the system tray. What I want you to do is disconnect the computer from the Internet." A.J. gave instructions on how to do that.

Odessa disconnected the cables. A.J. had her turn it back on and then walked Odessa through the procedure of finding the spy software. When Odessa finally found what A.J. wanted, she felt an iciness that made her vibrate with deep dread. What had her father been into?

"Do you want me to explain how to deactivate and remove the software?" A.J. offered.

"No, too late. Whoever wanted to know my activities now knows what I did. I don't want to alert them that I know about their spying."

"Good luck," A.J. said, "but don't use that computer again unless you have to."

They disconnected and Odessa powered down the computer and replaced the cables.

Something smelled rotten in Phoenix. Come morning, she was going to pay a little visit to Wyatt Whitaker.

CHAPTER TWO

Sergeant Wyatt Whitaker hunched over his desk filling out his weekly 'transfer request' form. He had all the particulars filled in—name, badge number, address, phone. He was stuck on 'reason for transfer.' This was the fun part of the game. After two years in Cold Case, he had used every reason he could think of, including his most outrageous one—arm bit off by lion. He'd had Marco Jackson tape his left arm to his chest and had gone around for a whole day with his sleeve hanging empty.

"Whitaker, are you done yet?" His boss, Cher Dawson, glanced pointedly at her watch. "I'm on a time limit here. I need to get your form filed before I leave." By filed she meant in her trash can.

He glanced at her leaning against the door jam. She wore a black evening dress that just about concealed her pregnancy, and a diamond choker that ringed her neck. Damn, it had just occurred to him that she was a woman and that she didn't look half bad. Then he shuddered. What was he thinking? The woman carried a Smith and Wesson and she could hurt him in places he might need later on in his life.

Every Friday at four-thirty P.M., he started filling out the form. "I'm working on it." He had his reason now. *I am requesting a transfer from the Cold Case Unit, because tomorrow I am flying to Sweden for my sex change operation. Since it would be uncomfortable for my fellow detectives in this unit after said operation, I believe that it would be in the best interests of the squad to be transferred, post haste.*

Cher tapped her watch. "I'm having dinner with the governor, Whitaker. Get a move on." She went into her office.

He reread his reason. Not bad, he thought. He was almost as creative as Jackson with his Tiger Lily comics. Picking up the paper, he kissed it for luck. Then he stood and walked into Dawson's office and handed it to her.

She took it, glanced at it and then burst out laughing. "I'm having this one framed to hang on the wall."

Not exactly the response he wanted, but Wyatt bowed. Even he was impressed with himself. "Glad I amused you, L.T."

"Why do you think I keep you around?"

He refused to let her get the last word. "Because keeping me under your thumb feeds your ego." He turned before she could frame a reply. Rarely did he get the last word in with her and that irritated him no end.

He started for the door, but a small, slender woman blocked his way. She stared at him and it took him a moment to catch his breath. *Very nice. Very nice, indeed.* Her skin was the color of toffee brittle. Her eyes were light brown, almost gold. Cat's eyes. She wore tight black jeans, motorcycle boots and jacket, and her hair was close-cropped and dyed into a blonde Afro. She had sexy, tough chick written all over her, but her eyes stopped him cold. They had a dangerous glint that told Wyatt this was the real woman—no party girl facade.

"Can I help you?" Wyatt asked politely.

"I'm looking for a Detective Wyatt Whitaker." Although she had a familiar look, he couldn't place her.

He'd almost made it through the door and into his weekend without all the complications that seemed to crop up at the most unexpected moments. "You found me, but I'm on my way out the door for a beer."

She smiled slightly and took a step toward him, close enough to make him back up. "I can buy you a beer."

Her subtle perfume wafted toward him—an enigmatic, sensual scent that sent his pulse into overdrive and made promises no good girl ever made. For a second Wyatt closed his eyes and inhaled. He liked her smell. And she wanted to buy him a beer. He couldn't turn that down. No way. His weekend could get delayed for a beer and a beautiful woman. "I can't let a strange lady buy me a beer."

Her smile dazzled him. "My name is Odessa Ripley and I'm no lady. Just ask my mother."

Just the kind of woman he liked. But then he remembered where he'd seen her before. "You're Phil Ripley's kid, aren't you. I saw you at the funeral."

One eyebrow went up. "Do I look ten years old to you?"

Taken aback by her aggressive answer, he backed up another step. This baby had attitude. If she wasn't so small, he'd be afraid she could kick his ass. He wisely retreated to politeness. "Sorry for your loss. Phil was a good cop."

Her bottom lip quivered for a moment before her chin came up. "Thank you."

He had the feeling that vulnerability was not an easy reaction for her. She had an air about her of supreme toughness. Like you could jab a needle in her eye and she wouldn't even flinch. That really intrigued him. "What brings you here?"

She stuffed her hands in the pockets of her leather jacket. "My dad had a meeting scheduled with you for the day after he died. Do you have any idea what he needed to talk to you about?"

He hesitated. She looked totally relaxed, but he had the impression she was a snake waiting for the perfect moment to strike. And frankly that wasn't a question he'd been expecting. Hell, it almost felt like an interrogation to him. "I've had a long day and if we're going to talk business let's do it over a decent burger and an ice cold beer."

"I'll drive," she said and turned on her heels and headed back out the door.

She was one of those I-have-to-be-in-control-of-everything women. He resisted the urge to sigh because that would be unmanly.

In the parking structure, she stopped in front of a black BMW Roadster and glanced carefully around.

She did everything except drop to her knees and check under the car for a bomb. Which was really too bad because he could have gotten a better look at her ass. "Nervous?" he asked.

She flashed him a smile. "Cautious."

Which was kinda on the same side of the street, if you asked him. I'll protect every inch of you, he wanted to yell. Wyatt shook his head. "I'm six foot three, I'm not goin' to fit in that itty-bitty thing." He pointed to his black F-350 truck. "We'll take mine."

She glanced at his truck and gave him a lopsided grin. "Are you compensating for something?" She held her thumb and forefinger about an inch apart.

Wyatt stopped short. *I get that—big car and little penis.* He almost grinned. "I'm a big ole strappin' ranch boy. Maybe after a couple of beers, I'll show ya." Hell, he was gonna have a great time with her.

She frowned. "This is business, Detective. Not a date."

Shit, he was almost ashamed of himself. "My business is crime. What's yours?"

"You'd be amazed."

For a second he let his imagination run wild. "Does that come with a good dental plan?"

"Better than yours. Actually I'm a personal trainer."

He unlocked the truck and opened the passenger door. She scrambled in nimbly. "Nice ass," he mumbled. Damn, he didn't mean for that to slip out.

She glared at him. "What did you say?"

Busted. *Come up with a quick answer, Whitaker.* He smiled, hoping he looked innocent. "I'll bet you have nice abs."

"I'm not here to talk about my abs. I'm here to talk about my dad."

This was getting better every second. He closed the door and hurried around to the driver's side. "I'm all ears." He started the truck and backed out of the parking spot and then out to the street.

"I'm assuming," she said, "the Cold Case Unit investigates unsolved cases?"

"Yeah." He made a right turn on the street.

"Why did my dad have an appointment to see you?" Though she stared straight ahead, her voice had an odd intensity to it.

And why do you care? That was the question of the moment. "I don't know. He didn't elaborate, but it could have been anything from an overlap on a case to wanting to grab a beer. And as much as I like a beautiful woman to buy me a drink, I got to ask myself where all this is going." He turned at the next stop light.

"I don't know either," Ripley said with a sidelong glance at him as though she were dangling a carrot in front of his nose. "But I do have a list of names I found on his computer."

He turned into the parking lot behind his local watering hole and parked the truck next to a rusty old Dodge with a bobble head Santa in the rear window. "What kind of a list of names?"

"Of dead people," she replied as she stared at the bar in disbelief. "I can't go in that place."

Dead people. Wyatt wasn't surprised. After all, Phil Ripley was a cop and he majored in dead people. That was his job. "What's wrong with Billy-Buck's? This is my favorite bar. It's quiet. People don't bother me while I eat and they have the best burgers in town." *Pretty waitresses, good food, and cold beer, everything a guy could want.*

She rolled her eyes. "Don't take this wrong, but that bar just screams redneck."

"You're a fake blonde, you'll blend in fine. No one will notice."

"Right. Are you always this charming?"

He shrugged. "It's a gift."

"All right," she said, opening the door, "let's get this over with." She stepped out of the cab, jumping down to the concrete, and carefully checked the landscape again.

Damn, she was paranoid. Obviously the fact that she was with a seasoned cop did nothing to make her feel safe. He could handle any trouble that might mosey their way, but he didn't tell her that. "Don't do me any favors." Wyatt turned off the motor and opened the door. As they walked toward the bar, he thumbed the remote and locked the truck.

The bar was smokey, dark and smelled of stale booze and sweat. The only concession made to the Christmas season was a bedraggled Santa Claus behind the bar and a row of blinking lights taped to the front window.

Odessa paused a moment as she entered and checked the room. A half dozen men sat on stools arranged in front of the long bar. A dozen booths hugged the wall. Country and western music blasted from a jukebox near the back. Cute little cowboy and cowgirl silhouettes indicated the restrooms. Everyone in the bar stopped what they were doing and turned to stare at her. Oh yeah! This was a happening place all right, and she felt as if she had "kick my ass" tattooed to her forehead. Thank God she was carrying.

She hated the bar, from the waitresses clad in skimpy fringed skirts, and low-necked blouses that revealed way too much cleavage to the bartender with a torturous maze of tattoos down his arms and dirty blonde hair pulled back into a greasy ponytail.

Actually, she hated all bars. When Odessa drank, she did it home and alone.

The cop guided her to a shadowy table at the back of the bar, one hand on her arm in a protective gesture. She sensed a prickle of hostility from the men as they watched her in the mirror. She had invaded their territory. She promised mentally not to let any black rub off.

He started to help her remove her jacket, but she shrugged him aside and slid it off and seated herself on the side that faced the door.

Whitaker sat across from her and angled his chair so he also faced the door. Typical cop, she thought, but then again, that was typical spook behavior, too. For a moment she imagined a bar full of agents all angling to sit with their backs to the wall and facing the door. She almost chuckled.

Odessa studied Wyatt as he signaled a waitress. Tall, blonde, broad-shouldered, blue-eyed, he was not what she'd expected. He had that sexy Harrison Ford back-in-day look working for him. He was right about being a strappin' healthy boy. His mama and daddy had done good in the DNA department.

She liked his mouth, full and pouty with a sensuality that made her want to touch his lips. For a second, an image of those lips on hers distracted her. Then a small spurt of anger erupted. She didn't want this man kissing her. He was not the kind of man she wanted to have personal business with. Men were exercise for her. Keeping one around for longer than a few weeks got complicated. She couldn't explain things about her life, her long absences. One thing usually led to another, and they would walk away, their little egos bent all out of shape.

Where the hell was that waitress?

Finally, a tall, slender woman sidled up to the table. She had long blonde hair teased into epic proportions beneath the coyly tilted brim of her Stetson and she wore enough makeup to hide a thousand wrinkles and a million sins.

She winked a heavily lashed eye at Whitaker. "How ya doin', darlin'?" The waitress leaned on the table to give him a glimpse all the way down her loose blouse to her Merry Christmas and Happy New Year. Odessa repressed a snort. She hated trashy women.

"Doing good, Willa." He smiled at the woman and she rested a long-fingered hand on Whitaker's arm.

"The usual, Wyatt?" she drawled in a come-hither tone.

He patted her hand. "You know what I like."

A good swift kick in the butt. Odessa swallowed impatience at the way the woman ignored her. Finally, she said, "Listen, honey, take your tried, dyed, and fried hairdo on over to the bar and get me a single malt scotch—double and no rocks."

The waitress glared at Odessa and waited a moment before saying, "Anything else, sugah?"

The tone rankled and Odessa wanted to slap her. "No," she replied brusquely.

The waitress flushed and sashayed away after giving Odessa an evil scowl.

Whitaker started to laugh. "The next time you invite me out for a drink, we'll stop at the Quicky-Mart and drink in the truck."

"I hate being ignored," Odessa snapped back at him.

"Tell me you're jealous. Do my ego some good." Whitaker patted her arm and she jerked away.

"Let's skip to business. Who's investigating my father's murder?"

He nodded as though he'd been expecting exactly that question. "Homicide. Specifically, Mike Banner."

Amazingly, she'd never heard of this guy. "What kinda cop is he?"

"He's okay." Though his voice was non-committal, his eyes went vague and unfocused for a second. Odessa knew the look. Whoever Mike Banner was, he wasn't Whitaker's favorite guy, but he would never give him up, or ever say anything the least bit suspect to a person outside the job. Mentally, Odessa substituted *lazy* for *okay*.

She knew the type. In her line of work, these were the jerks who kept her employed and in some cases very busy. "The kinda guy you want to beat up just because it's Tuesday?"

For a second Whitaker looked surprised. "Maybe," he said in a cautious tone and then looked away while he fiddled with a spoon.

She leaned her elbows on the table, knowing she'd get no other statement out of him. "Tell me about the robbery. Give me an insider's view."

He hesitated for a moment, "It was a robbery that went bad. Your dad was in the wrong place at the wrong time. When your dad died, we were having a rash of convenience store robberies. We called our suspects the Ding Dong Bandits."

Who the hell thought of that crap? "The Ding Dong Bandits? Do you know how ridiculous that sounds?"

"Yeah! But whoever was committing the robberies would clean out the stores of every Ding Dong. They didn't take the cash. It was a big joke, until your dad took two in the chest. And after he died, the robberies stopped."

Her stomach tightened up. Maybe if these jerks had been on the job, her dad would be alive today. She forced herself to remain calm. "So until my dad died, the robberies weren't a big priority."

"No one was getting hurt and the robberies had all the earmarks of some sort of college prank. The only thing we could do was file reports and put out a description of the thieves." He frowned as he stared around the bar. He appeared to be looking everywhere but at Odessa. "The odd thing about the robbery when your dad was killed was that it didn't fit the profile of the previous ones. The killers didn't take Ding Dongs. They took Ho-Hos."

"Ho-Hos?" In her job no evidence was left behind unless it was supposed to send a message. "Why is that important?"

He shook his head. "Not taking the Ding Dongs broke the pattern. Scoring Ding Dongs was the purpose of the robberies."

"Copycats or nervous because they shot a cop?"

"Maybe." His voice trailed off. "But Ho-Hos were racked on the next aisle."

She could tell he wanted to say more, but didn't. What wasn't sitting right? "Do you want to just tell me instead of beating around the bush? Cards on the table, Detective Whitaker. We have to share what we know. Hearing you, I'm thinking my dad's death might not have been the random act everyone keeps insisting it was." Which made her wonder how the list of names fit into everything.

"Who the hell would kill Phil Ripley? Even the bad guys liked him."

Her lips trembled and a welling of tears appeared in her eyes. Oh God! She was going to cry. *Please don't cry.* He couldn't handle weepy women.

She sniffled and wiped her eyes. He saw a ripple in her body, and she went from grieving daughter to super-chick. Her eyes hardened and her lips firmed. "My father sent me some information. Have you ever heard of the White Lions?"

"Never heard of them."

"They're a hate group out of Alabama. I checked their website and found something interesting."

He leaned forward, his interest caught, wondering what she'd found. "What did you find?" And how did it tie itself to a cop's murder?

"I'll be honest, Detective Whitaker. I think my father trusted you. If he thought you were a stand-up guy, then you probably are."

"Thanks. Frankly, I didn't know I was on Phil Ripley's radar until he asked me for a meeting."

"Do you know who Rabbi Jacob Tannenbaum is? Or Juan de Cordova, Martin Borland, Donald Lambert, Joanne Summersby."

He knew. Each death had made the headlines. "All dead in the last five years. All activists for their communities. Are they the names on the list you teased me about earlier?"

She nodded. "My father sent me a note that gave me access to his computer and an encrypted file. Along with this list of names, he also gave me the White Lions website."

Wyatt frowned. What had Phil gotten himself into? "Why would your father send you that information?" More importantly, why hadn't he shared it with the Hate Crimes people the moment he became suspicious, unless…he was killed before he had the opportunity. That put a new spin on Phil's death.

"Probably," she replied, "because I've got connections in D.C. in the Attorney General's office and in the FBI. I think Dad wanted me to find those names in case something happened to him. I think he knew he was a marked man and wanted me to finish it. My dad hated loose ends and so do I."

Oh hell no. He wasn't having some babe investigating a cop's shooting. He didn't care if she helped the president do pushups. "You are not a cop. If you want to turn all this information over to me, I'll be happy to check it out for you."

She tilted her head and studied him. "How do you feel about the FBI, Detective Whitaker?"

Funny Business Incorporated? He just loved working with suits every chance he got. "No cop worth his balls likes to work with the Feds."

"Good," she said with a slight smile. "I thought you might say that. If my father was investigating a series of hate crimes, then it falls under domestic terrorism. One can make the argument that the FBI needs to be running the show. With the new Patriot Act and the changes in domestic terrorism policies, I would be happy to make a case for the FBI." She took her cell phone out of her jacket. "I could call them right now."

"Okay, I get the picture. You don't have to draw me a map." He drummed his fingers on the table. "You're telling me I either keep you in the loop or you're going to push me out of the loop."

She batted those long eyelashes at him. "Don't take it personal."

His food came. He stared at it, his appetite gone. This woman looked like a fox with her sharp features and big brown eyes. As for the way she smiled, he couldn't decide between the words sexy, devious, or wicked. Maybe it was all three, but she had him by the short hairs. He didn't want to give up anything to the Feds. He wanted to be the big man in the department. If what she was saying went this deep and this dark, this was the kind of case that would make his career and he could write his own ticket right out of Cold Case.

Hell, yeah, he wanted to keep this himself. He decided to throw the lady a bone. Look at the big picture and go for the big play. He stuck out his hand. "All right, I'm in."

Now that she had Wyatt Whitaker tucked firmly in her hip pocket, she was ready to proceed to the next level. "I don't know how I'm going to prove it, but I believe my father's death is linked to those people. When we find out why my father was interested in them, we'll find his killer."

She'd spent so much of her life on a need-to-know basis, she found it difficult to lay all her information out on the table. She'd intended to find out what Whitaker knew, without revealing what she had, but things weren't working out that way. She suspected that behind that good-ole-boy grin, great body, and pretty boy face, an incredible mind was at work. She'd done a little checking on his record and found that he was a very good cop. Plus, she found him sexy. Too sexy for her own good. He'd probably be a lot of fun in bed. Too bad she didn't have time to find out.

Wait a second. Back on track, girl. Focus. Focus. You have no time to get the muffin buttered.

"What was that for?" he asked.

"What?"

"You just got this weird look on your face, like you just ate something bad."

God, was she slipping? She used to be as easy to read as a rock, but the CIA had trained her to mask her feelings and she'd gotten pretty good at that. "I had an inappropriate thought."

His eyebrows wriggled and he rested his elbows on the table. "I like inappropriate thoughts. Tell me everything."

Odessa had the urge to slap him upside the head. "Stop thinking below your belt buckle. Focus." She snapped her fingers in his face.

He snapped his fingers right back at her. "Give me something to focus on."

He was a feisty one. She could tell she was going have to be extra good on the bullying with him. "You need more than what I've already told you?" She could almost smell his ambition. She just had to nudge it in the right direction. "Think of your career track. Find Phil Ripley's killer and you'll be a god in the Phoenix P.D."

Whitaker nodded. "Now I have something to focus on."

The waitress brought their drinks. She plunked Whitaker's beer down in front of him and slapped Odessa's drink on the table in front of her, just barely avoiding splashing it. "That will be seven dollars."

Odessa dug out money from her jacket pocket. She separated the tens and twenties, then counted seven one dollar bills, refusing to give Willa any more than what she'd asked for. The waitress took the bills and stared hard at them before crumpling them and dumping them all on her drink tray. Willa mouthed the word *bitch.*

"Thank you." Odessa gave Willa a bright grin.

Willa sashayed away again without a backward look.

Odessa took a sip of her scotch. "Finally." Not good, but it took care of business. Warmth spread through her and she imagined a mellow glow forcing away tension she hadn't been aware of until she'd started to relax.

"So," Whitaker said after a long swallow of beer, "you're thinking your dad might have sniffed out something that alerted the white supremacists in this area. I remember Donald Lambert. He died in a drive-by shooting. Witnesses said the shooters were black."

"That doesn't mean anything. Dark outside, a little Revlon, a cheap wig." Odessa had once gone undercover as a white woman—a wig and some good pancake makeup could work wonders. Unfortunately, she'd had an allergic reaction to the makeup, but she did get her assignment done.

He leaned his square chin on his fist. "How do you know this?"

"One of my neighbors is a bigwig makeup artist in D.C. and I know all his secrets."

He leaned forward. "Who else are you neighbors with?"

Everyone always asked this question, she was used to it. "You know who Raven Hathaway is, don't you?"

His eyes lit up and he sighed. "The model who holds hands with the jet set. Of course, I know who she is. She's in *People* almost every week."

"I'm her personal trainer. If not for me, she wouldn't have that ass."

Whitaker leaned forward. "Can you get me naked pictures? I'd even settle for an introduction."

You and every man in the free world, stud. "Why am I not surprised?"

He shrugged those broad shoulders. "I'm a guy."

All guy from the tips of his blond hair to the really big feet stuffed inside his fancy, snakeskin cowboy boots. Wyatt Earp Whitaker had the whole man package.

"I'll make you a deal. You share everything you know with me, and I'll have her jump out of a cake." Raven would do anything for her.

"Don't think I'm freaky," Wyatt said, "but can you get her to wear a whipped cream bikini?"

Odessa stared at him and nodded her head. "As long as it's low fat and doesn't mess with all my hard work."

He sighed, a look of longing on his face.

Odessa felt a little twinge of jealousy. She never inspired that kind of response in a man. She loved Raven like a sister, but just once, Odessa wanted a man to drool over her the same way they salivated over Raven. What the hell! Like she had time for this crap. "Then can I get a peek at your evidence? Just so you know, I'm not agreeing to anything just yet. I want to see how everything pans out; then you can see everything I have that my dad sent me."

"Done. But let's have some rules here."

Odessa took another sip of her scotch. "You don't seem like a rule-following kind of boy, Whitaker."

"Normally, I believe rules are guidelines for me to follow or disregard at my will. But something tells me, if what you're saying is true, that this could go all the way up a very long food chain, and since I'm kinda hanging around the bottom of said chain I want to cover my hiney."

She could understand that. Just by talking to him she was breaking about eight hundred CIA rules. Freelancing like this could get her the unmarked grave retirement plan if the wrong people ever found out. "I can understand that."

"As long as we understand each other. Now here are my rules. Number one, no Feds."

"Agreed."

He pointed at his chest. "Number two, I'm in charge."

Odessa didn't like that rule, but she could play along until she got what she needed. "Not to worry, I don't know anything about investigating homicides."

"My gut instinct tells me that you are a dangerous lady." He pointed his fork at her. "How dangerous you are, I don't now, but I get the feeling trouble follows you like a pack of hound dogs."

She raised her half empty glass to him, then took a sip. "I'm going to take that as a compliment."

"You take it any way you want." He had a smug grin on his face. "Rule number three, if this investigation doesn't go anywhere, I have the right to call it quits. And rule number four—"

"You have four rules?" Good God, was this man ever going to shut his pretty mouth and get on with the investigation? She had only so much vacation time. Lord love a duck, he could work for the Company.

"I'm making them up as I go along."

"Wait, time out." She held her hands up. "You've barely agreed to investigate and you're setting up all these stupid rules." This guy was worse then the brass. Rules! Rules! Rules! She hated rules.

He laughed. "I'm kind of an egomaniac."

What was my first clue?

"Rule number four," he continued, "I pay for drinks next time."

Did she have a choice? She needed a front man who knew the territory. "Agreed." She felt a little thrill that there would be a next time and for a second her imagination took flight until she harnessed it.

"When do we get started?"

"Now." She finished her scotch and Whitaker downed the last few gulps of his beer and shoved the last two french fries into his mouth. Odessa slid out of the booth and headed for the door, Whitaker following.

She slipped her jacket on before opening the door. The sun was gone, replaced by a heavy damp chill. The street lights had come on. She turned toward the truck.

The parking lot had a dozen cars in it. Wyatt led the way to his truck. The rusty Dodge was gone.

As Odessa paced along after Whitaker, she had the odd feeling something wasn't quite right. The street lamp near Whitaker's truck was out and the truck hung in deep shadow.

As they neared the truck, four men stepped out of the shadows. They were dressed in jeans, white T-shirts, leather jackets, and thick soled boots. She'd thought she was being followed. One raised a baseball bat and she saw a swastika tattooed on his hand. Great, she thought, skinheads. She heard a chain rattle. One of them swung a crowbar at her and out of the corner of her eyes she saw the glint of a knife blade.

Odessa stopped herself from reaching for her gun. Gun play was loud and bullets could be traced. She'd have to handle this low tech. "I'm going to have to whip me some ass."

Wyatt spread his hands out. "Stand back, little lady. Let the nice police officer handle this."

Oh yeah, right. Odessa burst out laughing.

CHAPTER THREE

Wyatt reached for his gun, but Odessa was already in action. She grabbed the chain with her left hand and yanked it out of Chain Boy's hand, bringing up her right hand palm first to cold-cock him. He slammed back against Wyatt's truck and left a dent as he slid down to the concrete.

Odessa twirled the chain around the bat and jerked it out of Bat Boy's hand. She caught the bat and brought up her knee, nailing Bat Boy in his special place. Then she swung the bat around one-handed and smashed Crowbar Boy in the knee. The sickening sound of bone shattering filled the darkness. Wyatt shuddered. Damn, she was good. He stepped back to let her have all the space she needed.

She held the chain in one hand and bat in the other. She glared at Knife Boy. "Want a shot at the title?"

Knife Boy shook his head, turned and ran like the chicken shit bastard he probably was.

Wyatt took a breath. He was impressed as hell. She didn't even look winded. Come to think of it, he was kinda turned on. Now that was freaky.

"You gonna say anything, Whitaker?"

He stared at the three guys moaning on the ground. Hell yeah, he had plenty to say. "You know, you have violated rule number two. I told you I'm in charge." He felt really ridiculous with his gun out and no one to use it on. Obviously she didn't need him or the horse he rode in on. He holstered the gun and reached for his handcuffs.

She opened her mouth to speak, but Crowbar Boy started to get up. She kicked him in the side of the head and he fell down, groaning.

He wished he could do stuff like that, but his boss would frown on such behavior. "What the hell was that?"

"I was helping him invoke his right to silence."

Wyatt pointed at his truck. "Look at the dent in my hood. Do you know how much that's going to cost to fix?" He could call his insurance company, but his rates would go up again. How did he explain the car-hit-by-man scenario?

"Sorry." She didn't look one bit contrite.

"How the hell did you do that to my car? Are you on steriods?"

"Would you believe," she held up her fists and did the Ali shuffle, "that I teach tae-kwon-do?"

"Damn it all to hell." He glanced around and saw Willa standing at the back door. Her mouth hung open with her cigarette dangling from the corner. All Wyatt could think of was that Odessa would be getting great service here from now on, 'cause no one in that bar would be willing to piss her off once word got around. As for himself, he wouldn't be able to show his face in the bar again. Everyone would know that Odessa had beaten up three men while he'd stood there with his boxers in a twist. "You know that I'm going to have to call this in. How am I going to explain that you kicked three guys' asses and still maintain my manly dignity? You have screwed me for life in the police department."

She swung the chain around a few times. "My ego is not an issue. You can have all the credit."

He pulled out his cell phone as he reached for his handcuffs. Glancing around he saw Bat Boy and Chain Boy struggling to their feet and Crowbar Boy sniveling on the ground. He headed toward the other two, but she grabbed his forearm. He was surprised at the strength in her tiny hand. Actually in her entire small body.

"Let them go." She pointed to Crowbar Boy writhing in agony. "We only need one. He'll talk." She planted a foot on his broken knee. "Won't you, sweetie?"

Crowbar Boy screamed and tried to move away.

Wyatt held the cell phone between his shoulder and chin and grabbed Crowbar Boy by the arm. He dragged his arms behind his back, trying to cuff him. Considering his position on the ground it was a difficult endeavor.

"Why did you do that?" Odessa said. "He's not going anywhere. He'll be lucky if he walks without a limp. I am good."

She took off her jacket, and handed it Wyatt. "Here, I don't want to get any blood on it." She grabbed Crowbar Boy and propped him against a wheel.

As she bent over, her sweater rode up, and Wyatt saw the butt of a semi-auto tucked in her back of her jeans. Jesus, she could have killed all these guys. He put his hand over the phone receiver. "Do you have a license to carry that gun in the state of Arizona?"

"I have the papers." She squatted down and glared at Crowbar Boy. "What is your issue, dumb-ass?"

"I want a lawyer."

She backhanded him across the face. "Guess what, I ain't no cop." Blood trickled down his lip from his nose.

Wyatt liked the way she worked. Old school.

Crowbar Boy's eyes went wide. "I want a lawyer."

Wyatt finally got through to dispatch. He reported the incident and asked for a patrol car and a ambulance to pick up Crowbar Boy.

Odessa grabbed Crowbar Boy's face and made fish lips of his mouth. "What's your name?"

He mumbled something and Wyatt assumed that he'd asked once more for his lawyer.

Odessa boxed his ears. "What's your name?"

He mumbled again, his face turning purple. "I want a lawyer."

She closed her hand into a fist and Wyatt grabbed her by the back of her sweater and yanked her back. "Exactly what are you doing?"

She yanked herself away from him and pulled down the hem of her sweater. "Interrogating the suspect."

Somehow he had to marshal back control of this situation. "Listen, this isn't going to look good on my record since you already broke his knee. Why don't you move over next to the Buick and chill out on the citizen brutality and let me handle this."

She stared at him, her face contorted with anger. "I need—"

"If he doesn't want to talk, there's nothing you can do to make him," he interrupted her. "Unless you want me to haul you in too." Though he had no idea how he would explain her.

"But I—"

"Them's the rules, Ripley." That was all he needed, some chick going vigilante on him. He'd be lucky if they let him work in the office counting paper clips.

The look of savagery on her face threw him. "I can make him talk. Five minutes and a nail file. He'll sing like the Vienna Boys' Choir."

His gut told him to believe her. This woman could drag a man through all twenty-four levels of Hell. "This isn't D.C. We don't do things that way here in Phoenix." *Although I'd like to every once in a while.*

Odessa rolled her eyes and crossed her arms over her chest. "And that's the problem."

He heard a siren in the distance. Thank God, Crowbar Boy was safe.

Odessa unbuckled her seatbelt as Wyatt parked his truck outside the police station. Neither one of them made a move to get out of the truck. She'd finally calmed herself down enough to think. Oh, had she crossed the line! Her instinct had been to kill those guys. If Whitaker hadn't been there she had no doubt she'd be dumping bodies in the desert outside of town by now. God, she had to get a grip on herself.

Someone had made her a target. She hadn't been hunted in a good long while and she didn't like the feeling. Casting a sidelong look at her new partner, she wondered how he might feel about it. He didn't seem like the type to take it well. She considered her options. The most immediate need was to get their story together. "How do we want to play this?"

He glanced at her, his blue eyes full of sarcasm. "I don't know, a random attack?"

Good, but they had to work on the details. A believable lie was built on details. Of which they were sorely lacking at the moment. "Okay," she said, "that's good. How do you suggest we explain Crowbar Boy's busted knee?"

"What's wrong with the truth? I smashed him in the knee with the baseball bat after I took it away from Bat Boy."

She folded her arms across her chest. Good, they had their lie together. She needed to stay off the CIA radar more than she needed the ego stroke. Of course that would require the need to call in some favors. "Okay, let's run with that."

"When you and I are done with the paperwork, we're going to have a long conversation."

"About?" she asked, as if she didn't already know. She'd worked those guys like the trained killer she was. Any cop worth a dime was going to know the difference between what she did and someone who took a Saturday afternoon defense class at the YMCA.

"Maybe it's just me, but this random attack didn't feel all that random to me. How about you? All night you've been looking over your shoulder as though expecting something to happen. And I'm curious why you carry a gun."

Guess this guy thought women who carried were only going to shoot themselves in the foot or get it taken away from them. "Lots of women pack heat."

"Okay, then I want to know who taught you to be Jackie Chan's sidekick."

She shrugged. "I live in D.C. It's a rough town."

Wyatt shook his head. "Sorry, that answer is not working for me."

"I have a friend who taught me a few things about fighting. He was ex-Special Forces." That was sorta the truth. She did have a friend who was from the Special Forces, but she'd taught him more than he'd taught her.

Wyatt still didn't believe her, she could tell. "Really. That sounds good, but I'm still not buying your story."

"If I tell you the truth, I'm going to have to assassinate you." That option would make her life easier, but he was cute and she needed a contact in the police department and he was the best she had at the moment.

He'd seen the predatory look in Odessa's eyes when she'd gone after those guys. She'd been all business. He had the feeling that if he hadn't been there, homicide would be dealing with four dead men instead of a man with a broken knee.

For a second Wyatt felt a small shiver travel down his spine. She had known what she was doing and hadn't raised a sweat or broken a fingernail.

What the hell was she? He'd remembered hearing department gossip that Phil Ripley's daughter had been a wild child who'd done a few things that had never been put on the books. Admittedly, she'd been a juvie at the time, but word usually got around. And then she'd disappeared and Phil had stopped talking about her. For all Wyatt knew, she could be a bag man for the mob. When he had some time alone, he was going to put her name through the system and see what fell out of her tree.

"Are we going to sit here all night?" Odessa asked. "If doing all this paperwork is going to keep me here till midnight, I need to call and let my mother know so she doesn't get nervous."

"Are you staying with your mom?" She had a mother! She wasn't some genetically engineered super-babe bred to kick ass, turn him on, and make his life miserable.

"Why wouldn't I?"

He wasn't liking this. Especially the part where the skinheads attacked him, but he couldn't escape the paperwork. He led the way into the station hoping he didn't have a long night ahead.

Odessa sat at a battered steel desk writing her statement. Beside today she hadn't seen the inside of station house since Venice four years ago after she and her team extracted a high level terrorist suspect hiding in the Italian city. Police departments the world over were all the same—-bad coffee, uncomfortable chairs and unflattering lighting. Felt like home.

She listened to the annoying buzz of the fluorescent bulb over her head. She needed to get home and take care of her mother. If these guys knew that she was on their tail, her mother would be the next logical target. And her brother. What the hell was she supposed to do to keep them safe? Her mind raced. She had a few people she could call to help and keep quiet. Raven was number one. She could get to Andrew within an hour and get him out of town. Odessa would have to handle her mom herself. For a second she wondered if Whitaker would notice if she just got up and left.

"Odessa Ripley," came a voice, "is that you?"

She looked up. "Hey, Uncle Mick." Damn, now she'd have to sit and talk about the old days. Time to morph into helpless girl mode so she could make her escape.

Mick Thompson was one of her father's old cronies. He stood in front of her shaking his head and frowning. "Not again, Odessa. Didn't you learn anything when you were a kid?"

When would her past be buried? She held up her hands. "Look, I'm not wearing police issue jewelry. I'm a crime victim."

He gave her a wary sigh. "Does your mother know?"

She shook her head. "I didn't want to worry her. She's been through too much already." Translation: don't open your big mouth and make her start worrying. She has enough to deal with.

Mick's whole demeanor changed as he sat down on the corner of the desk. He went from big bad cop to sweet little kitty cat ready to believe her tale of woe. God, she still had the touch.

"What happened, kid?"

She forced a little tear down her cheeks. Her bottom lip jutted out. For added measure she sniveled. "I was attacked tonight." She glanced at Wyatt who sat at another desk and bit down hard on a pencil. "I was so scared."

Mick put an arm around her. "Tell me all about it, baby. Are you okay?"

"Uncle Mick," she glanced again at Wyatt, whose mouth was hanging open, "It was horrible. If it hadn't been for Officer Whitaker—"

"Detective," Wyatt put in.

"Whatever," she said with a wave of her hand. She glanced back at Mick, her eyes watering, her lips trembling. "I can't talk about it right now. I have to finish this paperwork and then go home to be with my mom."

Mick patted her shoulder. "It's okay, kid. If you need me, I'm here for you."

"Thanks, Uncle Mick." She wiped her eyes with the wrist of her sweater.

Uncle Mick kissed her on the forehead and headed back to whatever he'd been doing.

Wyatt clapped his hands slowly and deliberately. "That was an Academy Award performance."

She tilted her head in acknowledgment. "He likes me. He really likes me."

"You just broke down the toughest SWAT commander in the department. You stole his dignity. That's so not right."

As if this guy needed to know the truth. "What can I say?"

"Can you teach me how to do that?"

Odessa shook her head. "It's a girl thing." She needed to finish the paperwork and get on home and get her mom on a plane to parts unknown until this was finished. "And I really need to get home."

"Before you go, you need to tell me what you think is going on. You never answered my question and I want a straight answer."

Her first instinct was to escape and evade. She had to get home to her mom. "I forgot. What was the question? You've asked so many."

"You've been looking over your shoulder all night like you were expecting trouble."

She widened her eyes, hoping the innocent routine would work on this cop. "And it's a good thing I'm so cautious. We could have been killed."

"The scared little girl thing, not working on me. I've seen you in action."

Damn, she hated smart men. She took a deep breath. Time to throw the nice officer a bone. "After I checked the White Lions website, I also discovered that someone had dropped a software program into my dad's computer that traced every move I made while I was on the Internet. I think someone is worried I may know something that puts them in jeopardy. And I think the attack tonight was not a random coincidence, but designed to put me out of commission."

"What kind of Tom Clancy conspiracy theory shit is this?"

"I haven't a clue, but I want to find out."

Wyatt shook his head. "Look, lady, you may carry a gun and be kung fu princess, but that doesn't make you qualified to look into this."

Quite the contrary. She was exactly the right person to look into this situation. Her one advantage was that the people behind her attack tonight didn't know jack diddly about who and what she was. "Okay, I'm solo here. Since you don't believe me, I guess I'd better go."

Before she could gather her thoughts and leave, the door was flung open and a beautiful black woman entered as quickly as wearing a long evening gown and a pregnant belly would allow. From the look on her face, she wasn't happy. She stalked across the room and into an office. She pointed one finger at Wyatt and then slammed the door.

"Oh, God." Wyatt moaned.

"What the matter?" Odessa asked, although she knew this woman meant trouble.

"Someone must have called her. She's the wicked bitch of the west."

For a second she had some compassion for him. "Oh, your boss, right."

"My worst nightmare."

"She doesn't look too happy," Odessa said. "Are you her problem child, Whitaker?"

He shook his head. How much worse could the day get? "I don't mean to be, it just sort of happens."

She patted him on the arm. "I'm the problem child, too."

He glanced at her. "Do you know anyone who could help us now?"

"I know a couple lawyers and a Supreme Court Justice."

Wyatt took out his cell phone and handed it to Odessa. "Start dialing, I need a heavy hitter."

"I'm here to protect you, remember." Odessa grinned.

Wyatt glared at her. "It's going to look really, really bad if you break something on my boss. You'll have to kill her, because she'll seek revenge."

If it would get her out of here faster she'd consider it. "Come on, let's go do this."

For a moment Wyatt didn't move. "Give me another minute."

"You've had a minute and times a-wasting." She took off her black jacket and draped it over a chair and removed her nose ring, tucking it in her pocket. She took a deep breath and then seemed to slump over. "Okay, I'm good, I've got my victim persona back on."

He looked at her as she sat back down. She was a little hunched over, and her face seemed somehow more childlike. The only thing missing was a cute little dress and a doll under her arm. Damn, how had she done that?

Wyatt felt like a lumbering bear walking into Dawson's office.

Cher Dawson stood next to her desk. As Wyatt entered, she hung up the phone and glared first at him and then out the door at Ripley.

"Did you know," Dawson said, "that Emeril Lagasse is friends with the governor's wife?"

Wyatt shook his head mutely. Great. He was going to pay for the rest of eternity for this.

Dawson crossed arms over her protruding belly. "Did you know that Emeril was making a special dinner for us?"

Wyatt was afraid to say anything. Again, he shook his head.

"Do you know," Dawson's voice rose slightly, "how awkward it is to ask for a to-go box before dinner has even been served."

He reached into his pocket and withdrew his emergency candy stash. He held it out to Dawson. "I have a Snickers bar." Unfortunately, it had been smashed flat and one corner oozed chocolate.

She glared at him, then snatched the Snickers bar and broke it in half. "It's just not the same."

She tossed the two halves back at him. He caught them. "Not that hungry, huh?"

"Sit down," Dawson ordered in a voice that rattled the door glass.

He sat.

"Who's that woman waiting in my squad room?" Dawson asked.

Now it starts. "Is that any of your business?"

"When I have to be summoned on my personal time because one of my officers was involved in an off-duty incident, it damn well is my business."

This made him feel like some kid who was in the principal's office with his mommy. "Who the hell called you?"

She rubbed her forehead. "Some little piss ant rookie. But now that I'm looking at you, I can see you're still walking."

"I hope you're not too disappointed."

She rolled her eyes. "I'm glad to see you're not too dead, or I would have to torture someone else in the unit and I like them."

"L.T., you care." Wyatt couldn't keep the irony out of his voice

She scowled at him. "Replacing your ass would cause me extreme trouble." She gestured at Ripley. "Now about the woman."

He drew himself up and glared down at his boss. He couldn't tell her the truth, because he wasn't quite sure what that was. "She's my date."

Her mouth fell open. "You're dating her?"

"So?" Ripley was a hot-looking woman. Lethal, but still hot in a really weird sort of way. Damn, he was a man, he wasn't supposed to feel defensive.

Dawson chuckled. "She seems a little on the tanned side for your taste."

"You don't know my taste."

Now she snorted.

He knew what she thought about him, that he was a knuckle-dragging racist. His biggest problem was women on a power trip, not skin color. He liked women who were easy on the eye and easy on the nerves. He glanced out at Ripley. She had shown him all that attitude earlier, and yet given the chance he'd bed her in a heartbeat. Sometime between this afternoon's burrito and now, his life had taken a serious leap down Alice's rabbit hole.

Dawson sucked in her breath, an expression of disbelief still on her face. "Right now, I have a whole new respect for you."

He gave her a doubtful look. "What do you mean?"

"I thought you had a real problem with black people, but since you appear to be dating one, I guess it's not an issue anymore. She's very pretty. Is she over eighteen? Is she sane? Is she a working girl?"

Wyatt relaxed. His old insulting boss was back to herself again. He had been worried her getting knocked up would have taken her edge off. "She's street legal, has all her marbles and I've never had to pay for it. I'm a little too old to start doing that now."

Dawson tilted her head to the side. "I would have expected something a little fluffier. You know, like Barbie. Big plastic boobs and nothing but air between her ears"

Pinching the bridge of his nose, he remembered this woman could fire him any time she wanted to. "You're digging a little too deep into my personal life at this moment."

"That's a scary thought. Look, Whitaker, I have to go. Maybe I can get back to the party before the cheesecake. I want your paperwork on my desk by Monday morning." She opened the door and walked out.

Dammit, this was going to be a long night. This was not the weekend he'd envisioned. He saw Dawson stop in front of Ripley, who was sitting at Wyatt's desk. She held out her hand. "I'm Lieutenant Cher Dawson, I run the Cold Case Unit. From now on, please keep my detective out of trouble." Dawson swept out the door and was gone before Ripley could say anything.

"Look, Whitaker," Odessa said as he returned and she tossed her statement to him, "this isn't gonna work. I got to go. Maybe we'll get together and compare notes some day."

No, she wasn't walking out of here. He started afer her and then remembered the three skinheads moaning. When she did her thing she did bodily harm. Maybe he'd just let her go for the moment, but the partnership was far from over.

Odessa started the Beamer and as she backed out of the parking space, she dialed Raven Hathaway from her cell phone. Raven was home in Key West for the holidays. "I think my family is in danger. I need your husband," Odessa said when Raven answered.

"But I'm in the process of using him for something really important," Raven said. Odessa heard a low laugh in the background.

"Sorry, but I need him to get to Miami and put my brother and his family on a plane to D.C. As soon as I hang up, I'm calling A.J. to meet the plane and take them to a safe house."

"Is your brother going to volunteer for this, or is Derek going to have to get all commando on them?"

"They'll be packed and ready to go when you get there."

"Are you going to explain this to me, or am I hanging on a limb?"

"Get them safe and then we'll talk." She gave Raven the address and phone number.

"Done," Raven said, "but you owe me. Derek and I were going to make a baby this week. You owe me."

"Too much information."

When she'd disconnected from Raven, she called A.J. and made arrangements for her to meet her brother's plane when it landed in D.C. As she turned into her mother's driveway and got out, she called Andrew. Andrew's voice was sleepy when he answered.

"Andrew," Odessa said as she opened the front door and entered the quiet house. She wondered where her mother was. A glance at the clock told her she'd been at the police station for almost three hours. *My, how time flies when I'm having fun.*

"Odessa, it's after midnight."

"Shut up and listen. I need you to get everybody packed and ready for Christmas in D.C. I need you to not ask any questions. A man named Derek Lange will be at your door in about two hours. He's going to take you to the airport and—"

"What are you talking about?" Andrew's voice sharpened. "I'm not going anywhere."

He sounded annoyed, as usual. Her only option was to give him the "I've brought trouble to your door" speech. He'd believe that before he accepted she was a government agent protecting truth, justice, and baseball. Sometimes being the black sheep paid off. "Andrew, I really screwed-up big this time. I need to get you all safe. Please don't fight me. Just go with the agent."

He huffed. "What kind of trouble and why does it involve me?"

Only her brother could huff like their mother and maintain his dignity. "I did some business with some really bad guys. I stiffed them on a deal and they don't take rejection well. Okay. I mucked up. Now shut up and get packing. You're going into federal protection. There is no choice."

"I'm with the D.A.'s office. I can't just leave on a whim because you don't know how to—"

"Shut up, Andrew, I'm trying to make this right." *Do you need a gun to your head? For once in your life, believe me.*

"What are you talking about?" He started to laugh. "This is your best practical joke ever. You got me, Odessa. You got me good."

She wanted to reach through the phone and slap him. "I'm not joking." Desperation edged her voice. "You're going into federal protection. I can't tell you any more than that. I'll tell you everything when you're safe."

"What about Mom?"

"She'll be on a plane to D.C. within the hour. As soon as she's safe with you, I'll tell you what I can."

The laughter faded from his voice. "You're serious, aren't you?"

"Deadly." Thank you, God. "Take what you need. A. J. Miller will set you up with the rest. Just be ready in two hours."

"What kind of trouble are you in this time?"

If he knew the truth, he'd be on a plane to Phoenix before he hung up. "The kind that involves bodily harm…if I'm lucky. I'm sorry."

"You're always sorry."

More than you will ever know. "Just be ready." She disconnected. Just as she turned toward her mother's bedroom, someone pounded on the front door.

Odessa froze, wondering. She reached behind and took her gun out and carefully approached the door. She glanced through the spy hole and saw Wyatt Whitaker standing on the other side. She took a deep breath and put her gun back in the waistband of her jeans. She unlocked the door and cracked it open. "What are you doing here?"

Without preamble, he said, "Your skinhead is dead."

"I didn't do it," Odessa replied and slammed the door. She was busy and didn't have time for him. She had started down the corridor to her mother's bedroom again when the door slapped open and Wyatt Earp Whitaker entered.

"I'm not done with you, Ripley," he said in a flat tone.

She whirled. "You're trespassing. You know what trespassing means?" She grinned. "I have the right to kick your ass."

He didn't look impressed or scared. "You think you can?"

He'd give her some competition. She liked that. "Yeah, I do."

Her mother's bedroom door opened and Celeste appeared in the doorway. "What's all the shouting about? Do you know what time it is? It's after midnight."

"Mom, go back to bed," Odessa said. "Better yet, don't go back to bed. Start packing."

"I am the only one in this house allowed to take that imperious tone, Daughter."

Odessa sighed, feeling five years old again with mother ordering her to change her clothes. She glanced back at Wyatt and saw the light of amusement in his eyes. "You need to leave."

"Detective Whitaker?" Celeste looked him up and down. "What are you doing in my house at this hour?"

Wyatt looked chagrined. "You remember me! I was only here for the funeral."

Celeste gave Detective Cutie Pie her enlightened despot smile. "How could I forget? You were very kind."

Odessa narrowed her eyes at him. He looked as if he'd just won the biggest toy at the carnival. Celeste had a way of doing that to people, just not her daughter. But they didn't have time to play meet the queen. She had to get her mom out of this state. "Mom, we have to talk." She glanced back at Whitaker. "Hit the road, Whitaker."

Her mother folded her arms over her chest. "Don't be rude, Odessa. He's a guest in this house. Fix him something. A cup of tea would be nice. Don't you agree, Detective?"

"I would love a cup of tea right now."

He didn't look like the tea type. Odessa grabbed Whitaker by the arm and dragged him down the hall toward the kitchen. "Stay out of my way and fix yourself something." She had planned dozens of missions that had gone off like clockwork down to the last detail. Dammit, why wouldn't this man leave her alone and let her get her mother the hell out of here?

She marched back to her mother. "Look, you need to leave. Pack some things. You're going to Washington, D.C."

"No." Her mother's face was set in stubborn lines.

If she thought she could live with the guilt, she'd hit her mother over the head, stuff her in a trunk and mail her to D. C. She planned to tell her the Andrew lie. "Listen, Mom. A month and a half ago, I stole some secret documents from this Albanian guy." A good lie required details. "I was supposed to sell them to this Russian mobster. Instead, I sold them to an undercover FBI agent thinking I'd make more money. Now the Russian is coming after me. He knows where you live. He knows where Andrew lives and he's already attempted to kill me. I need to get you some place safe."

Her mother skewered her with a long look. "You stole something?"

Trust her mother to fixate on the obvious. Odessa shrugged and threw her hands in the air. "That's what I do. I steal stuff."

"Really? I thought you were a personal fitness instructor." Her mother's eyebrow rose in such a daunting manner Odessa almost trembled.

"That's just my cover." Didn't this woman understand the word *panic?* Did she have no fear? Hitting her over the head was looking better by the second. "Mom, bad men are coming to kill you. You need to pack your clean underwear." Why did her mom have to be so difficult at a time like this? "I need to put you on a plane to D.C. in an hour."

Her mother shook her head and stuck out her bottom lip. "Washington is so cold this time of year."

Wear a coat. You have about sixteen. Odessa smacked her forehead. "Mom, these people will blow up an entire neighborhood just to get one guy."

Her mother shrugged. "Perhaps they will take care of Mrs. Barlow across the street. I never cared for her taste in landscaping."

"Mom," Odessa almost screamed. If this were not such a life-threatening situation, this would be funny.

"You're lying to me."

That caught her off guard. "What?"

"You are lying." Celeste enunciated every word clearly.

"No, I'm not," Odessa objected. "I'm the bad seed. Remember? I'm the one you said would never get anywhere."

Her mother gave a smug smile. "I always know when you're lying."

"Oh yeah?"

"Of course and not *yeah*. The word is *yes*." Her mother's voice held a final tone.

Odessa put her hands on her hips and pulled herself up to her full five-foot-nothing height. "Then how about this one? I'm an agent with the CIA and I travel around the world assassinating really bad people."

Her mother paused for a long second and then smiled. "That I believe. Though I'm disturbed that you would kill people. I raised you better than that."

Odessa rubbed her ears just to make sure she was hearing correctly. "You believe that?"

"It's the truth, isn't it."

Well, where did a girl go from here, but straight into the truth. "Yeah."

"Yes," her mother corrected her.

Odessa dropped her hands from her hips, feeling totally defeated. "How do you know?"

"Your father talked in his sleep."

"*Mon Dieu*," Odessa muttered.

"Government trained assassin? I should have known."

Odessa whipped around and found Wyatt leaning against the wall grinning. "Shut up before I pop you just for the practice."

CHAPTER FOUR

Watching both of the women, Wyatt knew he had stepped into one thorny situation. Both were equally determined to get their own way. And he suspected if he didn't intervene they would be here until the next coming of Jesus. "Which brings me to this next question," Wyatt said. "What the hell have you gotten me into?" As a cop he'd never run into anything he couldn't handle, but this situation he wasn't sure he could. At least now he knew why Ripley had been so efficient with the skin-heads. Though he was a bit surprised. Didn't the government like their spies a little bit taller?

Ripley glanced at him, her dark eyes appraising. "I'm not quite sure."

"That's not the answer I was hoping for." Wyatt shoved his hands into his pockets and grimaced. He forced his tense muscles to relax. Now was the time to be cool and think his way out of this situation. "Right about now I'm needing something a little more concrete." *Like is this going to get me fired, embarrassed, maimed, or killed.* Not that it would stop him for investigating; he just needed to make more plans.

Ripley scrubbed her hands over her face. "Then I'm concretely not sure."

"A part of me knew you were going to say that."

She gave him a sarcastic grin. "If it's too much for you handle, you can leave at any time."

"I'm not going anywhere, lady." This woman was dangerous. Dangerous in a way Wyatt had never encountered before. He felt…excited. His pulse raced. Later when he had a moment, he was going to analyze his reaction.

"It's your funeral." Ripley turned back to her mother. "Mom, pack some bags. You're getting the hell out of Dodge."

Ripley's mother put her hands on her hips, stuck out her chin and said in a quiet, firm tone, "No."

Ripley looked truly surprised. "What part of 'you are in danger' don't you understand?"

Mrs Ripley took a step toward her daughter. "You will not take that tone of voice with me, young lady."

Wyatt held his breath, thinking these two might go to blows. Ripley might be a trained killer who could kick King Kong's ass, but he was putting his money on the mother.

Seconds ticked off with neither of the women giving any ground. Wyatt couldn't take his eyes away. This was better than a SWAT standoff any day.

"Sorry, Mom," Ripley said.

He stopped himself from laughing. This woman probably knew six hundred ways to kill somebody, yet her mother scared her. He knew the feeling, his mother could twist him like a pretzel. And then another thought occurred to him. Mom Ripley liked him. So that meant that Daughter Ripley might even be more inclined to keep him in her loop just to keep the peace. Oh yeah, I can use this, Wyatt thought.

Mrs. Ripley tightened the sash on her robe. "What we must do is go into the living room, sit down and discuss this calmly. Jacques will bring tea."

Sounded like a good plan to him. All except for the tea part. At this point, he needed something a bit stronger.

"Mom," Ripley said through clenched teeth, "we don't have time for tea or to talk about this rationally. Someone tried to kill me and they probably know your address."

Mrs. Ripley put her hand in the small of her daughter's back and gently urged her toward the living room. "We have plenty of time."

Odessa groaned, but didn't voice any further protest.

Wyatt let Mrs. Ripley and her daughter lead the way back to the living room. As he walked, all the evidence swirled in his head. He had to make sense of everything before he picked a course of action that would let him solve the case. He had a murdered cop, five executed civilians, one dead skinhead who wasn't going to tell him squat about what was going on, a CIA assassin out for blood, and the assassin's mother who thought all the world's problems could be settled over a cup of tea. He needed a real drink, something from his good friend Jack Daniels. And if he smoked, he'd light up two at the same time.

Then again, this was just like the TV shows about wolves he'd watched the other day. They had nothing to discuss. This was just Mama Wolf re-establishing her superiority over the pack. Mrs. Ripley wasn't leaving. He could already tell that by the rigid set of shoulders and the imperious way she handled her daughter. He wondered if Odessa had figured that out by now. Stealing another glance at the younger woman, he could see she pulsed with suppressed rage. Nope, she didn't have a clue. This was gonna be great.

They all sat down in the living room. Mrs. Ripley ordered tea from a hastily dressed elderly man who was obviously a butler. Wow! A butler. Wyatt never knew Phil Ripley lived so well. But then again, Phil Ripley had always played his cards close to the vest. Wyatt had a feeling Phil had known all about his daughter's career and probably approved of it.

"Okay," Ripley said to her mother when they were all seated, "Dad got caught up in something. I don't exactly know what, but I do know a couple of things. One, Dad was murdered. Two, he was involved in something bad. And three, your life is in danger and I brought it to your door."

Mrs. Ripley folded her hands in her lap and looked at her daughter expectantly. "Dear, let the police handle this. I know you think you have to be a part of bringing in your father's murderer, but I don't like you putting yourself in any more danger."

Ripley groaned. "Mom, I get paid a lot of money to deal with danger. I can handle it just fine. I just need you out of the way. For a little while. I can't be worrying about you while I'm doing my job."

Did Wyatt just hear a hint of pleading in Ripley's voice?

Mrs. Ripley patted her daughter's knee. "Detective Whitaker is very good at his job. Your father spoke about him fondly." She smiled at Wyatt. "Phil missed you very much after you transferred to Cold Case."

Wyatt had fond memories of Phil as well. They'd worked together on several cases. He'd been a good cop and a good man. Wyatt had missed Phil after his transfer, but he'd ticked off too many people in authority and being kicked over to Cold Case had been their way of solving the problem of Wyatt being Wyatt.

Ripley put her hand over her mother's. "You don't believe me. Mom, Dad's death wasn't an accident. The robbery was a cover-up. Dad was marked for execution because he knew something he wasn't supposed to."

Mrs. Ripley paled and shook her head. "No, it was a random shooting. That's what the chief of police told me."

Ripley shook her head. "Then why would they come after me when I started nosing around?"

Doesn't everyone want to kill you, Wyatt wanted to ask. That would have been naughty. Wyatt could see that Mrs. Ripley was considering that piece of information, but she was going to need a lot more than the crumbs her daughter was tossing at her before she packed up her Samsonites and got out of town.

"I don't know how Dad stumbled onto this piece of information," Odessa Ripley said, "but there have been five murders of prominent people in Phoenix the last few years and Dad connected them in some way. I need to find out what's going on."

Mrs. Ripley turned to Wyatt. "Why does it matter that this skinhead is dead?"

Wyatt knew the answer. "Because your daughter kicked the crap out of him and that's the kind of thing that looks bad."

"I felt physically threatened," Ripley said defensively with a glare at Wyatt.

"You know six hundred and forty-two ways to kill someone. You weren't threatened at all."

"I'm little," she returned, "I'm a girl. I can fake threatened really well."

"I saw your acting job at the station house..."

"Children," Mrs. Ripley said, clapping her hands, "stop squabbling."

Wyatt started laughing. "Damn! You're good, Mrs. Ripley. You make me feel like I'm five years old."

"Mothers are supposed to do that," she retorted, but a pleased smile spread across her austere face. "Back to the situation at hand. About this skinhead, how do you know he was sent to hurt you."

"Dad was checking out a link to a white supremacist group."

Mrs. Ripley shook her head. "We've been having that sort of problem in Phoenix for a while, dear. It could have been a coincidence."

"I don't believe in coincidence, Mom." She turned to Wyatt. "Did you get a chance to interview him?"

"No, I was with you. Remember? Paperwork, reports, my boss."

"Why not? I didn't ask you to stay and hold my hand."

This woman was breaking his balls. What did she want him do? Split himself in half? She was too much work, no matter how hot she might be. "You're the one who let the other three go."

She stood. "We had a live one."

He stood, too, not wanting her to get the better of him. Besides, he was over a foot taller and he should have the advantage. "You're the one who said let them go, that he'd talk. The only talking I got out of him was screams of agony."

She jabbed her finger at him. "If you'd let me slap him around some more, I'd have gotten everything we needed. You're one with the stupid rules."

He jabbed his finger back at her. "This isn't Iraq"

She glared at him. "So in other words, we have nothing."

"I have nothing," Wyatt replied. "There is no more 'we' in this equation."

For moment Ripley looked shocked. "What do you mean?"

Wyatt inclined his head toward the door. "You're going to D.C. with your mother."

"I'm not going," Mrs. Ripley said.

"Yes, you are," her daughter countered.

Mrs. Ripley shook her head. "No."

"Yes." Ripley walked over to her mother and stood in front of her mother, feet apart and hands on her hips.

Mrs. Ripley crossed her legs and leaned back in her chair. "No."

"Ladies." Wyatt held up his hands. "You're making my head spin and I'm a man. I don't like that."

The butler interrupted, holding a tray with a teapot and cups. He set the tray down in front of Mrs. Ripley and then backed out of the room.

"Tea," Mrs. Ripley said, holding up a cup.

Ripley sat again and said nothing. Tea wasn't what Wyatt wanted, but he nodded and Mrs. Ripley poured him a cup and handed it to him.

"I have a suggestion," Wyatt said. "This is a gated community, your mother is probably safe, especially with you in the house. In the morning, we'll take everything you have to my lieutenant and see what she has to say. And we'll proceed from there."

"Sounds like a plan." Ripley accepted a cup of tea from her mother and sat back. "Why you, though?"

He stopped moving the cup of tea toward his mouth. "What do you mean, why me?"

"We're dealing with a group of white supremacists. Why would my dad trust you, a white cop?"

That pissed him off. Did he have KKK tattooed on his forehead? Now he moved from annoyed to just plain blowing-his-stack mad. "I don't know. Maybe because they're breaking the law and it's my job to enforce the law."

"Yeah, but—"

"It's *yes*," Mrs. Ripley interrupted.

He liked her mother more and more.

Ripley rolled her eyes and ignored her mother. "Why you? You're tall. You're blonde and, frankly, you look like Hitler's wet dream. Hardly the person I would think to investigate white supremacists."

What did how he looked have to do with anything? She didn't look like a hired gun for the CIA. "Do you think I am one?"

"Did I say that? Did those exact words come out of my mouth?"

She didn't have to say the words but the meaning was loud and clear. A white cop couldn't investigate white racists. Wyatt almost grinned. Speaking of looks, she was cute when she was frustrated. Small, but mighty. Her body was well-toned and muscled. Perky nipples poked out the tank top she wore. Damn, she was really sexy in a slap-you-around, kick-your-ass kind of way. *I'd kind of like to sleep with her.*

"What *are* you looking at?"

Oops! He'd gotten side tracked by his libido. "Nothing." Nothing he'd reveal to her. If he so much as peeked at her sideways, she'd probably rip out his spine and wrap it around his neck, and that didn't seem like a particularly pleasant way to check out.

She pointed to the door. "So go."

"Go where?" he asked, momentarily confused.

"Go home."

"Oh!" He would give her this little victory for the moment. Mom Ripley was on his side. He wasn't going to get pushed out of this investigation anytime soon, no matter what Ripley wanted. "Then I guess I'll be heading out the door." He said a polite good-night to Mrs. Ripley, who gave him a regal nod, and made his way to the front door.

Once Ripley closed and locked the door behind him, he turned around to examine the neighboring houses. The place seemed secure. The Christmas lights gave the area a pleasant, family-cozy feeling. But Wyatt didn't have a warm fuzzy feeling left inside him. He had an itch that traveled down the back of his neck to his toes.

He opened the door to his truck and sat inside. Maybe he'd just stay awhile. Hell, maybe he'd just stay the whole night. One of the reasons he'd bought this truck was because it was so comfortable.

Odessa faced her mother. She couldn't make her mother leave unless she clubbed her over the head and drove her to D. C. herself. Frankly, she wasn't sure if she could take on her mom. So she was stuck for the moment, but she wasn't going to give up just yet. "There's nothing I can say to convince you to go to a safe place?"

"No," Celeste said quietly, firmly.

"Aren't you afraid?"

For an all too brief second, Celeste's lip trembled. "If what you tell me is true, I'm very frightened."

"And the appropriate response to that emotion is to flee."

Her mother calmly eyed her. "We're Ripleys. We don't run. We fight."

Odessa's cell phone rang and she flipped it open. Raven's name flashed across the screen.

"I just wanted to let you know," Raven said, "we're getting ready to leave for Washington, D.C. and I'm taking your brother to my father's."

Raven's father was the liberal senator from Florida. Maybe Andrew would have had a better chance of survival against the enemy—whoever that might be. She was never going to hear the end of this one. "Did I tell you my brother is a Republican?"

"No, or that he's so cute." Raven sighed. "Not to worry, my dad will have him converted in no time."

"Don't hurt him, okay? He's my brother and I do love him most of the time."

Raven laughed. "I'm a lover not a fighter. Call me when you can tell me all the sordid details. Love ya."

"Thanks for everything. I owe you." Odessa disconnected and turned to her mother. "Andrew is on his way to D.C. With any luck, he might get a job with a senator."

"Thank you for taking care of your brother."

She smiled at her mom even though she felt defeated.

"What are you thinking?" Celeste asked curiously. "You look like you just swallowed something really bitter.

She had. "Nothing, Mom," Odessa replied. "Go on to bed. Tomorrow is going to be a busy day."

"Good night, Odessa." Celeste kissed her daughter on the cheek. "I love you."

Odessa drew, back surprised. Her mother didn't say that very often. "Mom, everything is going to be okay."

"I know, dear." Celeste touched her cheek. "You're going to bring your father's killer to justice."

She was going to kill him. "Go to bed, Mom."

Her mother picked up the tea tray and headed for the kitchen. Odessa started checking the windows and doors to make sure they were all locked.

As Odessa walked down the hall the next morning, she passed the bathroom and heard a noise. She froze and reached behind her for her gun and eased to the door. Okay, the bad guy was in her house. She could kill him and no one could give her shit about it. Another bang sounded and Odessa, gun drawn, kicked in the door. "Freeze."

Wyatt stood in the center of the room in the act of putting a towel around his waist. The towel dropped as he eyed the gun cautiously. "It's just me."

She eyed him up and down. He was so gloriously naked. She couldn't take her eyes away from the smooth expanse of his chest and the rippling muscles of his broad shoulders and arms. A small black heart tattoo, zig-zagged in the center as though it were broken, was positioned over his heart. He didn't have much chest hair and she found a small smile crossing her lips. And he was perfect in all the right spots.

She put her gun away and reached out to touch the broken heart in the center of his chest. "What does this mean." His flesh was smooth beneath her finger.

"My ex-wife. Bettina broke my heart and this is a reminder to never fall in love again."

A touch of sadness and anger filled Odessa.

"As much as I would like to stand here and discuss body art with you, I think we need to move on. 'Cause your mom might come by and see me naked and get the wrong idea."

Odessa chuckled. "Legitimately speaking, I could shoot you and there would be no repercussions and you would be out of my hair?"

"What little there is of it."

"Are you talking shit about my hair."

"I think your hair is kinda cool."

"You know you can't talk about a black woman and her 'do."

He grinned. "Hon, a man can't talk about any woman and her 'do." He paused. "I'm feeling a little exposed here. Could you just turn around, or close your eyes."

"Shut up, Whitaker, you're not that impressive." She stepped back out and closed the door.

"You like what you saw," he yelled through the closed door.

Yeah, but she wasn't going to admit that to him. She turned around and bumped into her mother.

Celeste was standing in the center of the hall with her hands on her hips. "What were you doing in the bathroom with a naked man?"

Odessa reached for her gun and pulled it out to show her mother. "Protecting you." Heat wrapped itself around her face. Why was she embarrassed? Because her mom knew she had seen a naked man?

"Really?" Celeste's mouth curved upward. "Thank you for your concern. But I let him in earlier so he could shower."

She holstered her gun. "How could you do that?"

"He spent the whole night in that truck of his protecting us, like any honorable man would do. The least I could do was let him shower and make him breakfast."

"You made him breakfast!" Odessa didn't know her mother knew her way around a kitchen, much less where it actually was located in the house. All of her life in this house, her mother had always had household help.

"Actually, Jacques made him breakfast. I supervised. He gave me an opportunity to do something that I've missed since your father died."

Oh my God, I don't want to know! "And what is that?" Odessa almost closed her eyes.

"To fuss over a man." Her mother's face went sad with longing.

And Odessa felt cheap for trying to second-guess her mother's intentions. She reached over to hug her mother, but Celeste had moved out her reach. Odessa's stomach clenched. A moment they could have shared was lost because they were too unaccustomed to showing each other affection anymore.

"Breakfast is in five minutes." Then Celeste rapped on the bathroom door and repeated her message.

After breakfast, Odessa waited in her father's study while Whitaker stood near the window to get a good signal and got his lieutenant out of bed. When he finished Whitaker put his cell phone in the front pocket of his pants. "She said to come over." He grabbed his jacket and left. Odessa followed him out the door, pulled it closed and checked to make sure it was locked. Then she headed over to his truck.

"Do me favor, Whitaker," Odessa said as she approached the truck.

He stopped and turned around to face her. "What?"

She pointed to the truck's door. "Go open the door of your monster truck."

"Why?"

"I need a running start so I can perform a flying leap to get in there."

His broad chest rumbled. "Funny." He used his remote to unlock the doors. "I have a kiddie ladder. Want to use it?"

Odessa stalked past him. "I'm gonna kill you before this is over. I just know it." She yanked open the door and hoisted herself up onto the front seat.

"You're gonna try, Ripley." He laughed again as he climbed into the truck.

Clicking her seatbelt on, she realized what it was about this stupid piece of machinery she didn't like. The huge truck made her feel almost…insignificant. She hated feeling like that. She'd ridden in HumVees, planes, trains and automobiles, but this truck was like a monster on wheels. "Do you mind if I ask you a personal question."

He turned to her and flashed her a brilliant smile. "If I said no, would it stop you?"

My God he had the most beautiful mouth. Even white teeth. Full seductive lips that were almost too pretty for a man. And when he smiled, if she wore panties they would ignite. Why didn't she get one of her father's old cronies to help her? This young stud was making her think all kinds of wrong thoughts. "Nope."

"Shoot."

Don't mind if I do. "What does a single man like you need a truck as big as this for?"

His blue eyes twinkled with mirth. "We had this conversation. You saw me naked. I'm not compensating for anything."

No, he was not. His stuff was extra big man size. "You're right, you're not compensating for anything, but that doesn't answer my question. This is a gas guzzler that drives like a goat."

"I have a ranch."

Odessa slanted a glance at him. "You couldn't have said that a little sooner?"

He grinned. "Yanking your chain is whole lot more fun." He started the truck and headed out of the subdivision for the other side of town.

He had a few spots on him she wouldn't mind yanking, but she decided silence was the better part of wisdom. Or whatever her mother used to say. As they drove, she pondered her situation. Just how much did she want to reveal to his boss. Frankly, the woman looked like she had a great big bullshit detector and a simple trust-me line wasn't going to work.

As they drove through Phoenix, Odessa watched the passing scenery. The city had changed and grown since she'd left over ten years before. More traffic. Bigger buildings. More people. The wide open spaces she remembered from her childhood had given way to clusters of housing tracts surrounded by vast acres of open land.

Whitaker parked in front of an old turn of the century Victorian house surrounded by beautifully landscaped lawns and bare oak trees.

Odessa gazed at the white and blue Victorian house and the nicely manicured landscape. This neighborhood had a turn of century charm her mother's never would. "This is a little pricey for a police officer's salary."

He walked next to her. "What are you saying, Ripley?"

Why pull any punches? Cops can't hide money to save their asses. "Maybe your boss is on the take."

"That could be." He undid his seatbelt. "But then again, maybe she married one of the richest men in the universe."

"Really," Odessa asked doubtfully. Dawson didn't look like the type to marry a bank account, she had too much pride.

"It could happen." Wyatt shrugged.

"Smart ass," she mumbled. She could fall in love with this guy. She had never known any man who could out smart-ass her, not even her co workers.

"What was that?" Whitaker asked.

"Nothing," Odessa replied as she opened the door and grasped the handles, prepared to jump down. The ground seemed to get further away every time she got into this monster.

As they walked up the sidewalk, Whitaker said, "A little something to keep in mind. Let me do the talking and you try not to brandish your gun in her face."

"I don't brandish my gun unless I intended to use it." This didn't seem like that kind of situation. At least not yet.

"You do you have a permit to carry for Arizona?"

"I have a 'get-out-of-jail-free' card for everywhere." As least a forged one that defied anyone's test.

He gave her a wistful look. "How do I get one?"

"Join the CIA, see the world, meet interesting people and then kill them."

Before the conversation could continue, the front door opened to reveal a man and a teenage girl, both dressed in jogging clothes.

"Good morning, Wyatt." The man held out his hand and they shook hands.

"Luc," Whitaker replied.

As snippy as his boss had been with him last night, she couldn't see the two men being on such friendly terms. But then again, what did she know about mental guy stuff?

"Hi, Sergeant Whitaker," the girl said with a flirtatious little smile as she passed him.

"Hi, Miranda," Whitaker replied.

Luc inclined his head toward the door. "Go on in, Cher is waiting for you." After a few more stretching exercises, Luc and Miranda jogged down the sidewalk and down the street.

So Cher Dawson had hit the marriage jackpot after all. "I guess your lieutenant isn't on the take, I recognize him. He provides me with my cable TV."

Whitaker nodded his head. "You, me and just about everybody else in the free world."

Whitaker held the door open and Odessa stepped inside a huge foyer with dark wood floors and a wide, elegant staircase that ascended to the second floor. At the top of the stairs a stained glass window cast a rainbow of colors on the wood.

Whitaker led the way into the living room.

Whitaker's boss was seated on the sofa with her feet up, a newspaper across her pregnant belly and a cup of coffee on the side table at her elbow. She was dressed in baggy sweats and thick socks. "This is Saturday, Whitaker. I shouldn't have to deal with you today. It's my day off."

"And good morning to you, too, boss." Whitaker formally introduced Odessa, then pulled a chair close and plopped down. "Boss, have I got a story for you."

"Better than the sex-change operation?"

Sex change operation! Odessa studied Whitaker and wondered what kind of relationship he had with his boss.

Whitaker sputtered for a second. "This will blow you out of the water."

Dawson took a sip from the mug. "Will it interest me more than a dead skinhead?"

Whitaker grimaced. "Heard about that, did you?"

She nodded. "Is there something I need to know? Like the fact that you beat him up and then he died."

"Let's just say my tale is related."

Odessa watched the two interact. Behind all the aggravation was a respect between them. They might not like each other, but they did have a deference for each other that showed in their eyes and in the way Dawson listened patiently.

"I can't hardly wait." The woman glanced at Odessa and pointed to a chair. "Why are you bringing your date to my house?"

"I'm not his date." Odessa sat down across from the other woman.

"Like dating me would be such a bad thing?" Whitaker tried to look offended but failed.

Odessa spread her hands. "I only date nice men."

Whitaker shook his head. "If there's one thing I've learned about you in the last twenty-four hours, it's that you don't know any nice men except me."

Annoyance swept over her. He hadn't learned anything about her in the last twenty-four hours and here he was trying to tell her all about herself. She stopped herself from a sarcastic rebuttal. They had to appear to be on the same page in front of his boss.

Whitaker turned back Dawson. "My story begins—"

"Cut to the chase, Whitaker. You're horning into my free time here. I have a nap planned, followed by a little snooze, and then maybe a bubble bath."

"L.T., pregnant women aren't supposed to take baths," Whitaker said.

Dawson dropped the newspaper on top of the baby bulge and glared at Whitaker. "I took baths last time I was pregnant and I'm taking baths now. I don't care what the new research says. It's just another study probably conducted by men who don't understand the curative value of a warm bubble bath."

Odessa watched as Whitaker backed off and hid her amusement. Even though he acted intimidated, she could see the regard he held for his boss deep in his eyes. This man was complicated. Even though he did the simple good ole boy routine really, really well, inside he was as complex as a maze and as unsolvable as a Gordian knot. Whitaker was the kind of man she could get lost in for a while. And this bothered her. She didn't want to like him this much. Hell, she couldn't remember the last time she had liked someone as much as she was starting to like Whitaker.

"Spit it out, Whitaker." Dawson rubbed her tummy.

Whitaker started telling Dawson about the murders, Odessa's father's suspicions and how all that had culminated in the death of the skinhead in the hospital's prison ward. When he finished, Dawson closed her eyes and rubbed the bridge of her nose.

"Thank God I married a man with money because I'm going to get fired over this one."

"Not you, boss. You're gonna be governor."

"I don't want to be governor," Dawson objected.

"Sorry," Whitaker said with an evil grin, "it's your destiny."

Dawson closed her eyes and sighed. Odessa watched the woman think.

As Dawson struggled to sit up, the newspaper fell to the floor. "What are you saying here, Whitaker?"

He bent over and picked up the paper, then folded it neatly. "Five high-profile murders that have gone nowhere. Come on, the department is better than this."

That impressed Odessa. The man was neat and polite. Two points in his favor as far as she was concerned

Dawson seemed to think about his statement. "Do you suspect a police cover-up?"

Odessa raised her hand. "Oooh! I have the answer to that one."

Dawson glanced at Odessa not amused. "Okay. What do you suspect?"

"I don't suspect," Odessa replied, "I know."

"You're taking a big chance trusting me. I could be a part of it."

Whitaker shrugged. "Not really."

Dawson eyed him for a moment. "How do you know?"

He seemed to struggle for the words. "Let me put this delicately. You're of the wrong racial persuasion."

Odessa slapped Whitaker on the shoulder. "That was very tactful. I'm almost impressed."

Dawson burst out laughing. "Whitaker, even I'm impressed."

Then she fell silent, her face grim. "Why," she asked Odessa, "did your father go to you?"

"I work for the government."

"You're FBI?" Dawson said with a lift of one eyebrow.

"No."

Dawson gave her an appraising look. "So who do you work for?"

She felt she could trust Dawson. Time to reveal some of her cred. "My organization has more international boundaries."

Dawson's mouth formed an O. "You're CIA?"

Odessa smiled and used her pat line. "I can neither confirm nor deny my employment with the Central Intelligence Agency."

Dawson closed her eyes again and rubbed her temples. "Does anybody know you're here?"

"Not anybody who can make me behave."

Dawson's head lolled back on the chair. "You don't look like the paper pusher type. What do you do for the CIA?"

"This and that," Odessa responded.

Dawson looked her directly in the eye. "When you say this and that, specifically what does that entail? Or do I want to know."

Of course she wanted to know, Odessa thought.

Whitaker raised his hand. "I know. I know, teacher."

Dawson glanced at him. "I'm not asking you."

Odessa simply grinned. "I'm their main go-to girl when someone becomes a problem."

Dawson swung her legs down to the floor and stood up, pushing a hand in the back of waist. "But you're so…petite."

And that was her burden to carry. "I know. Nobody takes me seriously. It's a cross I have to bear." Odessa slanted a glance at Whitaker. Especially when she had to do a high jump to get into his damn truck.

"Whitaker," Dawson said, "I want you to go to the office right now and see if any of those murder cases have fallen into our laps. Then I'll think about what to do next."

"Thank you," Odessa said. At least this was a start.

Dawson turned her cool gaze on Odessa. "I'm not done. I may not know exactly how you do your problem solving. If we have a case to investigate, it takes precedence over your agenda. You think I don't know what you're planning?. I liked your dad a lot. I don't want to see you head down the wrong street on your own personal crusade. Am I understood?"

Odessa resisted the urge to gulp and she managed a tight nod. Not exactly the words she wanted to hear, but she could play along—for awhile. Its not as if she had to take of these guys quickly, she could wait until the heat was off. Cher Dawson was a little too much like Celeste to be comfortable around.

Dawson hauled herself toward Odessa with all the grace of a pregnant woman. Facing Dawson was like being toe to toe with Celeste. Dawson pushed her belly against Odessa. "I swear to God, if any suspect so much as slips on a bar of soap in the shower, or chokes on a peanut, after I pop out this baby, I will come after you like there is no tomorrow."

Odessa swallowed. "You don't scare me." That was a lie. Yeah, Dawson did scare her, but in a very different way than her own boss, Carlyle, or the higher-ups on the ladder who yanked her chain to their advantage. This was a woman who made a threat and followed up on it.

Whitaker put a hand on Dawson's shoulder. "Ladies, we can all play like nice little children. You don't need to fight over me."

Dawson growled at him, but she stepped back, returned to the sofa and picked up her newspaper, then settled back down. "Go. Both of you."

Back in the truck, Whitaker sat behind the wheel staring at Odessa. "You're gonna kill them all, aren't you?"

Odessa didn't reply. She didn't have to share her business with him. But the need to act on her father's behalf was a curling snake in the pit of her stomach.

"Look, Ripley," he said, "you think Cher Dawson is scarey. You don't know me. I stand for justice."

"She hasn't decided to investigate yet."

"Yeah, she has. She just hasn't played all her cards yet. But I do know this. If we open an investigation and you murder anyone, you'll be in jail before you can think of a lie to get yourself out. Don't look at me like that. Murder is exactly what you intend. I don't care what your people let you do, I'll come after you. This is my playground, so we play by my rules. Do I make myself clear?"

Odessa took a deep breath. "You have too many rules." Dammit, why did she have to fall in with the one man who believed in rules?

He gripped her shoulder. "That's not the answer I'm looking for."

She glanced at him. His face was grim and his eyes were cold. "That's the best you're gonna get."

"I'll be watching you."

She shrugged his hand away. "I'll play by the rules. For now. But they are subject to change. Without notice"

Whitaker started the truck and put it into gear. He pulled out of the parking spot and down the street. Odessa leaned her head against the headrest. She needed him. She couldn't afford to make a lot of noise right now.

Technically, she'd just gone rogue and she knew the punishment for that. She'd once taken care of a rogue agent for the CIA. For the moment, she'd play along and pretend to be a good girl; otherwise, Whitaker wasn't going to let her play in his sandbox. But somewhere down the line when everything was said and done, she'd be back to take care of business.

CHAPTER FIVE

Ripley sat across from Wyatt, her feet propped up on the edge of a desk, and her body slouched comfortably in the chair as though she hadn't a care in the world. She almost fooled him into thinking she was as relaxed as a cat lying in the sun, but he could see the tense way she held her mouth and the alertness in her eyes. She kept one eye on the door and the other on him as though urging him to hurry because time was of the essence.

She made him self-conscious. Self-conscious in a way that made him want to polish his boots, find a fresh shirt and get a haircut. Even his ex-wife Bettina hadn't made him feel self-conscious and Bettina had been good at the kind of pointed comments that made other people aware of their shortcomings.

He typed the names of each of victims into his computer to see if any were filed with Cold Case. Two of the names popped up. He scrolled down, reading quickly, repressing a smile. Both cases had been caught by Detective Ronald Archer. When a detective either died while on the job or retired, all his or her active cases were automatically forwarded to Cold Case. Archer had died from a heart attack two weeks after he'd caught the second case. No wonder the two investigations had gone nowhere. They'd been sitting in Cold Case and no one seemed to care.

Archer had been a good detective; not brilliant, but persistent. Once he sank his teeth into a case, he had been like a pit bull, never letting go.

"What did you get?" Ripley asked.

"Two hits," he said as he scrolled down the second case. "Donald Lambert and Joanne Summersby."

"So your unit can investigate legally?" Her feet dropped to the ground.

"Yeah." He couldn't help noticing the hungry gleam in her eye. A part of him wished it were for him and not for her father's killer. "Let's go find the case files."

She pushed her chair back and stood. "And those would be where?"

"In the basement." He exited the computer file and put the computer on stand-by. Then he stood, stretched and headed across the squad room to lead the way to the basement.

They searched for nearly an hour before finding everything they needed. As Wyatt set a box on his desk, he kept thinking the box was way too light for the type of investigation that should have been done on high profile cases like these.

Ripley put her box on a chair and glanced at Wyatt. She a had a dust smudge on her cheek. "Now what?"

He resisted the urge to wipe her face clean. "Let's take these boxes somewhere more private."

Ripley looked surprised. "You can take these boxes off site?"

"I meant someplace where there isn't any traffic. Like Dawson's office."

"Won't you get in trouble with the hall monitor," she whispered. Her eyebrows jiggled. "She's got a lot of repressed rage."

That described Cher Dawson to a T. Wyatt liked that Odessa could still have a sense of fun at a time like this. It was one of the necessary skills to be a good cop. "She's not here. She won't know."

He picked up the box and led the way. He held Dawson's door open for Ripley. She flipped on the light and they set the boxes on Dawson's tidy desk.

"What's this?" Odessa asked, pointing to a framed photo.

Wyatt stared at one of his computer art pieces, a picture of Cher Dawson's head on the body of Godzilla. "Haven't you ever heard of Bitchzilla, the monster who ate Phoenix?"

She suppressed a laugh. "That's your boss's head on the body of Godzilla?"

It should have been in the Gugginheim it was so perfect. "That's the point. She's Bitchzilla."

"That's funny. She must have a cool sense of humor to frame it and hang it on the wall." Ripley took a step closer to get a better look at the picture. "Who did it?"

"That has never been determined." Wyatt smiled.

"You did it?"

"Why would you think that?" He almost confessed to her but didn't. Dawson knew he did it, but to this day had never been able to prove it. He wasn't giving up his secret unless she did something extra special for him.

"I just know."

He opened the Joanne Summersby box. She stood next to him and started rummaging through it. Her hip grazed his thigh and her finger nudged his fingers out of the way. As she crowded him, he could smell the fresh, clean scent of her skin. No perfume. Of course not, she wouldn't want anything giving her presence away when she was on a job.

As he pulled reports out of the box, he found his thoughts wandering back to his ex-wife. Bettina had been a mistake from the word go, but he couldn't stop the roller-coaster. She had been an investigative reporter for a local Phoenix TV station. Everything about her had been perfect, from her dyed blonde hair to her surgically enhanced feet—yes, she had had her feet done though he wasn't certain what had been done—to her perfect smile. He hadn't understood what she'd wanted with him, and had been too flattered to ask.

Wyatt was a beer-drinking, football watching, pork and beans kind of man, not particularly complicated, and Bettina had wanted a project. If he'd known that ten years ago, he would never have married her. He didn't want to be any woman's project. He glanced at Odessa and found her staring him.

"Your lips are moving," she said, "but nothing's coming out."

Wyatt picked up a thick file of crime scene photographs to avoid her probing gaze. He worried that she would see the places in his soul he didn't want to share with anyone. "Have you ever spent a whole lot of years trying to figure out something, and suddenly find the answer right there in front of you?"

She shook her head. "No, I'm not that deep."

Oh yes you are, little lady. You're deeper than I can fathom. But God help me, I'd like to give it a shot. "If you say so."

Her head tilted to one side. "What earthshattering piece of knowledge did you come up with?"

Wyatt shoved a photograph at her as if to give her some kind of warning. "That I'm no woman's project."

Her eyebrows rose. "Well, my world is all put to rights again. But tell me how your new insight helps with my father's murder."

Hell if he knew. "Let me explain to you how I investigate a case. Normally, I'm a pretty linear thinking kind of guy. B always follows A and C always follows B. But when I'm investigating a case, I open my head to the possibilities and sometimes those possibilities take me to some pretty strange and interesting places. To keep up with me you're going to have to go with the flow and right now I'm processing."

"You watch Dr. Phil, don't you?"

"Why do you ask?"

"That was a shitload of psycho babble and it almost confused me."

He held up his arms. "My job is done. I've confused Odessa Ripley."

"I'm gonna kill you slow."

He shook his head. Damn, she was a lot of fun to hang with. "Promises, promises."

"Do you need some help? I can read." She took a folder out of his hands. "And I do have a college degree and can bring my linear analysis skills to this."

"How do you think?" Getting inside her head would be the ride of the decade.

"Sometimes when B is irritating me, I stick an ice pick in his ear and move on to C."

Okay, he thought. "Ever done that to somebody?" He sat down in a visitor's chair because he didn't have the guts to sit behind Cher Dawson's desk.

"What do you think? I know seven hundred and fifty-two ways to kill somebody and I'm determined to use them all."

"What number are you at now?"

She picked up a stapler. "I haven't ever killed anyone with a stapler, but I'm willing to try it now."

Wyatt burst out laughing. "You can do that? Get out of town."

She replaced the stapler on the desk with a look of disappointment. "You're not afraid of me, are you?"

"No. That's not how I'm feeling you." He wanted to feel her with his fingers.

She put her hands on her rounded hips. "How are you feeling me?"

"Wondering what kind of underwear you have on."

Her mouth dropped open and no words came out.

He'd left her speechless. This moment was going in his journal. "Thong," he continued, "bikinis, granny panties, but I'm hoping for commando." God, he loved commando. Bettina had worn lace and silk, no commando anything for her. She'd told him once she was a lady. But he knew she was only a lady in front of the camera.

Ripley's mouth opened and closed as though working around something. If it were possible, stream would be coming out of her ears by now.

Wyatt grinned and cupped his ear. "Your lips are still moving, but nothing's coming out. Why don't you just sit in that chair and let me do my job." He took the folder she held and pointed at the other chair.

She sat and he started pulling crime scene photos out of the box, trying to make sense of what he was seeing. The evidence techs had been thorough. No stone had been left unturned, so to speak.

Ripley shifted in the chair. "Let me help. I can't sit here all morning with nothing to do. Just tell me what to look for."

Good, she was recovered. He glanced up from a photo of the living room. "I don't know." How did he explain being a cop? Not that she didn't have her own instincts, but he knew that instincts weren't enough. He had to be able to spot the anomaly inside the crime. "Just something that doesn't feel right. If you want to help, get a notebook. You'll find one in the top drawer of my desk. I'll dictate." She got up and went into the outer office and returned with a yellow legal pad and a pencil.

Wyatt glanced at the photo in his hand. Joanne Summersby had had a nice house. Nothing special, just a middle-class house in a middle class neighborhood. He set the photo down on the desk and started arranging the others around it. He could feel his mouth starting to get dry the way it did when he'd seen something, but needed to think it through.

Joanne Summersby had been the victim of a home invasion robbery. Wyatt studied the photos. She'd been surprised in her bedroom and her body lay in the center of the floor. She had been a pretty woman with feathery blonde hair and a heart-shaped face. Wyatt studied the photo. Something wasn't right and that 'something' made his mouth go drier.

He handed the photo to Ripley. "Tell me what you see. What am I missing?"

She studied it a second. "Frankly, I see a body, a bed, a sliding glass door, and I see the door to the bathroom." She bent her head over the photo.

"You've killed your share of people, haven't you?"

"That's a fair statement."

He liked that she didn't even look ashamed of what she did. "How do you get in and get out without being caught, or do you just level buildings?"

She shook her head. "Collateral damage isn't my style. I'm up close and personal, in and out like a breeze."

"So you wouldn't stick around to make things look right, would you?"

"Nope, that's not my job."

"She was killed during a home invasion robbery, a big mess. Give me your expert opinion on this."

She stood and bent over the desk to look at the array of photos. Wyatt caught his breath at the way her butt stuck out. Low-riders. God, he loved low rider jeans.

Ripley opened the file folder that contained the notes from the crime scene techs. She wriggled her butt a little as she read through it, turning the pages quickly and scanning down with one finger.

Wyatt leaned back in the chair and crossed his legs. He grabbed a file and opened it over his lap, willing her not to look at him. But if she did, he was prepared to look like he was working and not savoring that perfect specimen of booty. Bettina had spent fifteen thousand bucks to get an ass like that. And he doubted Odessa was the plastic surgery kind of girl. If anything had been done to her butt, it was the result of a healthy workout. And he wanted to play in her playground.

Ripley suddenly went stiff. "Oh, jackpot." She whirled around. "I caught you."

Wyatt gripped the edge of the file. "I wasn't looking at your—"

"What?" she interrupted him.

He'd jumped the gun. "I didn't say anyhing. What did you find?"

She held the photo under his nose. "Look at that."

He crossed his eyes, trying to figure out what he was supposed to see. "Okay, what am I looking at?"

She grabbed the other photos and flashed each one in front of his eyes. "These guys could work for The Company."

"You mean the bad ones."

"We have a few of those." She flapped the photos down hard on his lap.

Wyatt tried not to wince. Big Willy was at attention now and having those photos slapped down so hard was going to definitely cramp his style. When Ripley started to slap the last one down, Wyatt caught her hand. "I get the picture. Just tell me what you saw."

"Someone vacuumed the carpet in every room of the house."

"Let me play devil's advocate here," he said, already knowing where she was going. "She could have been a good housekeeper."

"No way. Personal experience tells me that a home invasion robbery leaves a whole lot of traffic. These people vacuumed their way out of the house. See how the vacuum tracks all lead to the door?" She tapped the evidence tech's report. "This house was cleaned. Professionally. The forensics report states no fibers, no hair, no fingerprints. Now you tell me what home invasion robber brings along his own Hoover and bottle of Windex?"

"Tell me something." Wyatt said. "Have you ever done something like this during the course of your 'employment' with The Company?"

She leaned back against the desk. "You're really fascinated with what I do, aren't you?"

"That and a few other things." Wyatt gathered up the photos and handed them back to her. He hoped she wouldn't notice the file was still covering his lap.

"Yes. Nine times out of ten, I'm on my own, but occasionally I get 'special' orders from my bosses."

Don't leave me hanging, babe. "Tell me the details."

"There was a French Algerian arms dealer who needed to be handled in a particular way. I did him in his house and then the crew came in and trashed the place and littered it with evidence to make it look like one of his competitors did the job. We got two of biggest bad guys off the street at once. It was a beautiful thing."

Wyatt gulped. "I'm sure it was." *Remind me to stay on her good side.*

She tapped a finger on the photo. "Who are the kind of people who clean up after themselves like this?"

"Professionals."

"But why this house? It's nice, but it's solidly middle class. Professional people hit big targets. I looked at the list of what's missing and only about four or five thousand in jewelry and some moderately high-end stereo equipment. Pros hit big targets—art work, stereo equipment you can't pronounce, and six figure jewelry."

"Someone wanted to see this woman dead for some other reason."

She nodded her head slowly. "If this woman were on the CIA's radar, I'd say we did it. But I can tell you right now, she wasn't."

"How do you know?"

"Because if the CIA wanted her dead, I'd have gotten first crack at her. She's on my home turf and no one would have questioned my being in town. I could have dropped into Phoenix, killed her, and dropped in to have a family dinner with my parents. In and out like a breeze."

"Let's take a look at Lambert." Wyatt replaced all the photos and files into the Summersby box and put it on the floor. He lifted the second box and opened it.

Donald Lambert had died in a drive-by shooting. His box contained even less information than Summersby's. As he and Ripley went through the file, she made notes as he dictated. No car had ever been recovered, no gun, and there had been no evidence of any kind at the scene. Nothing jumped out at him, but still he felt a dryness in his mouth. Usually with a drive-by, they shot up neighborhoods with bullets flying in all directions and usually a lot of innocent people got hurt or killed. This hadn't been a gang-style drive-by. The target had been Donald Lambert and only Donald Lambert had been shot. This had been as cold and professional as the Summersby case.

He thought about the TV shows where all the evidence was neatly recovered and eventually led to the perpetrator in an hour. Real life wasn't so neat and orderly.

When he felt that they had enough, he called Cher Dawson and told her what they had.

Dawson was silent for so long that Wyatt thought she might have gotten lost in her thoughts.

"Be here in an hour," Dawson finally said in a tone that told Wyatt she'd made a really big decision, "and bring enough pizza for everyone. And tell your friend to bring what she has on this situation, too."

When Wyatt relayed Dawson's orders to Odessa, Odessa's face clouded. "What do you mean, back to her house? Let's get on the road and do something."

"You don't understand. You're on the team now. That means you have to play in the sandbox with the other children."

An incredulous look crossed her face. "I don't have time to talk."

"Mommy gets very angry if you don't keep her in the loop."

Ripley crossed her arms over her chest. "What is Cher Dawson going to do to me?"

In the black jeans and thick green sweater, she looked tough. She was tough, but no one had more attitude than Cher Dawson. It was one of the rules. "You scare me, but that woman makes my blood run cold."

She made a small hissing sound through her teeth. "I could kill her for you."

He held up his finger. "Let me take a rain check on that. Dawson wants your dad's files, too."

"Everything is on his computer." She picked up her jacket and put it on, then stuffed the photos back into the box.

"Then we'll go back to the house and get the computer." Wyatt held the door for her then locked Cher's office. He didn't want anyone snooping around those boxes.

Odessa chewed at her thumbnail as she watched the passing buildings. This whole thing had snowballed into something bigger than she'd expected. She should have spoken to Carlyle instead of getting on her white horse and coming to Phoenix to look into things, but then again, the CIA was funky about personal vendettas. If her dad had been CIA, no rock would have been left unturned. But he wasn't and Odessa worried about what he'd found that had gotten him murdered.

She glanced at Whitaker. Except for his taste in country/western music, which was blaring at her through the speakers and made her want to put a needle through her eye, she liked this man. She liked his smart-ass sense of humor. She liked the way his brain worked. She liked the way he was with her mother. He showed a respect and a gentleness that reminded her of her father. And God knows, she liked the way he looked, from his over-grown blonde hair to his long, lean, muscled body. And oh my God, his little friend was very impressive, too. He was the kind of playmate she'd keep for longer than one night.

His face was drawn in concentration as he drove. She figured he was thinking about what she had involved him in.

"You're staring at me," Whitaker said as he turned a corner and headed back to the freeway. He ran a hand through his hair. "You like what you see?"

"The package ain't bad, honey."

"You like me in that special way, don't you?"

Her eyebrows drew together. How could he tell? She thought she had kept her attraction under the covers. Not that she was going to let him think he'd gotten one by her. "How did you make that leap?"

He smiled. "It wasn't a big one."

The wattage on the sexy grin could have lit up the entire city. Okay, she was ready to confess. "So what? It's not as if you can pull to side of the road and leap on me."

"You want to?"

"No!"

"Are you sure?" He steered the car into the slow lane. "A little romp would take the edge off."

Odessa forced herself not to grab the wheel and steer them away from the curb. That would be too easy. "Sexy though you might be, you're not my type."

He glanced at her. "To be honest, I've never been a coffee man before, but I think it's time to expand my horizons and take a trip to Starbucks."

"Did I say anything about your being white?"

He stopped at a light. "Will it be an issue for you? You ever date someone like me?"

"I've never dated a cop." She knew that's not what he meant, but she didn't want to admit she'd never dated a white man before. Not because she thought it was wrong; it had just never come up.

The light changed and he drove on. "You think I'm interested because you're black and not because I find you attractive?"

"That's a legitimate concern on my part."

"I'm thirty-seven years old and have already been married and divorced. I've seen a good chunk of the world and done a lot of things. I don't want to sleep with you because you're black, but because you're the sexiest woman I've seen in about twenty-seven years."

How did we get from investigating my father's murder to diving into my panties? She was mildly attracted, but the timing couldn't be worse. "We don't even have a relationship and you're thinking about sleeping with me."

"I'm a guy. You're a girl. Of course, I'm thinking about sleeping with you. You smell good. You make me laugh. You're pretty."

He just laid it all out there and frankly she had to admit she appreciated his honesty. Not that she was going to sleep with him. "Are you saying that all you want is nothing more than to have sex with me?" To be honest, that was all she needed—to jump into bed with a guy. Sex, for her, was just another form of exercise. Not that she was going to drop that bit of information; she had way too many other things to think about.

"You know what's so cool about you, Ripley? You're a beautiful woman who thinks like a guy. That's sexy."

Odessa didn't know whether to be flattered or not. "Are you saying you have a man crush on me?"

He shook his head. "No."

She liked that she couldn't fluster him. He was cool under pressure. A good skill to have when hanging around her. "So that was a compliment?"

"Yes."

Wow! That was an curious admission from him. She'd always been a love and leave 'em kind of girl by her own choice. She couldn't help being taken aback by the fact that Wyatt was just like her.

"Silence from Odessa Ripely," Wyatt said. "This is a new side of you. I kind of like it."

Odessa backhanded him on the arm. "Shut up, dumb-ass."

"There's my Odessa back. So how about it? Are we gonna sleep together or what?"

"No."

"Don't play hard to get, Ripley. I'm not about the chase. I want to catch it, stuff it and mount it."

Did this guy ever get a clue? "That was a huge sexual innuendo if I ever heard one."

He grinned, a winsome grin that added a roguish look to his face. "That wasn't an innuendo. That's my style, direct and to the point."

"Does that work for you?"

"Most of the time."

Whitaker parked in front of her mother's house, then put an arm along the back of the seat and grinned at her. "Ripley, let's not lie to each other. I've got the hots for you and I know you have them for me. So should the need arise, don't complain, just go with the flow."

Before she could answer, he opened the door and jumped out of the truck to collect her father's computer.

A couple blocks from Dawson's home Whitaker stopped at a pizza place and ordered ten pizzas.

"How many people are coming to this meeting?" Odessa asked when he carefully placed the pizzas in the back seat.

"Seven, maybe eight. Depends on who she finds."

"You need ten pizzas for maybe eight people?"

"Cops are big eaters."

"Do we need to chip in?"

"That would be the polite thing to do."

A half dozen cars were parked in front of Dawson's house. When Whitaker found a parking space, and Odessa prepared to jump out of the truck. She getting tired of the constant struggle getting in and out of the Monster Mobile, as she had privately dubbed the truck.

Dawson's living room was crowded with people. A tall black man paid court to a classy looking blonde woman who blushed when he leaned over to whisper something in her ear. A handsome Native American man, with hair pulled into a ponytail, sat in a chair reading a newspaper. Another black man sat at a table and typed on a notebook computer while Dawson dictated to him.

"Pizza's here," Whitaker said.

Dawson pointed at a card table set up behind a sofa. "Paper plates and utensils on the table here. Soft drinks are under the table in a cooler. Coffee on the sideboard."

Whitaker introduced everyone. The black man with the blonde was named Leland Davenport and he was a county attorney. He had a broad open face that showed a touch of humor. The blonde was Beatrix Hunter, a member of the unit. The Native American was named Jacob Greyhorse and he had a stoic, unreadable face, and dark eyes that missed nothing. He was the kind of guy The Company would hire. The other brother in the room was Marco Jackson, who had a slightly rumpled look to him, as though he'd been pulled away from some game. He grumbled at being called back two days early from his honey-moon.

Odessa stood out of the way as everyone went after the pizza. They were all comfortable with each other as they jostled for a position at the card table. When everyone was repositioned with pizza in hand, Odessa sat in a corner to stay out of the way as she observed. Dawson half lay on her sofa, a plate balanced on her stomach. Beatrix Hunter sat on a sofa with the lawyer and from the way their hands kept touching, Odessa figured they were an item. Odessa wondered how often this living room had been substituted for their office. She had the feeling that these were people who worked well together in and out of the office.

Whitaker brought in her father's computer, set it up on another card table next to the fireplace and fiddled with it, a perplexed look on his face. "Where does this plug go?"

Beatrix Hunter finished a slice of her pizza, went over to Whitaker and shoved him out of the way. "I'll do it," she said as he fumbled around behind the computer.

Whitaker went back for a second helping of pizza and sat on the floor next to Odessa's chair, his legs crossed and the paper plate balanced on one knee. He leaned against her, his back hot against her leg.

"Report," Dawson said as crisply as she could with her mouth wrapped around the pizza.

"Dead people," Whitaker said. "Lots of dead people." He recounted the five names Odessa had given him.

Odessa watched Hunter turn on her dad's computer and then frown. She walked over and handed her the encryption disk, then stood beside her watching. Hunter's hands darted over the keyboard with the same skill as A.J's. In the background, Whitaker recited all the names Odessa had given him. As each name was given, Jackson typed furiously on his laptop. At the end of his list, Whitaker hesitated and glanced Odessa. She nodded and he added her father's name. Leland Davenport wrote notes on a yellow legal pad and Greyhorse frowned as he too jotted notes down in a small spiral notebook.

"I'm up and running on the Internet, L.T." Jackson typed a few more words. "And I'm in our database."

Dawson nodded. "Search our records and find out how all these people died, Marco," Dawson commanded. She finished her pizza, licked her fingers, then wiped them clean with a napkin.

Marco Jackson's fingers flew over the keyboard of his small laptop. Obviously, he'd already hooked into the police computers. "Cordova was a hit and run," Jackson said as his fingers flew quickly over the keys. "Borland was an apparent suicide. Lambert was a drive-by shooting." He paused, typed a few more words and waited for a few seconds. "Summersby was a home invasion robbery and Tannenbaum is missing."

Dawson frowned, her glance roaming around the room. "What's the link between these people?"

Greyhorse looked up from his spiral notebook. "Community activists who had their run-ins with the police at one time or another."

"Jackson," Dawson said, "link these names together and find out what else they had in common besides run-ins with the cops and their political activity."

From her confident manner, Odessa figured Hunter knew her way around a computer. The screen had rearranged itself from gibberish into a readable format. Odessa watched as Hunter scrolled down. Odessa didn't have much use for computers. They were a tool, but Hunter acted as though the computer were her lover. Leland Davenport glanced up and Hunter smiled at him, a faint color washing across her pale cheeks. Yeah! Those two were definitely an item.

An icon started blinking at the bottom corner of the monitor and Odessa tapped the screen. "Spyware," she said. "Found it yesterday. Unfortunately, I activated it and someone knows I used this computer and what I was doing at the time and where on the Internet I went."

Hunter nodded. "I saw that. Someone wanted to know what your dad was doing. But as long as the computer isn't hooked into the Internet, nothing we do can be traced." From the set look on Hunter's face, Odessa had the feeling the spyware wouldn't be operational too much longer.

"What have you got, Hunter?" Dawson asked.

Hunter half turned. "Lots of files on all the victims. Phil Ripley must have had his scanner working overtime. I have police reports, evidence reports, interviews, backgrounds on all the victims all the way back to kindergarten." Hunter glanced at Odessa. "I never met your father, but he was a very thorough man." She tapped the keys. "And I have a list of every cop in Violent Crimes who worked on all these cases and exactly which cases they worked." She twisted around. "Whitaker, did you know you worked the de Cordova case?"

Whitaker looked up from his pizza. "Yeah, everybody in Violent Crimes worked that case. The whole Hispanic community was up in arms over the shoot. We needed to look good and did lots of little things that looked good in the media, but nothing much ever came of the investigation."

"I didn't work it." Jackson looked up from his notebook.

"That's because you worked on your Jamaica vacation investigation." Whitaker cleaned his hands and crumpled the napkin and tossed it on his empty plate.

"Right," Jackson replied.

"I didn't do much, just ran a couple of car license numbers," Whitaker said. "The lead detective was Ralph Stuart."

Hunter glanced through the list. "I have Ralph Stuart here and his fingerprints are over all five cases in one way or another."

"That's not unusual," Greyhorse said. "Violent Crimes isn't exactly the most populated bureau."

Dawson said to Jackson, "Where is Stuart now?"

Jackson consulted his computer. "Stuart took an early retirement about eight months ago. Says here he moved to Flagstaff."

"Convenient," Odessa murmured. Out of sight, out of mind. Who was the lead detective on her father's murder? Whoever he was, he didn't seem terribly pro-active in investigating the murder of another cop. In fact the whole department hadn't put out much effort for Phil Ripley.

Dawson frowned. "How is Phil Ripley involved in all this? Involved in such a way that he's on the list, too."

"He found something," Whitaker offered.

"Something damaging enough for him to end up dead," Greyhorse put in.

Leland Davenport tapped his yellow legal pad. "Something damaging that points back to the department."

Everyone swivelled their heads to look at him. Dawson's face was sharply curious. Greyhorse nodded slowly and Jackson stared at the attorney, surprise on his face. Odessa wondered how Davenport had come up with that conclusion. Not that she hadn't already thought about it herself, but she had wondered if these people would come to the same conclusion. Why else would her father hide all this information behind an encryption code? He'd known something so dangerous he couldn't take chances that the information would end up in the wrong hands. Odessa hoped that Dawson wasn't the wrong hands.

"Explain, please, Leland," Dawson said.

"One," Davenport held up a finger, "we have a lot of unsolved cases of people who were active in their respective communities. Two, not all of those causes were nice and neat, like working for the Red Cross which everyone pretty much admires. Three, these are not the kinds of people who make a lot of friends in certain communities."

Dawson tilted her head at the man. "I remember that Cordova was pretty determined to make certain illegal aliens were given due process under the law. I also remember that his grass roots program fell apart after he died."

"So did Martin Borland's demand for a legal same sex partnership law," Greyhorse said.

Hunter turned to face the room. "Five years ago Joanne Summersby was very active in supporting a bill that would make it easier to hold cops more accountable for protecting victims of domestic violence. The bill never did pass."

Odessa rarely paid attention to Arizona politics. She was too used to an international playground with bigger stakes. "Who wants to silence these people?"

Dawson glanced at Odessa, her face thoughtful. "Whitaker and you were attacked by skinheads last night."

"That's a group that belongs on the list." Davenport wrote something on his legal pad. "Any other suggestions?"

"Right wing religious fanatics," Greyhorse added.

"You mean Fundamentalists, don't you?" Hunter asked.

"No, they're not the same," Greyhorse replied and then said nothing more though his eyes went darker and more unreadable.

"I think cops have to be at the top of that list." Odessa felt the hositily level jump up about one percent as soon as the words left her mouth. "Hey, people in authority on any level, local, state, or national, don't like anybody who makes waves. Stop trying to pretend that every cop on the beat is squeaky clean."

Dawson glared at Odessa. "Don't pretend the people you work for are all squeaky clean either."

Odessa shrugged. "It's the nature of the business. That's why I work for them, because I don't have to be either. If my people were squeaky clean, I wouldn't have a job." Odessa could see that everyone besides Dawson and Whitaker had polite expressions of curiosity on their faces, but no one was willing to ask about her job. Whitaker grinned, letting them know he was in on the secret.

"Miss Ripley," Dawson swung her feet down to the floor and pushed herself to her feet, "may I have a moment with you?" She hooked a finger at Odessa and started out the arched doorway to the hall beyond.

Odessa followed reluctantly. Dawson was a little too much like Carlyle for her to be comfortable. There were times when Carlyle scared the shit out of her.

Dawson led Odessa partway down the hall, just far enough away to not be overheard, then turned to face her. "I know about you, secret agent girl."

Odessa folded her arms over her chest. "Oh?"

"Oh yeah! I spoke to someone who used to work in the same ball park as you do."

Her gut clenched. "What interesting little tidbits about me did you happen to find out?"

Dawson's eyebrows rose. "Your code name is Nemesis. Need I say more?"

A ripple of alarm swept down Odessa's spine. "Who did you talk to?" A handful of people knew her code name.

"Don't look so worried, Ripley," Dawson said with a chuckle. "My source had nothing bad to say about you. Though he did say that you're the kind of person who is a good friend but a worse enemy. I intend to stay on your good side. I don't want to end up dead."

Odessa almost chuckled. "I've never done a pregnant woman before. I am kind of curious."

"Don't let this pregnant body fool you. I can still give as good as I get."

Odessa believed her. Dawson might be pregnant, but there was a coiled spring look to her tight muscles that told her Dawson still worked out. "Who did you talk to?"

"Porter Anderson."

Odessa grinned. "Yeah! I know him. European operations. We worked together a time or two. I hear he retired. What's he doing now?"

"He works for my father's security firm. He's highly appreciated and would be missed."

"I got that clue." Odessa was really starting to like this woman. She was direct and honest. A person knew where they stood with her. If Whitaker's opinions were anything to go by, she'd be a great asset to The Company. Odessa wouldn't mind working alongside her. "Next time you see Anderson, give him my best. If he wants to get together, have a drink, talk about 'back in the day,' I'm open."

Dawson's voice was dry. "I'll tell him. Now, shall we get back to the others?"

Odessa nodded. The threat was well taken and she had no intention of pissing Cher Dawson off.

"What was that about?" Whitaker asked when Odessa returned and sat down next to him.

"Girl talk."

"Girl talk about what?" he persisted.

"How large your endowment is?"

A look of confusion settled on his face. "You were talking about my…"

Odessa glanced down at his crotch. "Told her I'd had a chance to check you out and she wanted to know how you measure up."

A broad grin spread over his face. "Every girl is crazy about a well-hung man."

"Children," Dawson interrupted their bickering, "let's get back to the subject at hand. Okay, everyone, right here, right now, we concentrate on Lambert and Summersby. Those cases are already in Cold Case and we can legitimately look at them. Greyhorse, what are you working on?"

"The Michaelson stabbing."

"Put it on hold. You and Jackson take the Lambert case. Nose around and see if you can dig up anything on Whitaker's skinhead." She turned to Whitaker. "What are you working on?"

"My transfer papers back to Violent Crimes."

"That's an every week thing. Put aside whatever you're doing."

Whitaker spread out his hands. "Send me wherever, boss."

Odessa almost laughed out loud at the answering look on Dawson's face. She knew exactly where she wanted to send Whitaker and it wasn't pleasant.

Finally, Dawson sighed, casting a look at the ceiling. "You take the Summersby case." Obviously, she and Whitaker had been having this same conversation for a long time. "Hunter, you're the computer guru. I want everything off that computer and printed out in nice neat piles for everyone to read. Legitimately, the only cases we can investigate are Lambert and Summersby, but we can follow any lead we need. What I'm thinking is, all these murders are all linked somehow. Since the department is not following through, we keep this in house. I am not letting Phil Ripley's murder go un-avenged."

Odessa didn't intend to let the murderers go either. She knew exactly what she intended to do them. She was going to make them suffer, make them understand their sins against humanity.

She glanced around the room. Everyone was busy with their own thoughts or writing in spiral bound notebooks. They were doing the grunt work for her and afterwards she would get to do the fun part.

Dawson glanced at Odessa. "I'm allowing you to accompany Whitaker as a courtesy. Don't make me regret my decision."

"I promise not to hurt anybody before clearing it with you." Odessa grinned.

"I'm gonna lose my job," Dawson said with a long-suffering sigh.

"Look at the bright side. You'd just get fired. Let me tell you what would happen to me."

Dawson held up a hand. "I don't want to know."

"Don't worry, my bosses know how to dispose of bodies. Your department won't be compromised." Odessa glanced around and realized everyone was looking at her, curiosity again in their faces.

Whitaker picked up the Summersby file and started toward the door. Odessa tagged along after him.

CHAPTER SIX

Feeling at loose ends, Wyatt stood on the lawn trying to work out what to do next. The truck chirped at him as he pointed the remote at it.

"Can I drive?" Ripley stood at the driver's side door, one hand resting against the chrome racing stripe.

After all that bitching she'd about his truck she wanted to drive? Wyatt shook his head as he ran his hand around the dent she used the skinhead to make. "Nobody drives Baby but her daddy."

She wedged her body between him and the truck. "You named this humongous truck Baby?"

"What's wrong with Baby?" He really didn't call the truck Baby; he just thought it would be fun to mess with her head. "She comes when she's called."

Ripley stared at him, open-mouthed. No reply. He it loved when he could get the upper hand. He felt he had to take advantage of it because he doubted he'd be in this position too often. "Nothing to say, huh?" He pushed her out of the way. "I like silence in my women."

She glared at him. "You are never going to enter the promised land now."

Wyatt couldn't keep the grin off his face. "Sure I am. I know a lot about seduction."

"I'll bet you do. But what makes you think it'll work on me?"

He slid a hand down her arm to her butt and patted it. Considering she could dismantle his entire body in five minutes, it was not his smartest move. But he just had to touch her. "I'm halfway there already." Her butt was sublime, tight and full of promise. He felt for underwear and didn't feel anything. He'd known she was a commando kind of girl.

Ripley turned her head. "What are you doing back there?"

His fingers squeezed, ever so slightly, the firm muscle in the warm denim. This one touch was worth dying for. "I'm copping a feel, I thought that was obvious."

She grabbed his nipple through the thin fabric of his shirt and twisted.

Pain radiated through him. He let go of her butt, backed up to his truck, and tried to stifle the scream building in him. This was war.

She let him go and smoothed out the wrinkles from his shirt. "Now that was copping a feel."

He reined in the pain. "You're going to make me work for this." He twisted her around and backed her up against the truck. "Good." He bent over and kissed her, his lips tight on hers. Her mouth opened under his and he felt her arms come around his waist as their tongues danced around each other. His senses reeled and he pressed himself against her. Her body was so delicate and fine-boned. His hands roamed to the skin of her neck. She was so soft so velvety smooth. God, he ached for this woman. He lifted his head. "If you sleep with me, I'll let you drive my truck." His voice was thick with arousal. He didn't care what he had to do to get her in his bed; he'd do it.

Her eyes were smokey with desire. "I'm not that easy."

"I didn't think so, but I had to give it a shot."

She twisted away from him. "You're going to have to work really hard to get that close to me again."

He put his hands on either side of her. "I'm up to the task."

She glanced down at his crotch. "Yes, you are. But I'm still not sleeping with you even if you dangle your truck in front of me." Then she ducked under his arms.

"I will find something that works, Miss Ripley." He pulled open the door and she stepped around the truck to the passenger side and pulled herself in.

Ripley latched the seatbelt and sat staring out the windsheild. "Find my father's killer, then leave me alone with him. Afterward I'll do anything you want."

He should have expected that from her, but he was still surprised. "You'd sleep with me if I let you kill some guy?" Wyatt asked. Let her be joking with him.

"I've done a lot of things I'm supposed to be ashamed of, but I never traded my body for anything. I was just seeing how desperate you were."

Funny, it hadn't seemed like a joke to him. She leaned back in the corner of the truck cab with a smirk on her face, waiting for him to answer. "Ask me in two hours." He turned on the ignition. "I'm going to find your father's killer and get you into my bed."

"But your boss told you to look into the Summersby case. Aren't we breaking her rules?"

Wyatt shrugged. "I can multi-task. I can tell you right here and right now, I'm going to find zit diddly-squat on Summersby. You know why. Whoever did that killing planned it out to the smallest detail. They knew what they were doing and didn't make any mistakes except for being too clean. Unfortunately I can't hang a case on carpet. But they made one huge error with the Ding Dong Bandits. If I eliminate the real Ding Dong Bandits, I have a better shot at the guys who killed your father. Let's face it, you don't give a shit about these other people. They're a means to an end for you."

Ripley was silent for a few long seconds.

Good, he had her on the run. Her conscience was playing some wicked games with her. Every once in a while, he reminded himself, he should play on that. "Don't be embarrassed," he continued. "A lot of times I've had cases land in my lap where I didn't give a shit about the victim other than catching the killer."

Her head lolled back on the headrest. "It's not that I don't want to care, I just can't. That's how I was trained. That's why I can do what I do. The second I start caring is the second I hang up my gun and get another life."

He saw a flicker of something cross her face and she turned away before he could identify it. He wondered if maybe she'd started caring about something and was angry with herself. "I can understand."

"How do we go about eliminating the real Ding Dong Bandits from the fake ones?"

"We have a conversation with the cop in charge of that investigation."

She rubbed her eyes. "But Dawson said—"

"Dawson knows I never listen to her."

"I can't afford to let you get your ass in any trouble, I'm doing so well on my own. So let's do this clandestine."

Now that sounded interesting. "Meaning what?"

"Point me in the direction of the information you need and I'll liberate it."

"You want to steal from the police department?" He was going to have a heart attack. He'd done some things that were almost unethical, but stealing evidence wasn't one of them.

She slanted a glance at him. "Once I stole information from the FBI. This will be cookies and milk."

Wyatt waved his hand. She was going to get him fired. Or worse, stuck in the same shit hole where he'd put a lot of people. "I don't want to know because this is the kind of trouble that comes knocking on your door at two in the morning."

"If I'm not badly mistaken, doesn't every convenience store have surveillance film these days?"

"Most of them do."

"Fine. All we need are the tapes of the robberies."

Wyatt turned onto the expressway, already thinking of a way to get the film without going to the lead investigator. "I know exactly how to get copies of the surveillance tapes." He shuddered to think that he was going into his ex-wife's lair.

The TV station was a large building in downtown Phoenix that looked as though a child had designed it with a set of colorful blocks. The building was a little too *avant garde* for Odessa.

Wyatt parked in an adjacent parking garage and led her into the building across a bridge leading to double doors that whispered open as they approached.

The closer they got to wherever Wyatt wanted to go, the more nervous he acted. He looked around warily and she noticed that he was clenching and unclenching his hands. He cleared his throat and took off down the hall with his long strides, as though anxious to get done whatever was making him so edgy.

Odessa trotted to keep up with him. "Who are we going to talk to and why are you so nervous about it?"

"I'm not nervous." He was about five minutes from a panic attack.

"Oh really?" She glanced at his hands.

After a second, he said in a strained tone, "Bettina Ellison Whitaker."

"Your mom?" If he could bait her, she could bait him. She loved the started look on his face.

His mom he loved. "No."

Guess number two. "Your sister?"

Didn't have one of those either. "No."

And behind the third door, she knew she'd hit pay dirt. "Then who could this mystery woman be in your life?" she half teased.

He gave her an annoyed look. "You've already figured it out. Stop yanking my chain."

She couldn't help the grin spreading across her face. "So tell me about your ex-wife."

"No. You'll know everything you need to know about her when you meet her."

She stopped. "I'm not going to like her, am I?"

"As my mother used to say, the jury is still out on whether God likes her or not."

"That's deep," Odessa said as they turned down a long corridor. "Why did you marry her?"

"If I could figure that out, I could figure out cold fusion. Not that once upon a time life with Bettina wasn't good. She could be fun, loving and stimulating. But when she decided she wanted to be co-host of the *Today* show she went sort of weird."

"That doesn't explain why you married her," Odessa probed. She was really curious about the kind of woman Whitaker would marry.

"I was drunk. We were in Mexico. She has really nice boobs." He raised his hand palm up and a dreamy expression crossed his face.

"Big knockers. How typical."

"I have to admit that in my advancing years, I've grown to appreciate," he gave Odessa's chest a quick look, "…more compact packaging."

"You make me feel as though I'm a Hot Wheels car."

He sighed, "Those were my favorite toys when I was a kid."

"From Hot Wheels to monster truck! Now there's a transition." Odessa wasn't the least bit surprised. Whitaker was the kind of man she could read a mile away and never get bored with the book. Every page was a surprise and she loved surprises. Her favorite snack was Cracker Jacks.

He stopped in front of a door with a window in it. Inside Odessa could see a dozen pre-fabricated desks. People moved hurriedly around the office. Some carried files, were on the phone or typing away on computers.

A grey-haired woman with pencils tucked into her hair and an unlit cigarette hanging out of her mouth hurried past. She gave Whitaker a quick up and down look then patted his butt. "Good to see you, Wyatt." She gave him a huge hug.

This definitely wasn't Bettina.

"Myrna, you are still the sexiest woman on God's green earth. When are you going to marry me?"

She grabbed his butt. "You had your chance, stud. I don't do sloppy seconds."

"I'll regret that mistake every moment of every day for the rest of my life."

Myrna patted his cheek. "You were bamboozled by blonde hair, big boobs and a toothy smile."

Wyatt grinned. "But I learned my lesson."

"The hard way," Myrna said with a laugh and tossed a glance at Odessa. "Who's your new flavor?"

"I'm Odessa Ripley." Odessa liked this woman.

Myrna glanced back and forth between them. "Are you two *special* friends?"

Odessa grinned. "He's trying."

"Make him work hard, honey." Myna winked at her and slapped Whitaker's ass one more time. "God, I love your ass."

"I almost feel cheap," Whitaker said with a wicked gleam in his eyes.

Odessa patted his ass, too. "You're not enough man for her."

Myrna shifted the cigarette in her mouth. "You got that right, honey." She turned around and yelled, "Hey Bitty, your ex is here.

The newsroom went dead silent and Odessa saw a blush creep up Whitaker's cheeks.

Odessa started whistling the theme from *Jaws* as Whitaker stalked across the newsroom.

A tall woman sashayed out of an office. She wore a light brown skirt suit and had artfully cut blonde hair, a perfect oval of a face, and a light golden tan on her creamy skin. Everything about this woman was too perfect—she had to be fake. The woman glanced at Whitaker, annoyance in blue eyes that owed their startling color more to contacts than the original shade.

Myrna gave a rude snort. Odessa got the feeling that Myrna had little respect for the blonde.

"Actually, Myrna," Whitaker said, "I didn't come to see Bettina. I came to see you."

Bettina Whitaker was almost across the newsroom when Whitaker's words sailed out. She paused, anger darkening her perfect face. Then she straightened her shoulders and teetered across the remaining space on four inch Manolo Blahniks. "Wyatt, darling. How are you?"

Odessa was proud of herself for recognizing the designer shoes. The fashion knowledge from Raven was paying off.

Bettina air-kissed Whitaker. "What can Myrna do for you that I can't?"

Odessa leaned forward, waiting for the answer. She elbowed Whitaker. "Go ahead. Answer that question. I want to know the answer, too."

Whitaker frowned at Odessa. To Bettina, he said, "I'm on official police business."

Disappointment filled Odessa. She'd been hoping for a more fun answer. But obviously, Whitaker wasn't in the mood for fun anymore.

Bettina gave an elegant shrug. Odessa was starting to be very irritated with her. She had all the classic model gestures, but she missed the mark. Odessa had seen perfect and it was a little more relaxed than this. Bettina was as fake as a three dollar bill. There was a desperation about her. The kind of desperation that came from someone who hadn't realized their dreams.

What had Whitaker seen in her? He wasn't a stupid man, which meant he knew something about Bettina that others wouldn't recognize.

Bettina's clear blue eyes gave Odessa a shrewd appraisal as she looked down her thin, aristocratic nose. "Who's your…ah…little friend here?"

Odessa's eyebrows rose. She felt as though she were being dissected beneath the magnifying lens of a microscope. This wasn't the first time she'd felt this way, but it was still uncomfortable.

"I'm Odessa Ripley." She held out her hand and Bettina took it in a limp grip that Odessa couldn't resist crushing.

Bettina pulled away.

Myrna poked Bettina in the side. "Be polite, Bitty, the man is moving on."

Bettina's face clouded. "I told you to call me Bettina."

Myrna waved a hand. "Whatever. Wyatt said he came to see me. Don't you have an appointment to groom something? You've got that uni-brow thing working again."

Bettina wet her lips with a tiny pink tongue. "I'll just let you all get down to business."

Myrna simply smiled and shooed the blonde away. "It's time for the grown-ups to play." Bettina teetered back to her office and closed the door forcefully. At her exit from the field, the newsroom went back to its ordered sense of chaos and Myrna drew Whitaker and Odessa to an office with photos on every available inch of wall as well as awards on a cluttered table.

"I hate that woman," Myrna said as she closed the door.

In unison, Odessa and Whitaker said, "So do I."

Odessa glanced at Whitaker and grinned.

"Worst thing that ever happened was when you left her, Wyatt." Myrna sat herself down behind a desk piled high with papers, file folders and envelopes. "She went totally off the deep end. I had hopes for her when you married her. Though I could never figure out why you married her, I do know why she married you."

Odessa leaned up against the wall because there was no place to sit. She had to hear all about this one. "Tell me everything."

Myrna sighed. "Bettina likes fixer-uppers. Not that there is anything wrong with Wyatt. He's USDA fresh Grade A man flesh. He's why women read romances and men buy Marlboros. If I had been thirty years younger I would have taken you from that bitch and kept you all to myself." She shook a finger at Odessa. "You listen to me, little woman, this one is a keeper."

She remembered Wyatt saying that his ex wanted a project but Myrna was right. Wyatt was all man and pretty damn near perfect the way he was except for his smart mouth. It was hard to get much past him.

"Damn, Myrna," Whitaker said. "I'm standing right here."

Myrna threw an orange stress ball and hit Wyatt in the shoulder. "Shut up, Wyatt. I'm talking to her, letting her know the lay of the land."

Odessa couldn't keep the smile off her face. These two were like squabbling toddlers. Myrna was a kick-ass kind of broad, Odessa's kind of people.

Myrna slapped her desk with her palm. "Okay, let's get down to business. What do you need and what are you going to give me for it?"

That sent a shot of panic through Odessa; she needed to keep a low profile. She hoped Wyatt wasn't going to promise her an interview or some crap like that.

"Why is there always a price for love?" Whitaker asked.

"Because in my business," Myrna said, "love don't come free."

Wyatt sat on a corner of the desk. "Always the pragmatist, aren't you?"

Myrna sighed. "Well, if you'd married me instead of the bimbo—"

Whitaker cut her off. "Bettina isn't a bimbo. I know she's different, but there's quite an intellect under all that blonde hair."

Odessa thought it was pretty cool that he defended his ex even though there was obviously bad blood between them.

"You know that and I know that," Myrna said, "but I'm never going to let her know that I know."

Odessa pushed herself away from the wall. *Whitaker liked smart women, just not ones that were threatening. Hell, what does he see in me?* "So that's why you married her?"

Whitaker half turned on the desk to answer. "Bettina was a whole different person once upon a time. And I liked that person."

Myrna laughed, her whole body shaking. "Yeah, that was before she discovered anesthesia and plastic surgery." Myrna leaned her elbows on the desk. "Again I ask, what do want from me?"

Wyatt blushed. Odessa liked that he could still be embarrassed. Sometime in the future, she'd have to use that.

Wyatt leaned over and gave Myrna a dazzling smile. "I need the tapes of all the Ding Dong convenience store robberies, including the one where Philip Ripley was killed."

A glint of recognition showed in Myrna's eyes as she turned to Odessa. She slapped the desk. "Ripley. I knew I recognized that name." She gave Odessa a sharp glance. "You're Phil Ripley's daughter. I saw you at the funeral. I'm sorry for your loss."

Odessa didn't remember Myrna, but then so many people had turned up at the funeral and she had been in a daze over her father's death. Touched by Myrna's remark, she replied, "Thank you."

"Where are you going with this?" Myrna tapped her fingers on the arms of her chair.

Odessa stole a peek at Wyatt. He looked as if he were stuck between a tank full of great white sharks and a firing squad. Myrna could browbeat a confession from a statue. She almost had sympathy for him. She knew they had to throw Myrna a bone to get those tapes, but just how big a bone was up to Wyatt. And frankly, she had confidence that he would get what they needed without spilling the entire story.

"Fair question," Whitaker said, "but I can't really answer."

Myrna fingered a pencil sticking out from her hair. "But you're going to, aren't you?"

He flashed her that million dollar grin and Odessa was a bit jealous. For some strange reason she wanted that smile to be only for her. No, she couldn't go there. She'd come to Phoenix to do a job, not get involved with a man. When this was over, she was returning to D.C. and her life.

Whitaker leaned over the desk. "I share all my best gossip with you, Myrna."

"I don't want gossip." Myrna took the pencil out of her hairdo and jabbed it in the air. "I want something that spells 'ratings.' "

"Right this second, Myrna, I'm working in some murky water. Let me get to shore and your hand will be the first one I reach for."

Myrna was silent for a long second before nodding. "Okay. I'll get you a copy of the tapes." She picked up a phone and punched numbers on the pad.

Odessa was amused at Whitaker's ability to flirt his way out of anything.

Whitaker stood up, leaned over, and kissed Myrna on the cheek.

Myrna gave a half laugh. "I would have given you anything you wanted for a good steak dinner. Why not get these tapes from your department?"

"It's Saturday," Whitaker replied.

Good lie, Odessa thought. She almost believed him.

Myrna drummed her fingers on the desk, her eyes shrewd. "I smell national coverage here."

Whitaker smiled. "Play your cards right, you could end up at CNN."

Odessa had a moment of terror. She didn't want national coverage of anything. She didn't know what they were going to find. The Phoenix PD would look really, really bad when people started turning up dead. Not to mention that her bosses would start questioning her about her vacation. If anyone could recognize a Ripley 'hit,' they could.

He stopped before he opened the door. "Thanks, Myrna. Just for the record, we were not here."

"Got it," Myrna said and started talking on the phone. She put a hand over the mouthpiece. "VHS or DVD?"

"DVD," Odessa answered, "we can play it on my laptop."

They left the building, the DVD in a plastic case tucked into his jacket pocket. Whitaker pointed his remote at the truck.

Ripley trotted along next to him. "You're taking this investigation in a direction I'm uncomfortable with."

He knew exactly what she meant, but he asked anyway, "What do you mean?"

"Coy doesn't look good on you," she said, stopping next to the truck and glaring at him.

He was going to be on top when they had sex. Just for once he wished she would just let him do his thing without questioning his every breath. "You want the investigation done right. I'm in this to win. I want to know who killed a cop."

"I want to know who killed my father." Ripley poked him in the chest. "Everybody else doesn't have to know the business, too. You made promises to Myrna."

"Excuse me, refer back to rule number one—I'm in charge. And If I'm in charge and you have a problem with how I investigate, you can go home any time."

She crossed her arms over her chest.

Wyatt jabbed at her arm. "Don't pout at me."

"I don't pout."

"Yes, you do," Whitaker said. "You have that 'I'm taking my toys home' pout on your face."

"What happened to that good-ole-boy, go-with-the-flow detective? I want him back. I liked him better."

Well, that was just his persona. Now that things were heating up, she was going to get the bastard. Play time was over. "You're not comfortable because we're not in secret agent territory. You don't like it when I don't play by your rules."

"You are treading in snap-your-neck territory."

The death threats again. "I'm not afraid of you. I don't care how big a bad-ass you are." He watched the emotions play over her face. She wasn't happy. Apparently nobody ever told her no. "Let's go back to your house and watch these tapes."

"Don't you need to show them to your mommy?" Her voice was snide and insulting.

"Ripley, you keep on the trail, you're gonna find out how big a bad-ass I can be."

She mock shivered. "I'm so scared. Oh, that's right! You're breaking the rules. Bad boy. What would Mommy Dawson say?"

He jabbed a finger at her. "I'm done arguing with you. Let me tell you something about the rules of evidence right now. You're a career killer. Not only are you not a licensed law enforcement agent, but you're not even authorized to be my partner. If you screw up the investigation, the whole case could get tossed out of court so fast, the blonde would get knocked out of your hair. You didn't actually roll into town all undercover. You've already been involved in beating the shit out of skinheads, one of whom died in police custody. You need to take a back seat for awhile and play by the rules. If you want your father's killer brought to justice, then you pay attention to what I tell you." Telling her that felt good. Like he'd recovered his manhood. Damn, she was gonna be hot in bed.

"Okay, fine. I'll be a good girl and play by your rules. But I get to go freelance if things don't work out right. Are you okay with that?"

Am I okay with that? Hell no. "Then you make sure I don't catch you."

He opened the passenger side door and tossed the DVD in. Ripley pulled herself into the cab and he closed the door with a slam. How did he get himself into this? He liked playing the bad boy, but this was way over the limit. And he was too pretty to go to jail.

Odessa locked her mother out of the study. She and Whitaker prepared to study the different Ding Dong robberies over and over again. The first four robberies showed three men entering a convenience store brandishing guns. The picture was a grainy black and white with detail hard to distinguish. The men were laughing and acting like kids. Too bad they wore ski masks, Odessa thought A.J. had great face recognition software.

After the fourth robbery had been studied and dissected, Whitaker paused the DVD and ran a hand through his hair. "You realize that watching this next one, you're going to see your father die."

Odessa felt an odd catch in her throat. She'd already known that going in. Though not one to believe in karma, a flicker of a thought occurred to her. This was the price she had to pay for her past. "I'm tough, I can take it." The words rolled off her tongue more easily than she thought they would.

Her throat went dry. She could do this. How many times had she watched people die before and felt nothing? But she didn't really know if she would be able to hang on to her objectivity. Her father…she didn't know how she would react. She'd only let herself cry once. When she'd returned for the funeral, she'd carefully avoided watching the news during her three-day stay, because the tape of the robbery was playing on every station. She hadn't wanted to see her father's death. She wasn't sure she was ready now. But if she didn't watch she might never catch his killer.

"Ready?" Whitaker asked.

She gave a sharp nod, and he started the DVD playing again.

On the screen, her father entered the convenience store, grabbed his beers and stood in front of the counter and just as he started to pay for his six-pack, three men entered the store. Her father turned and after a second reached behind him for his gun. She watched the way the men surrounded him. One of the men shot the clerk and then another fired his gun. Her father slid slowly to the floor, clutching the edge of the counter. With her heart in her mouth, Odessa watched him die. She was frozen with grief, surprised at the depth of her feeling. She'd thought she'd come to terms with his death, but she hadn't. Not yet. Whitaker went back and viewed the scene again and then again. After the third viewing, Odessa managed to separate herself from her feelings. Being a blubbering mess wasn't going to accomplish anything.

"Something's not right," she said. "I don't know what, but give me a minute." She set up to make a copy of the DVD and went to her room to get her laptop. After she made a quick copy she slipped the copy in the other laptop and started them both again.

"Give me a clue," Whitaker said after they viewed the first four robberies yet again.

As she pressed the keys, she noticed her hands shook. She took a deep breath, trying to get her emotions back under control. "Look at these guys. They're having the best time of their lives. They walk in, point a gun at the clerk, roam around the store a little bit, take the Ding Dongs and call it a day." She pressed a key and set the DVD in that laptop to play only the scene where her father died. "Compare those guys with these." She pointed at the other laptop with the Ding Dong bandits on the screen going through with their robbery and grabbing the Ding Dongs off the shelf.

Once again she watched her father enter the store, greet the clerk and pick up his six-pack. Her father followed this routine every Friday night. He stopped at the same convenience store, and picked up a six-pack for poker with the boys.

She watched as her father set the beer on the counter. Then the door was flung open behind her father and the three men entered the store. First they killed the clerk and as her father reached for his weapon, they killed him.

"These guys are all business," she said. These men were pros, just like her.

"You do have a point. Did you notice something really odd?"

"I'm not sure, so much is already odd." Even though the killers wore the same ski masks and wore the same sloppy gym clothes, their attitude was different. She couldn't quite pick it up, but the Ding Dong bandits had slouched and moved in a careless, undisciplined manner. These men walked like soldiers, or cops, more straight-backed and efficient in their way of moving. Instead of Ding Dongs, they took Ho-Hos. "Restart the scene of your dad's murder again," Whitaker ordered.

She did as he asked and squinted, trying to see what he was seeing. "What are you looking for?"

He tapped the screen. "Anomalies. First, on the first four robberies there's only three men and no guard outside." He restarted the first robbery on Odessa's laptop. "Look here. The camera faces the entry door and there's no guard in any of those robberies. Just three men and they all enter the store. But in the last robbery there are four men. Three enter and one waits outside."

She followed his finger back and forth as he pointed at each screen. "The fourth guard could be standing out of range of the camera." She leaned forward to stare at the first robbery with the devil-may-care thieves.

"But the point is, if a guard is monitoring what's going on outside and inside, he needs to be at the door. And there is no guard, no fourth man standing outside. We have a discrepancy. We have the real Ding Dong bandits and pseudo-Ding Dong bandits who mistook Ho-Hos for Ding Dongs."

Tears threatened, but Odessa kept them under control. She wasn't going to give in to her feelings no matter how many times she had to view her father's death, even though each viewing was a knife thrust deep into her heart.

She watched her father fall again, seeing what was happening around him instead of just watching him. "Four men instead of three. Ho-Hos instead of Ding Dongs. And business instead of fun time." That was enough to tell her that someone had truly intended to murder her father and make it look as if he were just in the way of something else going down. Clever, but other questions came to mind. One of them being why the lead investigator hadn't noticed the same discrepancies.

"That shooter meant to kill your father," Whitaker said in a sad tone. "He was set up because I think he knew something someone else didn't want him to know."

"So what does this exercise prove?"

"Proves we have some smart bad guys." He stared at the figures on the screen as they left the store. Phil Ripley lay on the ground, a flood of blood staining the floor beneath him. "Restart that again."

She tapped a few keys, the screen went blank, and then she watched her father being killed yet again.

"Do you see that?" Whitaker said.

"I see a lot of things and none of them add up."

"Right there. Look at Mr. Gunslinger."

She bent close to the screen and watched. The shooter stood off to one side, almost completely out of view of the camera. He pointed his gun at her father. The gun went off, her father fell and the shooter waited a few seconds before twirling his gun like an old wild west gunslinger and dropping it into his pocket. "Nobody did that in the previous robberies."

"Yeah," Whitaker responded, his brow furrowed with concentration. "And I've seen that gun action before."

"Where?" She tried to keep the impatience out of her voice, but a little leaked through.

"Hell if I know. But I've seen that gun twirl before." He frowned with concentration.

"A firing range. Another cop. Another crime on tape." How could he not know? He was a cop trained to observe just as she was trained to act. She swallowed as her impatience slid toward anger.

"Don't rush me," he snapped. "I have to think about this."

"Think faster. Think harder. That guy killed my dad and I want him." She glanced out the window. The sullen afternoon overcast had given way to an early winter darkness. Her stomach growled and she realized they'd missed dinner. Though she vaguely remembered knocking at the door, they had both been so engrossed neither had answered and the knocking had eventually ended.

Her body was so cramped she felt shooting pains down the backs of her calves and across her shoulders, but her head was numb. She felt as though she should feel something more than the vague sense of anger that had started to build. "What now?"

"I'm still thinking."

Glass broke somewhere in the house. The alarm went off and Odessa heard her mother cry out. A popping sound came from the living room and Odessa smelled gasoline and fire.

She jumped to her feet and ran out the door. Smoke billowed down the hall from the living room, and her mother stood in the hallway crying. Odessa grabbed her. "Call the fire department," she screamed as she shoved her mother into the study.

Odessa raced for the kitchen. She found the two fire extinguishers her mother kept near the stove and ran back down the hall. Whitaker was tearing flaming drapes down from the broken windows. Cold air fueled the flames and they spread quickly from the drapes to the nearest chair and then hopped to the next chair. The carpet started to burn.

She tossed the second extinguisher at Whitaker as he stomped on the burning drapes. The sofa and another chair exploded into flame. Odessa pulled the pin and pointed the extinguisher at the sofa while Whitaker pointed his at the curtains.

"The fire department is coming," her mother called from the doorway.

"Get out of the house," Odessa yelled at her mother as she and Whitaker fought the flames. Her throat burned and her eyes blurred from the smoke, but she kept the fire extinguisher pointed at the burning sofa. As the flames sputtered, she heard the distant wail of the fire department siren.

CHAPTER SEVEN

Odessa watched the eastern horizon lighten. Standing on the cold, wet lawn, she saw the last of the fire trucks leave. The cops and the arson investigator had just left. Most of the neighbors who had come out to watch the fire had returned to their homes to get ready for the coming day.

Despite her exhaustion, Odessa faced her mother as she shoved her cell phone back in her pocket. "I called the airlines and made a reservation. Your flight leaves in two hours."

They stood on the lawn staring at the wreckage of the living room. Odessa could hardly bear to see the defeated look on her mother's face. Her long hair, which had escaped from the neat French twist she usually wore, hung down about a face lined with exhaustion and something Odessa couldn't quite name.

Celeste had wrapped a warm blanket around her shoulders. "I am not leaving my home."

For a brief moment, Odessa glanced pleadingly at Whitaker and he mouthed the words, What do you want me to do? The expression of confusion on his face should have told her he wasn't going to help. "You're a cop, tell her she has to leave."

He ran both hands through his blonde hair. "There is no you-have-to-leave-after-someone-tries-to-burn-down-your-house law. I think she should go someplace safer than here, but I can't make her go if she doesn't want to."

Odessa let out an exasperated breath. Why did she have to have such a difficult mother? Why couldn't she understand that by staying she was jeopardizing her life? Her brother got it. "Thank you for all the help."

"Don't be angry at Wyatt." Celeste tugged the blanket tighter about her shoulders.

Putting her hands on her hips, Odessa wanted to yell at the heavens. "I'm way beyond angry. Somebody tried to burn your house down and you want to stay. Do you want to give them a second chance?"

Celeste turned away from her. "I can hire someone to protect me. A security firm."

Like there was anyone in this city she was going to trust with her mother's safety. Maybe she should call Derek and have him come down. She bit her bottom lip, deciding not to. She already had enough people who knew her business to contend with. "If you get on a plane and go to D.C. you won't have to hire a security firm."

Her mother stared at the house. "I'm not going. I have lived in this house for twenty-one years. Everything…" A tremor in her voice stopped her. Celeste took a deep breath. "Everything that belongs to your father is in that house and I'm not running away."

Odessa put her hand on her mother's shoulder. She was about five seconds from falling on her knees and begging. "You're not running away. You're going someplace safe so that I can do what needs to be done and not worry about you." God, why did her mother have to be so obstinate now of all times?

Her mother turned to face her, tears running down her cheeks. "And that's what I'm afraid of. If I'm gone, you'll do something you'll regret."

Odessa closed her eyes for a second. Her mother was afraid that if she left, Odessa would go buck wild mad and kill everyone. Which had been her plan in the first place. Maybe it was time for a new path, at least on the surface. "I don't need you to keep an eye on me." She had enough to worry about because she didn't think she was going to get out of this situation without a jail sentence. "I don't need you to be my conscience."

Celeste said, "Yes, you do."

As she clutched her mother's shoulder, Odessa had to stop herself from shaking some sense into Celeste. "If I have to physically put you on the plane, I'll do it."

Celeste's chin went up. "You'll try."

Thank God terrorists weren't this hard to deal with. Odessa rounded on Whitaker, knowing she had just lost that battle. Without question, her mother was staying. They both knew it. "Say something."

"You're out gunned." Wyatt shrugged. "She's not going to budge. So we need to come up with a plan to keep your mother safe."

Thanks a lot, dude. "Arrest her. Put her in jail. She'll be safe there." Desperation called for serious measures.

"The skinhead wasn't," Whitaker said, reminding her of the skinhead so conveniently dead while in a prison ward at the hospital.

Odessa held up her hands. "No place here is safe. You need to go to D.C. Let's stop at Wal-Mart and get you some clothes."

Her mother raised her eyebrows. "I do not shop at Wal-Mart."

Sometimes her mother could be such a snob. "That's the only place I know where you can buy underwear and bullets twenty-four hours a day." She pointed at the burned out living room. "The house isn't safe."

"The house is fine." Celeste waved her hand in an imperious manner. "I spoke to the detective and the arson investigator and they both said I can stay, just not go into the living room."

A truck rolled into the drive with heavy plywood sheets in the back. The driver got out and approached them. Celeste started telling him what needed boarding up.

"Damn it." Odessa backhanded Whitaker on the arm. "I need to get that woman to safety, and you're not helping."

Wyatt grinned. "You can't make her do anything she doesn't want to do."

Odessa wanted to punch him again for his smugness. "Then help me persuade her."

"I don't know your mother from a hill of beans, and no matter how you cajole or threaten, she's not going anywhere. I've seen that look before."

"What am I supposed to do?" Odessa started pacing back and forth.

"Why not let the police handle the investigation and you protect your mother?"

Odessa stopped pacing to glare at him. "Hell, no."

"Your mother is your problem. I have a murder to investigate."

She jabbed him in the chest. "I swear to God, if you walk out and leave me alone to deal with this, I'll shoot you…you figure out the spot."

Whitaker grabbed her finger and held on tightly. "Listen, Ripley, your mother is not going anywhere. Hire someone to protect her."

His touch was warm. She could have pulled away anytime she wanted to, but she liked him touching her. "A bodyguard?"

As he glanced at the house and the surrounding houses, he let go of her finger. "You look like you could afford two or three bodyguards."

"I can see all my arguments aren't working. I'll hire a security detail, but only as long as they aren't white or ex-cops."

"What's up with that?"

She trusted him because her dad did, but she wasn't going to be taking any more chances. "This is a racist thing and a cop thing."

"So you're saying you won't hire white people or ex-cops! That's bullshit."

"Don't be offended, but cop loyalty runs deep. You all cover each other's ass. In my line of work, if my best friend messes up, I have no trouble putting two in the back of her head. In the CIA we trust nobody." Her little speech sounded good, even if it wasn't totally true. Odessa would kill herself before she killed Raven.

"Call Dawson's dad. He's an ex-cop, but he's black so that should make everything right with you."

"I guess I can overlook the ex-cop thing." Odessa trusted Dawson for the most part. Her father couldn't be too bad.

Whitaker whipped out his cell phone and walked a few feet away as he dialed and then held the phone to his ear.

Everything was spiraling out of control. Odessa's world did not spin out of control like this. She just wanted to hunt these people down and kill them in the most painful way she could think of. She wouldn't admit it to anyone else, but she was on the edge. Her hand itched to do something, anything.

The man from the truck started hammering plywood sheets over the broken windows. Odessa's mother stood off to one side looking haggard and tired as she watched.

Whitaker stood with his cell phone to his ear and Odessa realized he was taking care of things for her. While she felt a rush of gratitude, she also felt a bit annoyed. She tried to remember the last time she'd let a man help her.

She tilted her head and studied Whitaker. He wasn't so bad. He looked good even at this ungodly hour of the morning. And he cared, no matter how much he showed his macho side.

The sun had finally come up and it glinted off Whitaker's blonde hair. He was so tall and so broad, wearing those Wrangler cowboy jeans and fancy stitched boots. Damn! She was all hot and sweaty thinking about him. He flipped the phone closed and started walking toward her with that lopsided grin on his face as if he knew all her secrets. God, from the belt on down, he was built like a bull. She couldn't help the gusty sigh that escaped.

What the hell. She sighed, knowing that she was going to sleep with him before this was over, despite all her protests, and it was going to be some nasty, whipped cream, mind-blowing kind of sex. How long had it been since she'd had that kind of sex?

"Ripley," Whitaker said, "you're almost embarrassing me there."

"What do you want?" Damn, he'd just interrupted the best fantasy time she'd had in years. He was a smart-ass, macho, sarcastic kind of man. God, she could fall in love with him, but she wouldn't. Love didn't work for her.

"Dawson and her dad will be here in a hour. She wants to talk to you. And we're in trouble."

Yippie skippy, I can't wait. "I don't want to talk to her, I just want her father."

He shook his head. "We were playing outside of the sandbox without Mommy's permission."

"But how would Dawson know that unless you told her."

Whitaker put the phone in his pocket. "Give me a minute while I think up an answer that will get me out of trouble."

Odessa poked him in the chest. "You do that." She glanced around and realized that her neighbors across the street were going to work. A few cars had driven past, slowing to gawk at the damage. She felt too exposed.

Cher Dawson stood in the center of the study. She'd been yelling at Ripley and Wyatt for the better part of fifteen minutes. Wyatt had gone off to his little happy land and said yeah in all the appropriate places. He kept waiting for Ripley to whip out a little pen knife and gut his boss. She didn't seem like the kind of person who would take this 'you've been a naughty two year old' abuse with a grain of salt. He was used to Dawson's rants and raves. But in the end, he always brought his man home, and she would forgive him and he'd be back in the fold again. That was their relationship. He was comfortable with that.

"Are you done yet, boss?" Wyatt asked.

Dawson nailed him with a glare that said 'hell no.' "Whitaker, what the hell am I going to do with you?"

"Send me back to my old squad, cut me loose, let me be a real cop."

She ran her hand through her hair. "Let me get this straight. I tell you to stick to the Summersby investigation and you go off and do your own thing. What part of your anatomy do you want handed to you?"

"Wait a sec, Dawson," Ripley jumped in. "The man is coming to you with a hot lead and you're yelling at him. Where is a little of the 'job well done,' or 'Dude, you're a fabulous cop'?"

Wyatt was surprised Ripley would defend him, but he really didn't want or need her help.

Dawson took a deep breath. "You don't—"

"Wait a second," Ripley interrupted, "the man was thinking independently and doing a damn good job it." Ripley glared at Dawson, looking like a pit bull with a bone.

Wyatt was torn between retreating to someplace else or watching this. Why did he always end up with opinionated, hard-headed, obstinate women? He liked his fluffy, no brain dates with women who didn't make him think too hard.

David Dawson, Cher's father, checked his watch. "Whitaker, do you want to get a cup of coffee? Cher's got another hour or so of hot air inside her and your little friend doesn't look like she's going to give up ground anytime soon."

"This is so fascinating."

"I understand." Dawson clapped him on the back. "I had three sisters and this was my life every day. So let's go."

Dawson led the way to the kitchen where Jacques had left a pot of fresh coffee in a thermal carafe and arranged mugs on a tray with a plate of cookies. David Dawson poured two mugs and handed one to Wyatt.

David sat at the kitchen table. "So you think Phil's murder was premeditated."

Whitaker sipped from the mug. "Yes, sir. And I think it was a cop."

David frowned. "Why?"

Wyatt didn't have any authorization to tell David about the other murders, but he was Cher's father and if Wyatt couldn't trust David, who could he trust? Clearly and succinctly, Wyatt told David about the murders Phil Ripley had been investigating. "Because these murders were just too convenient. And the victims were the kind of people who are on our watch lists as agitators."

David tapped a finger on the table. "I knew Martin Borland. He was a good man. When his suicide was announced, I couldn't believe it."

"Why?"

The older man wrapped both his hands around his cup of coffee. "Martin and his partner had just been approved to adopt a daughter from China. They'd bought a house. His design firm was solidly in the black. That's not a man who commits suicide."

"What did the cops who investigated say?"

David sipped his coffee. "They acted as though it was a nothing case going nowhere. That was a bad year. We had a record high number of homicides. The police don't get pressured here the same way they do as they in San Francisco or New York when a gay man is dead under suspicious circumstances. Phoenix is not enlightened." He sounded sad and a little frustrated. He'd spent twenty-five years on the force hiding who he was. Even after he'd retied, David had been careful who he shared his private information with.

That shit ticked Wyatt off. All victims deserved the police's full attention. "Murder is murder. Who gives a shit who the person was? That's not our job."

"You can't tell me you don't look at the victim and form opinions."

"Whether I do or not, murder is illegal and my job is to find out what happened. There are a lot of people I think deserve to be dead, but when it's done in an illegal manner, I'm pissed. Phoenix is my town."

David half smiled. "You're a good cop, Whitaker, and Cher tells me all the time you're the best she's ever seen. You were her number one choice when she was given Cold Case."

Yeah, right, Wyatt thought. "Can you record that for me? I need independent corroboration."

David laughed. "Don't let Cher get your down. She's all bluster."

Wyatt sobered. Despite all that went on between him and the lieutenant, he really did like her. She was hard-nosed, but fair. She might threaten to fire him but she'd go to bat for him in front of any court in the land. "I know that and frankly, I like working for her, but don't tell her I said that. I don't want to ruin our relationship."

The door opened and Ripley walked into the kitchen and headed for the coffee.

"What did you do with the body?" Wyatt asked.

"Your boss is fine. She's watching the DVDs. We just needed to air some laundry between us." She poured coffee into a mug and selected a cookie. She munched the cookie as she leaned against the counter. "This is what I want," she said to David, "a twenty-four/seven detail with one man in the house and one man outside at all times. And I want guys who aren't afraid to clear leather and use their guns."

David nodded. "You've got it."

She planted her palms on the table and leaned over about an inch from Dawson's nose. "Parker Anderson works for you and he knows my rep. If I'm not happy nobody gets out alive."

David's eyebrows shot up, but he didn't back down. "What are you saying?"

Wyatt rolled his eyes. She looked so cute when she was threatening.

"If my mother chokes on a chicken bone, I'm coming after you all." Ripley straightened up.

"Fair enough." David held out his hand, and after a moment, Ripley shook it.

Wyatt wondered what he'd gotten himself into. He was going to die.

Odessa finished the cookie. "When will you have your men in place?"

"Within the hour."

"Good." She licked her fingers and finished her coffee.

Wyatt watched as Ripley wandered around the kitchen. She was fidgeting and looking anxious. What was bothering her? As David Dawson started outlining the procedures for protecting her mother, Ripley's eyes glazed over and she lost her focus.

Wyatt had the feeling that if David said one more word, Ripley would shoot him.

Ripley seemed to shake herself. She smiled at David and said, "I can see you have my mom's safety well in hand. Thank you for your effort." She glanced at Wyatt. "Let's roll. We have business to take care of."

Wyatt followed her out of the kitchen, down the hall to what was left of the front door and out onto the walkway. "What's up?" For someone who had been up all night, she still had a lot of energy. Wyatt was starting the feel the lack of sleep.

"You need to take me to the nearest Guns R Us store. Mama has to gear up."

She already had the biggest handgun this side of Chicago. What the hell else did she need? "And what does gearing up entail? Anti-tank hardware? Surface to air missile?" Wyatt asked as she stalked down the driveway to the street.

"I love when a guy talks dirty to me."

"Stop, I'm getting all excited." He held up his hand. "What are you going need?"

"I need the right toys because we are going after the bad boys." She stopped with one hand on the handle of the truck door. "David Dawson knows what he's doing; he doesn't need me around trying to second-guess him. I'm in a mood to kick some butt." She stared at the devastation of the house, frowning.

"And I have to come with you, risking my entire career and maybe my life?"

She blew him a kiss. "You're such a big bad-ass."

Wyatt unlocked the car. "Now you're trying to flatter my ego."

She slanted an amused glance at him. "Is it working?"

Always, he thought. "Tell you what, you can take me on a little road trip and we'll do whatever you want to do, but when all is said and done, you have to do whatever I want." And he knew exactly what he wanted.

"As long as it doesn't involve a roller coaster," she said. "I don't like roller coasters. I don't like thrill rides or jumping out of planes."

"The only thrill ride I had in mind for us is in my bedroom." All he had to do was get her to agree.

She rolled her eyes. "Okay, fine. You win. I'll have sex with you, but…if I need you to kill somebody, you'll have to do it, no questions asked. And don't worry about getting caught. I've covered up many a unexpected death and can make it look like anything you want it to look like."

Good thing she worked for the good guys. "Where is this Guns R Us you're looking for?"

"Downtown." She opened the passenger door. "This is Phoenix. There's always a gun show somewhere." She pulled herself into the cab.

Wyatt slammed the door. She was one prepared lady. She knew all about Arizona gun laws and that the best guns were the ones available at the gun show: no ID check, no waiting period, no records. No fuss, no muss. He would have offered the weapons he had, but he wasn't much of a gun nut. He had his service weapon, a couple rifles to shoot rattlesnakes and a shotgun. Nothing special and he had the feeling she was going after special.

An hour later, Wyatt couldn't contain his amazement. Ripley shopped like a pro. He'd been with Bettina once when she'd stormed through a store and racked up five grand worth of clothes in less than forty minutes. Wyatt held Odessa's purchases as she traversed the long aisles jostling elbows with gun dealers, collectors and the curious.

Ripley walked in front of him, a phone to her ear. Wyatt had no idea who she was talking to, but when she finished, she folded the phone and turned to him. "Do you have a couple guys you trust to cover your ass?"

"Jackson and Greyhorse. They'll do whatever we need." Though he hesitated to involve them. Greyhorse had a streak of morals and Jackson was newly married. Wyatt didn't know if Jackson wanted to risk his life after so short a time with his new bride. His new wife was a little on the fragile side after having a stalker kill her parents and attempt to kill her. Jackson didn't like leaving her alone for too long.

"It's too bad that skinhead had to die," she said as she stopped at a booth to examine a flashy looking red Glock. "I had some questions for him and I'd have only made him wish he wanted to die."

"His compatriots are unknown."

She waved her phone. "Not anymore. I know where they hang when they aren't beating people up."

He stopped dead in his tracks. "How did you find out?"

Sauntering over to him, she smiled. "Your problem is that you local cops aren't on a friendly basis with the FBI."

"And the CIA is?"

"We have access to all their information." She had a secretive look in her eyes.

He couldn't believe the Feebs shared anything, much less important info. "They share with you with no problems?"

She shrugged as she put the Glock down and shook her head at the hopeful-looking clerk. "Only a problem if we get caught. That's why it's so friendly." She'd told him she'd stolen information from them once before.

"When I have to deal with the Feebs, I'm coming to you."

"Happy to help."

"So why the skinheads?" he asked even though he already knew. He just wanted to hear her say it.

"Because," she said as she continued down the aisle, "they're at the bottom of the food chain and the bottom feeders are always easiest to rattle. Who else is gonna give us the info we need to start moving up the ladder of evolution?"

"Okay, but you have to make me one promise."

She rolled her eyes at him. "I already said I'd have sex with you. What else could you possibly want?"

"I'm too pretty to go to jail. So whatever you do and whoever you do it to, make sure it's not within earshot or view of me."

Waving her hand as if to dismiss his worry, she smiled. "These people aren't going to report us. Everything will be fine."

Fine for her, he thought. He had a career to think about and so did Jackson and Greyhorse. "Okay, but beating up skinheads is not going to look good at our trial."

"What trial?"

"The one that's gonna happen after they arrest you, me, Greyhorse and Jackson."

Ripley shook her head. "People like me don't have trials," she whispered.

He leaned in closer to her. "Who punishes the bad CIA agents?"

She grinned. "They send me after them. And since this is just me being bad, when this is over I'll have to shoot myself and dispose of the body."

That was funny in a dark, creepy, morbid sort of way, but he didn't laugh. "I want to watch you dispose of the body."

"You've never heard of the 'leave no witnesses' rule? You'll have to go with me."

"Just as long it's Mexico with lots of tequila."

She stopped at another booth and idly picked up a Heckler & Koch semi-automatic. She handled it like the pro she was, but the clerk, a kid who looked barely out of puberty, tried to give her all the fun info about the weapon. She glared at the guy menacingly and he fell silent. She whipped a wad of cash out of her pocket to pay for the Heckler & Koch. "I can go for Mexico," she said, "but I have a sweet little place in Martinique."

She had a house in Martinique! The CIA was well-paid. He could barely afford his ranch. If not for his brother, he would never have had the down payment. "Ah! De islands, mon. That's about the right speed."

She glanced up sharply. "I'm done here. Take me to your house."

"What for?" Hope flared up in him and he started wondering if he had enough condoms.

"What do you think? I need to clean my guns and I don't want my mom to see what I have. She'll start getting all moral on me and I'll start feeling guilty. And then I'll have to lie. Let's just go to your house. You should have what I need."

His mind went blank. Ripley at his house made his blood race. "Yeah! A bed, condoms—"

She held up a hand. "Down big boy. Business before pleasure. And you better have clean sheets on the bed. Because if not, there's nothing in this world that would induce me to do what you have in mind."

He'd known it was too good to be true. "Damn! I was getting all ready for that good time you promised me."

She left the building that housed the show and headed for his truck. He trailed behind her carrying her guns. His mama would have been proud of him for carrying her packages. Such was the life of a man in lust.

CHAPTER EIGHT

Odessa put the Heckler & Koch down on the dining room table. Each of the guns she'd purchased was cleaned, loaded and completely untraceable. She looked up to catch Whitaker staring at her. He leaned back in an overstuffed leather chair, his leg hooked around the arm of the chair. From her vantage point she could see a big ole erection just waiting for her.

Her heart raced and she found herself nervous. That was strange. The last time she had been this jittery was way back when she had still been a virgin. That was a long time ago. She wondered what had ever happened to…she couldn't remember his name, but he'd been a jock on the high school football team and so full of himself. Even at seventeen, Odessa hadn't been easily dazzled. She'd simply wanted her virginity ended and he'd been available. Poor guy. He hadn't even been important enough for her to remember his name, just the fumbling actions of his eagerness to prove he was better than the average Joe.

She came back to the present, aware that Whitaker watched her with avid expectation. What was it about him that made her so edgy? His magnificent body? His scintillating humor? His eager beaver attitude? She couldn't figure it out. Maybe she was more emotionally attached than she liked. He knew some of her secrets. The only thing she knew for sure was that she wanted him.

She stripped off the latex gloves she'd used to clean her new guns and walked over to the blazing fire in the fireplace, tossed the gloves into the flames and watched them melt. She took off her thick leather belt and dropped it to the floor. Then she lifted her sweater over her head. She turned to look at Whitaker.

His foot slid to the floor and he stood, open-mouthed.

"I smell like gun oil, I'm going to take a shower." She tossed her sweater at him.

He caught the sweater and stood holding it as though he didn't know what he wanted to do with it. "There's girl soap in the hall closet."

"Girl soap? You must have a lot of company." She regretted the comment as soon as it left her mouth. She sounded jealous and immature. She didn't want to know about him and other women. She doubted that he was a saint. He was desirable and could probably have any woman he set his mind on. So why did she feel such a stab of jealousy? She didn't own him. He didn't own her.

"My mother stays with me when she's in town. I keep a supply on hand; she's not the most logical packer." He dropped her sweater on the chair. "Besides, I don't want you smelling like Irish Spring."

She pulled off one motorcycle boot and dropped it to the floor with a thud. "What do you want me to smell like?"

He grinned wolfishly. "Sex."

"You intend to help me with that?"

He took a deep breath. "You've got five minutes to get all sparkly clean."

She took off the other boot. "You make that sound ominous."

He walked over to her and stopped just inches in front of her. "You and I have some serious business to attend to."

"You haven't even kissed me yet."

His arm snaked around her waist and he lifted her up until their eyes were level. His other hand slipped under her butt and she locked her legs around his waist.

She could see the lust and need plainly in his blue eyes. She felt the same way.

"Screw the shower." His lips claimed hers with rough intensity.

She didn't need a shower. What she needed was this man inside her. Odessa's lips parted and he pushed his tongue inside. Their tongues warred with each other. Sex was not going to be easy with him. He would want to be dominant. She wanted to be dominant. They were never going to see eye to eye.

He squeezed her buttocks as she circled her arms around his neck. He began walking. A few seconds later he lowered her until her back hit the solid oak dining table. She began clawing at his shirt. Buttons flew off. She had to touch his skin.

His hands went to her T-shirt. The hem lifted and he broke contact with her mouth to strip her of the soft cotton. As soon as her chest was bare, his lips went to one of her nipples.

Odessa's back arched as his tongue flicked the pebbled point of her nipple. A moan escaped her and her heart raced as his lips moved over her heated skin. She began to shake with anticipation as his mouth moved to her other breast.

"Perfect," she heard him say.

She liked the fact that her body pleased him, that she turned him on. The zipper on her jeans rasped down and his hand slid between her skin and the denim. She was on fire, out of control. For a brief second she felt exposed. She usually took command of her sexual encounters. But with Wyatt things were different. To feel so uninhibited was all new territory for her.

He chuckled as he nibbled her skin.

She tensed.

He slid his fingers down toward the nub of her sex. "I love women who leave their panties off."

Should she spoil it for him and tell him she'd abandoned her Lady Jockeys after he made the crack about what he thought she wore? Hell no, she thought. Let him think she always went without underwear.

His finger slipped inside her, easily reaching the most sensitive area. Her hungry internal muscles clenched around his finger. She wiggled, trying to get him deeper inside her. "Wyatt, I…"

"Oh baby, I can't wait much longer."

She didn't want him to. "Please."

He added another finger and flicked her clit with his thumb. "I knew you'd be sweet."

Odessa kinda liked his sexy talk. He made her feel naughty in a way no other partner she'd had the last ten years had ever done. When was the last time a man had made her feel as if they were more than just exchanging body fluids? Never that she could remember.

He started pulling off her jeans. First down one leg and then the other. His fingers were warm and teasing and her skin felt like liquid fire. When she was naked and lying on top of the table, her legs spread wide open to him, he pushed back and smiled at her, his gaze moving over her body as though caressing her.

He pulled off his shirt slowly, seductive and teasing. His chest was tight and taut and his abs were like steel. Muscles rippled as he slipped two fingers into his jean's pocket and pulled out a condom pack.

Odessa raised herself on her elbows. "Party favors."

He grinned. "Nothing says 'I care' like a Trojan ribbed for her pleasure."

She bit off a sigh threatening to escape. "You know what women like." A spurt of jealousy consumed her as she thought about the number of women he'd practiced on.

"Yes, I do." He peeled his pants down slowly, pausing dramatically before freeing that beautiful full, thick penis, already hard with the tip glistening. It stood tall and proud, touching his flat stomach.

Odessa couldn't help it. She sighed. "Bring that little somethin' somethin' over here." Before she died from the pleasure of seeing it.

"First, there is nothing small about my somethin' somethin'. Got it?"

She almost saluted. "Loud, proud and clear, sir."

He put the condom pack between his teeth and ripped it. Slowly he sheathed himself.

Odessa could barely stop herself from drooling as he rolled the latex down, covering his penis. All for me, all for me, she chanted to herself.

Slowly, he ran his hand up her leg, stopping to tickle her inner thigh before moving up her hip, across her flat stomach, to gently caress her breasts. "What do you like?"

"For you to shut up and get down to business."

His eyebrow rose. "No foreplay?"

"Next time."

He grabbed her around the waist and pulled her to the end of the table. Before she could catch her breath he buried himself so deep inside her she almost exploded. She bit her lip to stop from screaming out in pleasure. Her internal muscles spasmed, trapping him inside her. Odessa clamped her legs around his waist, trying to force him deeper. She wriggled her butt. He caught his breath. His chest rose and fell rapidly, as though he were running a marathon. The moment was sublime.

Slowly he ground his hips between her legs, stretching her, hitting the most sensitive spots inside her. She clutched his arms, keeping him close, feeling him deep inside her. Exquisite sensations raced up her body and she started to shake.

He began to slide in and out, pulling himself all the way out and than entering her as deeply as he could. He massaged and kneaded her nipples until they were so hard she thought she would die from the sensation of pleasure rippling through her.

He held onto her hips as he nibbled her ear. "Look at me," he commanded.

Odessa opened her eyes as he lifted her off the table without breaking the connection between their bodies. He thrust hard into her and she gasped. Her breasts ached, and her core was hot and pulsing.

Spasms began to work up her spine. Odessa could feel herself losing control as he impaled her on his shaft. She wrapped her arms around his neck and began to push herself down on him. His lips met hers in a furious kiss. Odessa knew that she was going to come soon. She wanted to hold out, but Wyatt had way too much control over her body.

The ripples started deep inside her, building and building until she felt poised on the edge of a cliff. Then she exploded into pleasure. She tried to catch her breath, she tried to have a thought, but nothing came. Her climax went on and on, each wave crashing into the next until she could barely stay sane. Seconds after she climaxed, Whitaker's body stiffened and he groaned. His climax fed hers and she erupted once more into the cascading waves that made her shudder and gasp for air. She pushed him deeper and the spasms continued on and on until she thought she might faint. A scream built inside her and as the last waves of her climax erupted, the animal inside her was released and she screamed long and loud until her throat was raw. She went as limp as a newborn. Her head fell forward against his chest and she sighed.

Slowly Whitaker lowered her onto the table. She rested her head against his chest. She couldn't think, couldn't breathe, couldn't focus on anything but the fading cascades of pleasure that left her shaken and wanting more. Whitaker gently caressed her cooling skin. Their harsh breath was the only sound in the room. If not for his arms around her, she would have fallen back on the hard wood of the table. She would have fainted dead away. Never in her life had she had sex like this.

She didn't know how long she continued to sit on the table with him still inside her. She felt him stir and would have gone another round except she was so pleasantly tired, so totally satiated. She pushed her hand through his damp hair. "That was—"

He stared at her through slitted eyes, groggy with the intensity of their pleasure. "I know."

"—not bad," she finished.

For a second he simply stared at her, and then he began laughing. His penis begin to harden. "Again?"

"Oh hell, yeah."

Wyatt listened to the sound of water running in the shower. Ripley had been in there for less than five minutes and already he felt as though he could go another round. He couldn't believe how terrific the sex had been. He was still stunned over the intensity between them, the way her body had reacted to his. Not the sex part. That was a given from about five seconds after he laid eyes on her. What sent him for a loop was how he felt about it. He couldn't remember any other woman who had satisfied him as thoroughly as she had. Not even with Bettina in the early days of their marriage when the sex had been outstanding.

He kept replaying the scene with Ripley over and over in his head. He didn't just find physical pleasure with her; he connected with her on another level. Shit. The last time he'd thought he had connected with a woman like that he'd married her and look what had happened there.

The problem with Ripley, despite the fabulous sex, was that she brought him a brand of trouble he wasn't sure he could skate over, nor was he sure he wanted to. But he liked hanging out with her. She was cynical, funny, and except for her disdain of country-western music, was great company. He liked trading barbs with her; he liked knowing she didn't defer to him about every decision. She just did what she had to and moved on.

The phone rang before he could get more deeply into what was going on in his head. "Yeah?"

"It's Jackson."

"You're still up for tonight?"

Marco Jackson laughed. "I'm even bringing company."

"Who?" Wyatt asked warily. The Jackson clan had ties to every major law enforcement agency in the world. Make that the universe. One of the Jackson brothers had just had a kid accepted at MIT who had a eye on NASA for the space program.

"Elena and Roberto."

Oh shit, was this going to be a big Jackson family affair? "Why?"

"Because if I don't, there's no telling who Elena will blab to."

Wyatt had only worked with Elena Jackson briefly before she'd left the force. "You're sure they're okay with this?"

Again, Marco laughed. "Elena is about to bust a gut, she's so excited to be back in the saddle again—so to speak. And who is Roberto going to tell? He's already at the top of his food chain, more or less."

True, SWAT Commander Roberto Jackson was not the most chatty of men even in the best of times and except for his captain, he was at the apex of his career. Elena was no longer on the force, since she'd married, become a mother and started her own private investigation firm. "This might not—"

"You never know when you're going to need another gun, my friend," Marco said. "You know Elena and Roberto are good at keeping quiet. You don't need to worry about them."

"I'm not," Wyatt said. "See you in about an hour." He hung up just as Odessa walked out of the bathroom zipping up her jeans. She hadn't put on her T-shirt and he had an unobstructed view of her small breasts. Who knew that her breasts would have given him more pleasure than he would have believed possible?

"The shower is all yours," she said.

"Damn, you're quick."

She pulled her T-shirt over her head and tucked it into her jeans. "I'm not like most girls."

He stood, then realized he was still naked when she smiled. "That's one of the things I like most about you."

Standing on tip-toes, she kissed him. "Hope you can still say that after tonight."

She didn't fool him. She didn't need him to do this. This was her way of playing safe. "I'm not worried about you."

"If you say so."

He wasn't going to get in an argument with her. She wouldn't have invited cops along if she intended to kill anyone. This was a sign she trusted him. At least in his skills as a cop.

CHAPTER NINE

Odessa parked the rented Suburban in the middle of the Wal-Mart parking lot. She searched the parking lot. "Is anyone here yet?"

"Not that I can see." Wyatt relaxed his fingers from the hand grip over the door. He hated the lack of control as a passenger. Even though Odessa was a reasonably good driver, she was a little too aggressive for him.

She opened the driver's door and jumped out. "I want to go inside while we're waiting for everyone."

"Why?" Wyatt asked.

"I have shopping to do."

He followed her across the parking lot. This was no time to go shopping. "The last thing you need is ammunition."

She shook her finger at him. "A girl can never have enough bullets and in D.C. I have to drive a long way to get to a Wal-Mart. I just love shopping here."

Now that surprised him. People with money usually didn't like mingling with the common folk that shopped at a place like this. "You do?"

She stopped and turned to grin at him. "Yeah! Under that roof you can get everything from furniture to zucchini. I love Wally World."

Wyatt hated Wal-Mart. The store never made any sense to him. He always ended up wandering for hours just to find one thing. He liked to shop on the Internet, basically he was a point and click man at 2 A.M. in his boxers.

The doors swished open and they walked into the chaos that seemed to be Wal-Mart. A greeter shoved a cart at Odessa and she took it with a gracious thank you.

Dammit, she was getting a cart. A cart only meant one thing: She was going to be there for hours. "What do you need a cart for?"

"This is an adventure. Look, just stay outside and don't bother me. I'll be back in fifteen minutes but if the line is long, make it twenty minutes."

He didn't care how great the sex was, it wasn't worth a trip to Wal-Mart. "Nobody gets out of Hell in fifteen minutes."

She tapped her watch. "Time me." She strolled off without another glance.

He was going to make her pay for this.

Fourteen minutes and forty-five seconds later, Odessa walked out carrying a bag. Wyatt studied the bag and decided she hadn't bought a gun. She led the way back to the Suburban and as they approached it, Marco Jackson parked on the other side. Elena Jackson-North popped out of the car, followed by her brother Roberto and then Marco.

Wyatt hadn't seen Elena in months and he admitted that he missed working with her. Her face was alight with anticipation.

Jacob Greyhorse pulled into another parking spot and got out. "Where's the party?" he asked as he approached Wyatt.

"On the outskirts of town where all the bad little boys and girls meet," Wyatt replied.

Marco leaned against the Suburban. "This had better be good. I'm giving up hockey tickets for this."

"Don't worry, we're gonna have a ton of fun." Odessa rubbed her hands together.

"What's in the bag?" Wyatt stared at the blue Wal-Mart bag in her hands.

"Just some assorted party favors." She opened the driver's door. "Saddle up, posse, and let's go." She climbed inside and Wyatt gritted his teeth. If not for the fact they hadn't wanted his truck on the scene of their forthcoming party, he would never have allowed her to rent the Suburban.

After everyone was buckled in, Odessa opened the bag and tossed ski masks to those in the back. "For the party." Then she reached into the bag and brought out a CD and hummed as she unwrapped it..

Wyatt tried to see what the CD was, but couldn't. He was hoping for Kenny Chesney, but didn't think he had a hope in hell of hearing something he liked. She pushed the CD into the player and the next second he was assaulted by an accordion playing polka music. He resisted the urge to put his hands over his ears. *She listens to polka music.*

He turned around and saw that the mouths of the others were hanging open in amazement. From the corner of his eyes, he could see Odessa bopping along with the tempo. Roberto tapped Wyatt on the shoulders and mouthed the words, "What is this shit?"

Wyatt reached over to turn the music off. Odessa slapped him on the hand. "I'm listening to that."

He liked to think he was a tolerant man about other people's taste in music, but this was inhuman. "I am not listening to this crap."

Her whole body bopped to the tune. "Hey, this is my car and my tunes. That's the rule."

"In whose rule book?"

She stopped moving and pulled the lapel of her of her black leather jacket revealing her shoulder holster. "Ms. Heckler & Koch's rules."

He didn't care if she blew a hole in the side of his head; it would be better than listening to her stupid music. "I'm not letting this one go, so put your weapon away. Do you know what this stuff is doing to us."

She nodded her head. "Pretty much the same thing it's doing to me."

If he was quick he could get the CD out of the player and only suffer a flesh wound. "It's irritating the hell out of us."

She grinned. "Me, too."

Did she just say what he thought she said? "Then why the hell are we listening to this shit?"

"Because it puts me in the mood to kick ass."

From the back Jacob said, "Rock on."

"Word up, my sistah," Elena Jackson North shouted from the back seat.

Wyatt started laughing. Once he started, he couldn't stop. In the back of the car, everyone else joined in.

Odessa turned the volume up and started the Suburban. She backed out of the parking space and headed for the freeway.

The sun had gone down by the time they arrived at their destination. The Roadhouse Bar and Grill was a dingy shack with a gravel parking lot and a row of motorcycles neatly lined up against the side. The rest of the parking lot contained trucks, a few sedans and a couple of SUVs. A few dispirited Christmas lights twinkled from the only window. A florescent 'open' sign winked drearily in one corner.

Ripley parked at the front door, and turned off the motor. To Wyatt's relief the polka music finally stopped..

She unfastened her seatbelt and opened the driver's door. "Give me a moment. I'm going in to warm up the crowd." She jumped down and headed toward the door while putting on her ski mask.

Wyatt glanced down at his crotch and looked up. "You know," he said with a glance at Roberto, "this morning I had my balls. I don't know where they are at this moment, but I want them back."

Marco patted Wyatt's shoulder. "You do realize that what we are doing could put us out of a job, get us killed, or worse yet, send us to prison with all the people we've put in there for the last ten years?"

It didn't bear thinking about. "Yeah." If he had to chose, he was going with dying.

"This is going to be so much fun," Elena chimed in, her voice full of excitement.

In unison, Roberto and Marco said, "Shut up, Elena."

Elena laughed. "Come on, you two. The most action I see nowadays is fighting my way to the Pampers aisle for a two for one special."

She pulled the ski mask over her face, opened her door, and jumped out. "I want to kick the butt of someone over eight months old."

Jacob stared at his ski mask. "You know, there's something wrong when the women lead the charge."

"Whitaker, I'm wondering where my balls are, too," Roberto Jackson said.

In all the time Wyatt had known Roberto Jackson, this was the most conversation he'd ever heard from the guy.

Elena was already at the door by the time Wyatt and the other men got out of the car. As Wyatt put on his ski mask, he heard two shots. Everyone ran toward the bar, pulling on their ski masks and grabbing their guns.

Wyatt burst inside and saw Odessa standing in the center of the bar with her guns out and one foot holding down the neck of a skinhead sprawled on the floor. A photo of Adolph Hitler hung over the bar with a bullet hole right in the middle of his forehead. The stereo system was smoking. She had stepped over the line, he thought. This was so not right.

Elena covered Ripley's back, her head moving back and forth as she scanned the crowd, her gun waving in the air.

Wyatt took up a position at the door. Marco, Roberto and Jacob fanned out behind the patrons, their guns drawn.

The bartender was reaching behind the bar for something and Wyatt trained his weapon on the guy. "Go ahead, give me a reason."

The bartender slowly raised his hands and backed away.

Ripley put her guns away. She reached down and pulled the skinhead to his feet. Wyatt recognized him as a member of the gang who had attacked them. He had been the one that had the knife, but instead of fighting he'd run away, escaping punishment.

She held Knife Boy by his shirt and sat him down in a chair. She slapped him on the back of the head. "I didn't get to beat up on you the other day. I'm here to rectify that."

Wyatt felt a tiny touch of sympathy for the guy, but was way more worried about ending up on Cell Block H as somebody's girlfriend.

Knife Boy was trying to act tough, but he'd already shown himself a coward when he'd run the first time they'd met. If there was one thing Wyatt had discovered about gangs, they were like dogs with a stare-down to figure out dominance. Faced with real opposition, they ran. And Knife Boy was a runner. His bravery came from numbers, not from anything he carried inside himself.

In less than a minute, Odessa reduced the kid to the slobbering, crying juvenile he was. What a sight to see. It was almost worth the possible trip to jail.

Odessa was talking to him, her arm around his neck in a friendly gesture with the exception of her thumb jammed in his windpipe. Tears rolled down the kid's face.

Glass broke behind him. Wyatt whirled in time to see Roberto walk through the door with a short, bald man in his grip, the man's feet dangling above the ground. "I caught a little one. Can I keep him?"

Ripley eyed Roberto. "Tag him and toss your trout back."

Roberto pointed to Ripley. "But you have someone to play with."

Wyatt pinched the bridge of his nose through the ski mask. "Just do as the lady asked. Please."

Roberto shoved the man away. The guy crashed into the bar, hitting his head, and slid groaning down to the dirty floor.

"Oops!" Roberto said.

"Yeah, oops," Wyatt agreed.

Roberto chuckled. "That's gonna hurt in the morning."

Wyatt wanted to say that was going to hurt into the next decade.

Odessa straightened, dragging her skinhead up by the scuff his shirt. She prodded him toward Wyatt. "This one is going to come play with us for awhile."

Wyatt took the kid by the arm and headed to the door.

"Don't hurt me," the kid whined.

"Shut up." Wyatt had no patience for anyone who didn't have the courage of their convictions. Hurting others was okay for the kid, but he wasn't much into his own pain. What a wuss.

Odessa walked over to a wall which held a large Nazi flag. Grabbing it, she tugged. The flag ripped and came down. She threw it on the ground, spat on it and walked on it, dragging her feet with each step For a few seconds she stood there almost as if she were daring anyone, including the renegade cops, to say anything.

Nobody did.

Then everyone started backing out of the room. "Enjoy the rest of your evening."

Out in the parking lot, the moon had finally risen, casting the desert landscape into eerie shadow. Wyatt guided the kid toward the Suburban. As he opened the door to throw the kid in, Marco, Roberto, Elena and Jacob backed out the door. Odessa followed.

Odessa closed the bar door with a firm slam. As she started toward the Suburban, she paused at the row of motorcycles. With one foot, she kicked the nearest motorcycle over and in a domino effect, they all fell down into a pile of metal. For a second, she just stood there admiring her handiwork, a broad grin on her face.

What a beautiful sight. Wyatt couldn't count the number of times he'd wanted to do exactly the same thing. Damn, she was definitely his kind of woman.

Jacob inclined his head toward Wyatt. "I know where your balls are."

Wyatt stared at Odessa sauntering over to the SUV as if she didn't have a care in the world. "Where?"

Greyhorse smiled. "In her left pocket."

Knife Boy snickered and Wyatt jabbed him in the ribs with his elbow. "Shut up, you asswipe." Wyatt had enough to handle without the enemy thinking it was funny.

Ripley climbed into the driver's seat, started the motor and headed down the dirt road back toward the city lights.

"I don't know anything," Knife Boy whined.

"I don't care." Ripley tapped the steering wheel.

He snarled at Ripley. "You can't do anything to me."

She snorted. "I'm gonna do to you what you and your buddies intended to do to me."

"Kidnapping is illegal," Knife Boy cried. He obviously knew something of the law.

Ripley shrugged. "Yes, it is, but I don't care."

"Dumb ass, shut up." Wyatt needed to bring both of them down.

"His name is Stan Blackman," Odessa broke in, "which is rather ironic, him being a white supremacist and all."

Laughter came from the back of the Suburban. Wyatt couldn't help thinking that everyone was having way too much fun and that he and Stan were the only white people in the car.

Ripley drove for a few miles and then pulled to the side of the road and parked in the shadow of some rocks. She turned in the driver's seat and smiled at Stan. "Stan, you have two choices. You can either tell me what I need to know and I'll only give you a little beat down so that it looks like I had to force you to cooperate, or I'm gonna kick the righteous shit out of you. I'll break a few fingers, crack a few ribs, maybe gouge out an eye, and then I'll pull your teeth out. And then you're gonna tell me what I need to know. Those are your choices, Stanley. What's it gonna be?"

Stan's eyes were wide and round. He looked like Bambi's stupid brother.

Wyatt felt himself start to sweat. What were the other cops going to do while she kicked the crap out of this kid? He couldn't let it get to that point.

Roberto leaned over the front seat and patted Stan's shoulder. "He must be processing the situation."

Ripley jabbed at her watch. "Ticktock, Stan. Who's your man in the police department?"

Stan's lips started moving, but no sounds came out. He began to tremble.

Odessa sighed. "Get him out of the car."

Wyatt grabbed Stan, not to get him out of the car, but to keep him inside. "No."

Stan turned to Wyatt. "I don't know who he is," Stan cried. "They just call him the Gunslinger."

Odessa grabbed Stan's chin and yanked his head around. "Ever see his face, honey?" Odessa asked.

He nodded his head.

She squeezed his chin harder and Stan yelped. "Well, describe him to us."

Wyatt was relieved Stan wasn't going to get his ass kicked.

"Tall, blonde hair, blue eyes. Old, real old, about forty."

"Forty's not old," Wyatt said, considering that he was getting close to that territory himself.

Another snicker sounded from the back and Wyatt felt as though he was the only stinking grownup in the car. Now that was a role reversal.

"All right," Ripley said, "time to take you out of the car, slap you around a little and call it day. Just tell us where to drop you off and we'll take you wherever you need to go." She pulled a wad of cash out of her pocket. "Even the bus station."

Wyatt grinned at Stan, finally comfortable enough to take his hand off the kid's shoulder. "Nothing says thank you like cash."

She waved the wad in front of Stan.

"Take the money and run, son," Jacob called from behind Stan.

Stan twisted around. "I'm not your son."

Jacob punched him in the nose.

Odessa threw the money on Stan's lap. "Stop that! I'm the one who supposed to beat on him."

"I'm sorry," Jacob said, though he didn't sound sorry. "My hand slipped. Old age, you know. I'm almost forty."

More snickering came from the back.

Odessa sniffed. "Well, I guess I can't beat on you now. All this foreplay and no action. Makes a girl all cranky."

Wyatt grinned. Finally. He knew just what to do with a cranky girl.

Odessa dropped Stan off at the bus station and then returned the others to their cars at Wal-Mart. Odessa drove back to Whitaker's ranch. They didn't talk. Both were lost in their thoughts. Though the evening had gone well, she felt a nagging in the back of her head, telling her that Whitaker wasn't happy for some reason. She parked next to his truck. In the morning they would return the Suburban to the rental agency at the airport. She turned to Wyatt. "That was fun, wasn't it?"

"No." He stared out the window at his home.

"Come on." She tried to jolly him out of his dark mood. "Don't tell me you don't think about doing things like that all the time."

"Maybe, but the point is, I don't. I follow the rules."

Odessa snorted. "Just barely."

He turned to face her, his eyes grave and almost sad. "I've never thrown a suspect around a bar."

Odessa leaned back in the driver's seat. "You can't tell me in all your years as a cop you never put a shakedown on some bad guy."

"Not physically."

Odessa knew he'd taken it to the line on more than one occasion, but she suspected he hadn't crossed it. "Look, I understand. In your world you have to play patty-cake with a suspect because they have rights, but in mine the rules are a little more flexible."

"Where did you get your training? Iraq?"

She leaned her head back against the headrest. "Those were the days."

He gave her an odd look. "You haven't tortured anybody, have you?"

That one made her gut clench. He'd touched on something she wasn't very proud of. "That's an odd question to ask someone like me."

"Maybe I just have to know."

Grudgingly, she said, "Would you think badly of me if I told you that I saved a platoon of American soldiers."

His face remained blank as he gave her the cop stare her dad had often used on her to try to break her down. "Did you enjoy torturing?"

She remembered the awful feeling in her gut and the way she'd tried not to show her disgust for what she'd done. "No. I didn't enjoy it, but it was necessary."

"But still wrong."

"The person I lit up was one of the men who trained little children to strap bombs on their chests, walk into a crowd and blow people to bits. If you think I've lost one second of sleep for what I did to him, then you'd be wrong. He was an evil bastard who spent thirty minutes in my company until I got what I needed from him. That was a fair trade for what he did. I might have tortured him, but he murdered hundreds. Not just Americans but his own people, innocent people who couldn't fight back. And when it came down to brass tacks, in thirty minutes he cried like a baby. I only had to pop him in the knee cap a couple of times." But she still hadn't liked what she'd done. Torture was the lowest form of terrorism, no matter who the person was or what they had done. Odessa had not been proud of what she'd done, but she had followed orders. "You're not my judge."

"But I am your lover."

Was that supposed to make her go all soft and girlie on him? This guy was out of his mind. "One roll in the sack does not a lover make, sweetie pie."

He drew back and she could see she'd offended him with her 'sweetie pie' remark.

"I'm not your sweetie pie," he said in a cold, icy tone. "Don't call me that again."

His quiet, firm tone sent a shiver down her back and she knew she needed to apologize. "I'm sorry, that was out of line."

Wyatt simply stared out the window. "I'm not getting anywhere with you, am I?"

"That little punk bastard was involved in some way with my father's death. Whatever rules I might have obeyed before are now out the window. My father was a great man and that little puke doesn't deserve to breathe the same air my father did."

"The Phil Ripley I knew wouldn't tolerate bad cops. Do you think he would like the way you're investigating his homicide? You're not above the law."

For a long moment, she turned that over in her mind. "My father knew what I do for the government and he accepted it. Maybe not because he wanted to, but because he loved me. And I'm the one he sent the disk to, because he knew I would see this through to the end." The bitter end, she thought. She would pay for her actions. She would sacrifice her soul for her father.

"Don't give me this 'end justifies the means' scenario."

"I'm not," she replied, "but you're dealing with bad cops. My dad used to say that one bad cop was worse than any crook on the street because when a person wears a badge he makes a promise to uphold the law and protect people. Carjackers, murderers, rapists are doing what they want to do and they don't pretend to be anything but what they are. But a bad cop hiding behind his badge, is the lowest form of scum."

"What makes you think you have the right to be judge, jury and executioner?"

Their actions have judged them already, she thought. She was just carrying out an appropriate sentence. "You're judging me. I've never judged anybody; I've just executed them. Good ole Stan should be happy. I could have just killed him. But instead, I gave him some cash and a brand new life. Maybe he'll take that chance to become a better man than he ever thought he could be." She doubted it, but she had to give him the opportunity. If he came back, he came back and could be dealt with, but if he left Phoenix and went somewhere where he could start new, then he had a chance to be something. A lot of people would kill for that opportunity.

"I'm not judging you. I'm commenting. And what happens if Stan's buddies catch up with him? Do you think they're going to let him go because he's a better man than they are?"

Not really her problem if he didn't have the right kind of friends. "He didn't have to talk." But he did, a little voice said in her mind. She'd threatened him, she'd forced him.

"What would you have done to him if he hadn't talked?" Whitaker said the words low, as if someone were listening to them and he wanted to keep the conversation quiet.

She studied her short, manicured nails. "Do you know why I picked Stan? Because Stan is a talker. Half of those people in that bar, I could have shoved needles in their eyes and they wouldn't have told me to go screw myself because that would mean they were talking. Stan was a little no fuss, no muss bastard from the get-go. I knew I could get what I wanted from him with minimum effort.

"The guy whose knee I busted wouldn't have talked. I knew that five seconds after I met him. Everything besides putting two in the back of his head would have been a waste of my time."

"How can you look at people and size them up?"

"Comes with the territory."

"What about me?"

"You wouldn't talk," she said. "And I respect that, more than you'll ever know."

"So you're not keeping me around for the sex?"

She laughed. "No, but the sex is outstanding. Speaking of which, I'm feeling a little antsy. I thought we might go work off some of my excess energy. Maybe this time we can make it to the bed."

Wyatt opened her car door. Instead of letting her out, he grabbed her and threw her over his shoulder. When she struggled, he smacked her butt.

"Ow!"

CHAPTER TEN

Wyatt took Odessa straight to the bedroom. When he set her on her feet, she reached up and touched his cheek. Instead of tossing her on the bed as he'd envisioned, he bent over and kissed her. When their mouths touched, she seemed to caress him with her lips. A dozen different feelings overwhelmed him. He still felt angry over the scene in the bar and wondered why he was spending so much time regretting what had happened. Clearly, Marco and Jacob had enjoyed their tussle with the bar patrons. But Wyatt hadn't. Sadness mingled with his anger. His attraction to Ripley warred with the sadness. How could he be attracted to her? At first he'd thought she was exciting. She'd aroused him in a way no other woman ever had. Even though he was now beginning to realize what a dangerous woman she was, he was already so deeply attracted to her, he didn't think he could ever shake lose.

An odd sweetness swept over him. Her touch sent searing heat through him. Their kisses were different than any others.

He deepened the kiss. Her lips were soft and yielding beneath his, and he could feel the strength of her passion down to his boots. At this moment it didn't matter that he was chasing her father's killer or that he wasn't sure of her or what she'd done in the past. He needed her. She made everything tolerable, everything right. Yet at the same time he was afraid. Afraid of her power over him. Afraid of what he might do to keep her with him. Because he wanted her with him for always, but she wasn't an abandon duty type of woman.

Odessa tugged at his T-shirt, pulling it over his head. Wyatt had to get her to the bed. The cool air night air blew in from the open window, chilling his skin. His nipples hardened as her fingers grazed their tips

Her tongue slipped inside his mouth, dancing with his. Wyatt could taste her passion. He pulled back, breaking contact with her.

Her eyes shone with heat and bewilderment. "Change your mind?"

Cupping her face with both hands, he stared into her eyes. "No."

Her lips trembled. "Then why did you stop?"

Wyatt palmed her cheek. Her satin skin warmed beneath his palm. How did he explain how he felt? How did he explain his fear, his anger, his sadness?

Odessa pressed against him. "Make love to me."

A shudder of pure desire rushed over him. Her breasts were crushed against his chest, her hands on his body. She rubbed against him like a cat and he lost all control. He grabbed her upper arms and took her mouth with an ungoverned need. His tongue ravaged hers.

Then Wyatt tore his lips from Odessa's. In one swift motion he bent over and picked her up. Her arms went around his neck. She opened her mouth, but he shook his head, not wanting her to ruin the moment.

He lowered her to the mattress.

"You are so beautiful," she said.

A hot flush crept up his neck. He didn't know how to take her compliment. "Men aren't beautiful."

"You are." She scooted further up the bed.

"You're saying this to throw me off."

She sat up and patted the spot on the bed next to her. "Never." She began to take off her sweater.

"Stop."

Her hands fell away. "Was I doing something wrong?"

"I like taking off your clothes." He held out his hand.

Slowly she touched her fingers to his. "I want you."

Her skin was warm to his touch, but he couldn't help noticing that her hands shook. He squeezed his eyes shut, and let her words echo in his head. "I need you."

Odessa slipped her arms around his waist and tilted back her head. "Kiss me."

He opened his eyes and for a second he could only stare at the classic perfection of her face. Muted light from the one lamp flickered off her smooth skin, casting soft shadows across her cinnamon-colored face. This was not the same woman who could kick ass, talk trash and back it up all at the same time. No, this was a desirable creature who stirred his imagination and gave life to his soul. "Anything you want." He kissed her. As their lips met, Wyatt undressed her. He heard the rustle of fabric over bare skin. Or maybe the sound was the rush of his blood through his veins. He wasn't sure.

Her hands moved over his skin. They were callused. He'd never thought calloused hands could feel so seductive.

She tasted of wine and chocolate. Their tongues entwined and he felt his knees go weak. He began to lick the side of her throat, then down the hollow between her small, firm breasts. Her skin smelled of vanilla and exotic flowers and was as soft as hot satin. He could feel the muscles of her back contract as he caressed. He couldn't get enough of the feel of her. She was in his blood, in his soul.

She touched his stomach. So potent was the impact, he moaned. Her hands dropped to the fly of his jeans and she began to unfasten it. He wanted to help her but that would mean he would have to take his hands away from her skin, and he was intoxicated by the supple feel of her body. And he had to admit to himself he liked that she was as desperate to have him as he was to have her

She broke the kiss. "Help me."

Wyatt grabbed her wrists and guided her hands down to her side. Her small breasts were firm and chocolate tipped. She had a tiny waist that flared into gently rounded hips. This was the body of a goddess. Wyatt reached out and touched the tip of her breast with his finger. Her nipple beaded on contact. He heard her sigh. When Wyatt completely cupped her breast, they both trembled.

He cupped the other breast. To touch her was sublime. Perfect. "I can't get enough of you."

"So are you going to talk all night?" She scooted over until she was nestled against the snowy white pillows. Wyatt undressed and then he removed the rest of her clothes. He could feel heat raging inside him. He was hard and ready for her.

Odessa pushed herself further back on the nest of pillows. Everything about Wyatt Earp Whitaker surprised her, from his obsessively neat house to his little rampage about playing by the rules. He was the last person she'd thought would insist on following the rules.

The mattress sagged beneath his weight. He slipped an arm around her waist, brought her to him and crushed her to his chest. He stroked her body, leaving trails of excitement all over her. Odessa whimpered. Her need for him was almost painful.

"So beautiful," he whispered.

His words thrilled her. "Love me, Wyatt."

The muscles in his throat constricted and he took a harsh breath before meeting her gaze. "As much as you want."

She grinned. "Good."

The lamplight glowed on his white skin. The shadows it cast across his face made his features seem sharper, his shoulders wider. Odessa slid her fingers into his silky hair and brought his mouth back down to hers. He rolled on her and their legs entwined. She could fell his erection jutting into her belly. A thousand new sensations attacked her all at once. She pressed closer to him, wanting to feel every bit of him against her.

Wyatt groaned, "Odessa."

She liked the way he said her name as his lips moved down her neck. He smelled like smoke and musk. Odessa couldn't seem to grab on to a single thought. Her body had taken over and was doing all the thinking for her. She liked the sensation.

Wyatt began to nibble at her earlobe. His gentle nips tickled and she forced herself not to laugh. An ache knotted her stomach. She closed her eyes, stunned by her powerful reaction as his hands roamed all over her body. His fingertips drew small circles on her hips. She liked the roughness of his palms on her skin.

His lips closed over the tip of one breast.

Odessa's back arched at the moist swirls. She rubbed her cheek in the springy softness of his hair. She watched him suckle her. His body was so white against her dark skin. The contrast was perfect, as if it was meant to be.

She could feel the strength and vigor just below the skin. He was a powerful man, yet so gentle.

His mouth moved to her other breast.

Odessa was transported by the depth of her feelings. This was what she'd always dreamed being in love would feel like. But she didn't want to think about love. Love changed things and she couldn't afford to let that happen. Wyatt's hands grazed the skin of her inner thigh and brought her away from thoughts of love. She parted her legs, hoping for more of the sweet sensation of his hands on her delicate skin. As he touched her, she moaned deep in her throat. Every touch, every kiss was more than she hoped for.

Wyatt's finger moved over her secret place. He stroked her gently until damp heat spread deep inside her. Her heart raced and she gave herself up completely to the moment. He buried his fingers in her curls, dipping a finger inside her. Shock went through her at his subtle invasion.

"Relax," he whispered as he began stroking her sex. Odessa bit her lip to stop from crying out. Her hips arched as she gave herself to the wild sensations racing through her. She was almost ashamed that she could be so easily swayed by his skill.

"Do you like that?" he asked.

Odessa stared at Wyatt. "More than you'll ever know."

He half smiled. "Good."

His eyes were filled with such passion and craving she wanted to cry. No man had ever looked at her with such emotion before. He continued his stroking. Pressure built inside her.

Odessa closed her legs to trap his hand there. Her insides grew tighter and tighter until she thought she would explode. His voice got huskier, deeper, more insistent. She couldn't hold back the tide and her body erupted. Spasms tore through her with such force she cried out, unable to stop herself. She seemed to float on air for endless seconds before going limp.

She drifted back to earth. He rubbed his hard cock against her. She had a hard time trying to catch her breath. "Now what do we do?"

He caressed her cheek. "The good stuff." He positioned himself over her and began to rain kisses over her body. Odessa giggled as he stuck his tongue in her navel. She grabbed a fistful of his hair to pull his head up, but he was too strong and she couldn't make him stop. Not that she really wanted to. His lips moved down her body until they reached the juncture of her thighs. Odessa squeezed her legs closed, but he didn't stop kissing her.

"Open for me," he commanded in a husky tone.

He positioned himself between her legs. Odessa closed her eyes and he put her legs over his shoulders. She felt exposed and vulnerable.

Again time stood still as she waited for his newest way at pleasuring her. He placed a kiss right at her center and a wanton shiver flowed through her. His tongue slipped inside her. Odessa groaned, helpless to stop her reactions. Again, the familiar tightening built in her body and instead of fighting it, she relaxed and let the warmth fill her. Her hips wriggled as she wanted him further inside her. Her body exploded and she cried again, an almost scream that bounced off the walls.

As she came back down to earth, Wyatt moved over her. She looked up at his handsome face, his blue eyes glittering like jewels. His powerfully muscled chest heaved with every breath.

"Put your legs around my waist."

She did as he commanded. She lifted her hips until his erection was nestled on her stomach. "Love me. Now."

He laughed and lowered his body over hers. His eyes smoldered as he entered her.

Odessa bit her lip to stop from crying out. A look of pure pleasure colored his face. She reached up and touched his cheek. Her muscles conformed to his length as if she had been made only for him. He began moving in slow, steady strokes.

Odessa threaded her fingers through his blonde hair and brought his mouth to hers. Their kiss was sweet and lingering. He whispered her name, softly and lovingly.

Sweat trickled down his skin and the light from the single lamp gave his body a look of slick ivory. As his movements increased, Odessa felt poised on a precipice. She chanted Wyatt's, name urging him on. He buried himself deep inside her, pushing against her and setting that secret spot inside on fire. When the first wave of pleasure washed over her, her whole body tensed. Then he thrust deeper inside her, and a surge of ecstasy crashed over her.

He moaned her name and went still on top of her. Their bodies melted together. They lay like that for long seconds. She was to afraid to speak, knowing it would end the moment. The one thing she knew was they would never go back to who they used to be. Then something odd happened to her as he lay spent on top of her. She felt a tenderness rise deep inside her and fill all the lonely places she hadn't even realized existed until this moment.

Odessa watched Wyatt sleep. He lay on his back one arm covering his eyes. He breathed deeply. The sheet lay across his stomach. Just as Odessa smiled and reached out to touch him, her cell phone rang.

The display showed her mother's number and she was tempted to ignore it, but felt guilty. "Hi Mom."

"You didn't come home last night," her mother said in an almost plaintive tone. "What were you doing?"

Odessa grabbed the blanket from the foot of the bed and wrapped it around her and padded out into the hall, the soft fleece of the blanket trailing behind her. "I was out torturing and maiming people."

"You're with Detective Whitaker, aren't you?"

I can't do anything, she thought, without my mother making me feel sixteen years old again, sneaking in past her curfew to find her Celeste sitting on her bed refolding her laundry the way she liked it folded. "I'm a grown woman, Mom. I'm allowed to have sex every once in a while." Take that, Odessa thought. *I'm a woman in charge of my life. Then why I do feel as though I've abandoned my mother?*

"I knew it," her mother laughed.

"Mom, you played me." Deflated, she could only admire her mother's ability to manipulate her.

"I'm glad to know I can still outsmart you."

Odessa leaned against the wall. "Mom, do you want a job with the CIA?" She'd be good. "You could be our secret weapon. We could send you to Iraq, bring all the troops home, and leave you to handle the situation. Everything would be solved in ten minutes."

"Thank you," her mother replied, satisfaction in her voice. Then the plaintive tone returned. "I don't like having bodyguards."

Although the comment was out of left field, Odessa wasn't surprised. Her mother didn't like living in a cage. "Mom, I'm concerned about your safety."

"I can't go anywhere by myself. I can't work in the garden alone. I can't go to the grocery store. I can't have friends over. One of them tried to go into the women's locker room at the gym to watch me change."

She had a vision of the Mexican standoff at her mother's upscale fitness center. "So what did you do?"

"I left. I wasn't going to jog the track in my Manolo Blahniks."

Only her mother got all dressed up to go to the gym to sweat, which didn't surprise Odessa. Besides designer labels on all her clothes, her mother also had designer sweat. "What do you need, Mom?"

"I'm just checking on you. Mothers do that, you know. Daughters aren't so good at checking in with their moms."

Dig, dig, dig. Odessa slid down the wall until her butt was on the hardwood floor. Her mother had her shovel out. "Mom, I might not have physically checked on you, or written, but I've always kept an eye on you."

"I accepted a long time ago that you were your father's child. I know that you love me."

You don't understand, she wanted to scream. She loved her dearly, just differently. Her father had accepted her for who she was. Her mother wanted her to be someone different. "Mom, I would die for you."

For the first time in all the years she'd been on her own, there was dead air on the phone. She'd left her mother speechless. And Odessa felt delighted. How sweet! Her mother didn't have a snappy comeback for that one.

After several long heartbeats, Celeste finally said, "How close are you to finding your father's killer?"

"I'm one more rung up the ladder."

"What will you do when you find this person?"

Odessa rubbed the back of her neck trying to alleviate the tension centered there. "I'm going to make him pay." Until she was satisfied.

"Exactly what does that entail, Odessa?"

Her mother didn't need the details of their eventual deaths. And Odessa wasn't going to give them. "That's between me and God, Mom. Let it go. Don't ask questions you don't want the answers to."

"I don't want you to do anything that will damage your soul."

That gave Odessa pause. For a second she was the one who was speechless. Odessa didn't think of herself as damaged. "I won't let anything damage my soul." But the death of her father had dented her soul a little more than she liked to admit. "Don't worry about me. I can take care of myself. You stay safe. Listen to your bodyguards and do exactly as they tell you. When you take a shower, one of them better be handing you the towel when you're done. That's the way this is going to be until everything is over."

"I don't like this."

"I offered to put you on a plane to D.C. There would have been no bodyguards there."

"They took my husband," Celeste said in a fierce tone. "They are not taking my home or the rest of my family. Especially not you."

Her dad had been a go-with-the-flow kind of guy. Nothing much upset him. He'd been flexible and malleable. He'd even been manipulate-able. Odessa grinned. She'd just made up her own word. But her mother was different. She had run their world like a benevolent dictator. And thinking back, no one had been unhappy with that deal. Her mother had grit. Hell, she should just turn her mother loose on these people. By Tuesday next week there wouldn't be a hate group left on the planet.

Odessa heard Wyatt stirring. "I love you, Mom."

"I love you, too."

Odessa disconnected and went back into the bedroom. Wyatt sat on the side of the bed, his hair rumpled, his face still vague with sleep.

"What's the matter?" he asked as she sat next to him.

"My mother just said she loved me." Odessa couldn't remember the last time her mother had been so honest with her feelings.

He slipped an arm around her and pulled her to his side. "Isn't that what mothers are supposed to do? Love their children?"

Odessa let out a long breath. How did she explain this? The only one who'd ever understood was her father. And he wasn't here anymore. "My relationship to my mother is complex."

"Mine, too."

For the first time she realized she'd never asked him about his family. Normally with guys she slept with, she didn't give a damn, but with him, she wanted to know everything about him. "Tell me about your family."

"I have a brother who owns a ranch in Tucson. My father is dead and my mom lives in Sedona. She's one of those new age, granola eating, chanting to crystal kind of women, but she's nice. I have two nephews and a niece. I graduated from the University of Arizona, became a cop, got married, got divorced, no kids. That's it."

Odessa stared at him, amazed. "How can you just sum all that up in a paragraph?" Her life would take up all the space in the reference section of the New York Public Library. Maybe it was a guy thing. She'd have to ask her brother when he decided to start speaking to her again.

"Easy. I just did. How did your father know what you do for a living?"

She shrugged. "He caught me. He was at this international police conference and he saw me going upstairs with this guy and he kind of caught me in the act of garroting him. My cover was blown. I wasn't going to kill my own dad to keep my secret. Who knew we were going to run into each other in Luxemburg? I'd never lied to my dad. I'd lied to my mother, and still do—out of necessity. But never my dad and I wasn't going to start then. He kept my secret, sort of. Who knew he talked in his sleep? It's a good thing my dad was faithful to my mother because he would never have gotten away with anything."

Wyatt grinned. "You know, you talk in your sleep, too."

Oh God, what had she revealed to her bed partners? "What did I say?"

"Something that sounded like 'No, no, no, Denzel. You're married.' I was a little offended since you were in bed with me at the time."

She gave him a sideways glance. "Did I make you feel cheap?" Not that she was sorry.

"The good kind of cheap."

He was good. "Did I make you feel easy?"

He started to unwrap her from the blanket. "I know you've been trying to distract me with sex and in the interest of harmony, I'm going to let you do it."

She pushed him back on the bed. "You're such a man-slut." She straddled him and he slid a hand up her rib cage. Her body was already humming. She needed him to help her forget what the future held for her.

CHAPTER ELEVEN

Odessa tapped her fingers on her thigh as she watched Cher Dawson sift through the stacks of papers and file folders surrounding her on her sofa.

Cher glanced at Odessa and then indicated for her to sit down. "I may have figured out who killed your father. His name is Randy Sorenson. He's an interesting man."

So the Gunslinger now had a name. Odessa chose the ottoman next to the sofa so she could look at the files too. "How so?" A fist of anger squeeze her heart. *Tell me more, so I can kill the murdering bastard.*

Cher opened a file and rummaged through it. "He's an unapologetic racist, sexist, homophobic, anti-Semetic, fascist, bigot pig. Who just happens to be a bad cop, too."

Odessa eyes widened at Dawson's breath control. "You said that all in one breath. For a pregnant woman, that's pretty damn impressive."

"An ex-smoking pregnant woman," Dawson corrected. "It's the Lamaze classes. And being my age means going to the doctor every two weeks to make sure everything is fine with this baby." She patted her stomach. "Now before you run off and kill Sorenson, I—"

"I haven't even formulated a plan yet," Odessa interrupted, though she had half of one in the back of her mind, just waiting to hatch.

"Yes, you have," Whitaker said as he entered the living room. He held a mug of steaming coffee in one hand and a Danish in the other.

Odessa tossed an annoyed look at him. *Let a man in your pants and they think they know everything about you.* "Don't interrupt. I may be sleeping with you, but you have no right to give away my thoughts."

Dawson burst out laughing. "Whitaker's got jungle fever."

Dawson and Whitaker had the relationship of rival first graders. Odessa couldn't help enjoying their banter. She'd had a similar relationship with her father.

Whitaker glared at Dawson. "So what?"

Dawson wiggled her finger at him. "Remember that time before I got married, and you heard me and Luc having that lovey-dovey conversation over the office intercom?"

Whitaker pressed his fingers into his forehead. "It's scorched on my brain. No matter how hard I've tried to forget, I can't. I'm scarred for life."

Dawson smiled. "We're even now."

Odessa glanced at Whitaker curiously. "Can we get back to the matter at hand?"

Dawson put down the file. "I'm not ready to bring Sorenson in for questioning just yet."

Odessa frowned. "I knew you would protect another cop." Cops protected cops. She should have known Dawson would come down on the side of the department.

Dawson mouth thinned to an angry line. "Don't interrupt me again."

Odessa knew to back off. "My bad." That was the best apology she was going to throw out there.

Dawson continued. "I hate this guy as much as you do. I want to burn him so bad I'd give up my left lung. But, and this is a big but, we have no proof. Sorenson may be a bad apple, but anyone could fake his little gunslinging habit just to make things bad for him. If we do anything to him right now with the evidence we have, the department is going to rally around him no matter how much everyone may dislike him. I don't want that to happen. I want him vulnerable."

"I want him neutralized." Odessa really wanted him so dead he'd never mess with anyone else's life. For a second the pain of her father's death reared its head and she fought against the grief. Not now, she thought. Later she would grieve properly for her father. Right now, only her need for revenge kept her from giving in.

"He will be," Dawson said, "my way."

Okay, Odessa could live with that for the moment. But if things didn't go right, she would be ready to step in and finish the job. This Sorenson would be dead and never know what happened to him. "For the time being I'll back off, but I'm putting you on notice. I have no problem picking up a phone and calling a buddy I have in the U.S. Senate who oversees Homeland Security. He'd love to send his boys down here and rip your police department apart. Busting bad cops and racist terrorists to boot is the kind of shit that could put a senator in the White House." And that was what an empty threat sounded like from a desperate woman.

Dawson wasn't moved. "Give me a minute and I'll write that in my diary."

Odessa felt her back go up. "I'm not popping some yang this time, boss lady." She whipped her cell phone out of her pocket. "I've got Senator Hathaway on speed dial."

Dawson held up her hand. "Give Phoenix a chance to make this right. If we don't, I'll let you use my cell to call your senator."

Odessa slipped her phone back into her pocket. "Out of respect for a sistah doin' a man's job, I'm gonna hold off."

Dawson inclined her head graciously. "Thank you. I know that cost you." Whitaker sat across from Odessa, one leg crossed over the other. He wriggled a booted foot. "What exactly do we have to do to make him more vulnerable?"

Odessa ignored his question. She had to get out of here for a moment and get her head together. "I have to think about this." Odessa held her hand out. "Give me the keys, I'm going to sit in the truck."

A look of sheer panic crossed his face. "You can't drive it."

Odessa snatched the keys and stood. "Hell, my feet don't reach to the pedals. You have nothing to fear."

"That's what I'm afraid of."

She stuck her tongue out at him, knowing her gesture to be totally juvenile and then walked out.

With Odessa gone, Wyatt looked expectantly at Dawson. "You have words for me, I can feel them."

"How tight a leash do you have her on?"

He wasn't enough man to control that woman and that was one of things that excited him the most about being with her. "Odessa Ripley is not the kind of a woman you put on a leash…unless she likes that kind of stuff." He'd have to ask her if she did.

Dawson covered her baby bulge. "Whitaker, not in front of the baby."

Wyatt couldn't restrain his grin. "You sort of found a sense of humor when you got knocked up, boss. I kind of like it."

Dawson rubbed her forehead. "Seriously, how is she holding together? I heard what happened at the bar last night."

"Who squealed?"

Dawson rolled her eyes. "Marco Jackson couldn't keep a secret to save his ass. All I have to do is look at him cross-eyed and threaten to tell his wife and he confessed."

Wyatt should have known, but more to the point, what was Dawson going to do to them. "You're not mad at us, are you?"

She rubbed her hands together. "Yeah! I would have liked to knock a few heads together myself."

About a hundred pounds of relief dropped off his ass. For a second he'd pictured himself in the state pen in a pink jumpsuit. "What are you going to do, give them the bum rush with that big belly of yours?"

"Be careful, Whitaker, pregnant women can be lethal. It's the hormones."

"Ripley's wound a little tight, but she's a pro. She'll obey your orders. The only time we'll have to worry about her is if her father's murder goes unsolved. When it comes down to brass tacks, she'll do the right thing." Or so he almost had himself conned into believing.

"For her, the right thing isn't the same as for us."

Wyatt glanced at his boot. "I'll explain it to her." For the tenth time, even though he knew that if Odessa took it into her head to kill Sorenson, she would. She didn't seem to care as much about the rest of the people who died; she only wanted the person responsible for her dad's death. "Look, when she went to that bar last night, she took cops with her. Not for backup. She could have jumped Stan anytime, beat the crap out of him and gotten the information she needed. I've seen what she can do and it's not pretty. She took cops because she trusts us enough to know we wouldn't let her get out of hand."

Dawson leaned back on the sofa. She might look relaxed but her eyes burned with that familiar intensity that made her a great cop. "How do you figure that?"

"Nobody died. That's how I know."

"Are you sure your skinhead's not at the bottom of some mine shaft right about now?"

She wasn't letting this go anytime soon. "I'm sure." The disbelieving expression on Dawson's face was not reassuring. "The more I get to know her, the more I'm realizing that she talks a good game about being some inflexible killing machine, but deep down inside, she has a damn good sense of right and wrong. I mean, it's a little more expedient that what we like, but she knows the line."

She crossed her hands over her expanded stomach. "And you know all this because you're bouncing on top of her."

Dawson had never been a person to pull punches. But she had a part of it wrong since it was sort of the other way around. "That's crude even for a guy."

Dawson shrugged. "So what?"

He didn't know how to explain why he trusted Odessa, he just did. Maybe it was connected to the sex. "I just know, boss. Trust me. Please."

"I'm going let you play watchdog, Romeo, but I'm having my father put a tail on Sorenson, just in case your logic is all in your boxer shorts."

"Briefs," Wyatt said. "Got to contain my monster."

She covered her belly again, "Whitaker, you're corrupting my kid and he's not even born yet."

"Any corrupting on my part is a moot point. You're his mother. And how do you know it's a boy?"

"Because my husband said so and he gets what he wants."

Wyatt stood. How could her world be so easy now? He wanted his easy non-complicated world back and he wanted it back today. He didn't care how boring it used to be.

Wyatt closed the front door and stepped out onto the porch. His truck was parked in the driveway and he could see Odessa in the cab of his truck. Her head was bent and she had covered her face with her hands. She looked so alone and vulnerable. His first impulse was to comfort her, but then he realized that if she'd wanted comfort she wouldn't have gone off on her own.

When she looked up, her eyes met his and she stared at him, her chin held high and a challenge in the tilt of her face. He wanted to comfort her, but suspected she would be angry if he did. He decided to let it be. He doubted that Ripley liked revealing her vulnerabilities.

He climbed into the cab and slammed the door. As he fit the key into the ignition, Ripley blew her nose and wiped her eyes.

"So what did she say?" she asked as she balled up a tissue and shoved it in her pocket. "I figured she wanted a private moment with you."

"She's worried you'll jeopardize the whole case. We know you don't care as much about Summersby, Lambert or the others. They are nothing more than a means to an end for you."

Her face went blank. "I want justice for them, too."

Oh yeah, he thought, she sounded real convincing. "Yeah, but you have no personal stake in their deaths the same as you do in your dad's."

"You're wrong. In the big picture, I do have a personal stake in putting these racist cops away. They undermine the very fabric of what this country stands for. They are no better than Osama bin Laden.

They want people who don't fit their ideals to just go away, and not in a vacation to Fiji type of way."

Wyatt shook his head. "That's a laugh. Or has the CIA become a kinder, gentler organization?"

"Their interests come first. Once you get on their bad side, you're gone. They're expedient. But in the last few years, I've seen a major change in The Company. It's not about governments anymore, but business. The CIA has no loyalty to anybody but itself. I play that game, too. I don't question my orders, I just carry them out, because that's what I'm good at."

He wondered if it was always that easy for her. "Do your orders ever leave a bad taste in your mouth?"

Her bottom lip twitched. "My last assignment was to kill a guy. It wasn't the killing but why I had to do it that bothered me."

So he was right. Not everything was all rosy on her side of the street. "What happened?"

"An agent turned and informed to the wrong people. Three agents and their entire families were obliterated. I'm sure you've seen photos of dead kids before, but nothing like what was done to those kids. It was horrifying. I think that was the first time I've ever enjoyed putting a bullet in somebody. I've never felt righteous before about killing, but this one felt good and that's a bad thing in my business." She fell silent, her face contemplative.

He started the truck and backed out of the driveway, thinking about what she'd said.

Odessa pulled tight black pants up over her hips and glanced at her reflection in the mirror. She looked ready for bear. She intended to take one down. She picked up the handgun she'd purchased at the gun show and checked it carefully. It would do.

The door to her bedroom slammed and her mother stalked into the room, looking for all the world like a wild panther. "What are you doing?"

"Getting ready to go out." Odessa hated it when her mother was in this type of mood.

"And do what?" Her mother stood in the center of the room, her hands on her hips and her chin thrust forward.

"What I'm really good at." Odessa placed the handgun into the holster snug against the small of her back.

"Did you find the man who killed your father?"

"I found the man who did the killing, but not the one who ordered the hit." Odessa balanced on the balls of her feet, ready for flight should her mother's intense grilling become too much.

"What do you intend to do?"

"I can't tell you that; you'd be an accessory."

Her mother frowned and pushed hair behind her ears. She leaned toward Odessa, peering into her eyes, getting into her face.

Odessa resisted the urge to take a step back. Her mom was in her space and making her acutely uncomfortable. She didn't like being intimidated by her own mother.

"Don't be a fool. Do you think your father would approve of your actions?"

"The day before he died, Dad mailed me the information that is allowing me to put this puzzle together. He knew what my job was with the CIA. If he intended this to be some sort of moral test, then he should have left well enough alone."

Her mother rocked back on her feet, her eyes narrowing. "Please, Odessa, don't do this."

"I have to. These are bad cops who killed a good cop. Do you think the department is going to follow through on this? No. They protect their own."

"Do you understand the price you'll pay for your vengeance?"

"I don't care." Okay, she did a little, but she wasn't going to let that stop her. Whatever came from her action, she would accept. Those were the rules she lived by and she was too old to change that.

"I cannot let you damage your soul. I want you to be in Heaven with your dad and me, not in Hell."

"I'll pay whatever the price is, Mom. If I'm doomed to hell, then I'll be there torturing those bastards and making them pay for eternity. I love you, Mom. Don't wait up for me." Odessa grabbed her jacket and walked around her mom to the door. She opened it to find the security guard standing on the other side. He took one look at her face and stepped aside. Odessa almost bolted down the hallway toward the kitchen.

Once outside in the cold night air, she looked up at the stars. She thought about her childhood and all the Sundays spent in church being lectured by the priests. She hadn't had much faith in God then and she didn't now. God had allowed bad cops to kill her father, a good man, who was doing his job because he'd taken an oath to protect and serve. She wasn't going to worry about her immortal soul at this late date. She climbed into the BMW and roared down the street.

The freeways were almost empty. She made good time across the city to the area where Sorenson and his family lived. She parked two blocks away and walked the rest of the way, keeping to the shadows.

Randy Sorenson and his family lived in a newer housing tract with wide streets and towering palm trees. The house was a one story ranch with a wide veranda that appeared to surround the house. Christmas lights adorned the eaves. A lighted Santa and two reindeer stood on the lawn. Two cars were parked in the driveway, one a late model mini-van and the other a Ford Explorer.

Odessa hunched down in the shadow of a row of large bushes until the lights went out in the house and the Christmas lights clicked off on their timer. She waited another two hours and then crept around the yard, sidestepping yucca plants and cactus. For a cop, Randy Sorenson hadn't given much thought to the placement of his landscape. The house was easy to approach despite the sticker in one window proclaiming that the house was protected.

Odessa found the alarm box on the side of the house and opened it. The alarm system was a cheap one that would be easy to circumvent. She whipped out her baby screwdriver and went to work. After she disabled the alarm, she listened at each window until she heard snoring. She tested the window and discovered it wasn't even locked. She opened the window by taking the casement glides off the track and removing the interior screen, then stepped into a bedroom and looked around. Night-lights gleamed in all the outlets. Was Randy afraid of the dark? Nice of him to provide her with just enough illumination to see him.

The bedroom was neat and tidy. A door opened to a small bathroom and double mirrored doors hid the closet. As she approached the king-sized bed, a cat glanced up sleepily, then curled back into a ball and went back to sleep. Worthless ball of fur. Now if Randy had a dog, things would be different. She'd brought doggie kryptonite—treats laced with a sedative. Not enough to hurt a dog, but enough to put it out of the way and not show any side effects in the morning.

Randy's wife, Janice, slept next to him. She was a pretty woman with delicate features and a no-nonsense mouth. She lay on her side, one hand curled beneath her cheek.

Asleep, Randy Sorenson didn't look at all like the ten-year-old photo Dawson had shown Odessa. He'd grown heavier, his cheeks had filled out, and his hair was showing gray at the temples.

Odessa sat down in a chair and watched Randy sleep. She felt the hardness of her handgun in the small of her back. She could do him right now, but didn't. Instead, she watched him sleep. His chest rose and fell and he snored gustily.

She'd once assassinated an Arab prince while his mistress slept in the bed right next to him. The poor woman had gotten the shock of her life the next morning when she woke up next to a dead man. If she'd awakened earlier, she would have been spared the shock because she would have been dead, too.

Randy slept peacefully. Obviously, his conscience didn't bother him. While she'd waited for dark, Odessa had contacted A.J. and asked for info on Sorenson. Randy Sorenson had been pulled in to account for several instances of police brutality. He'd tried to promote out of a patrol officer, but his test scores had been barely acceptable. So he stayed on patrol.

For the last few years of his career, this guy had watched people like Cher Dawson, Marco Jackson and Jacob Greyhorse get ahead of him. Odessa wondered how that had affected him and what had finally tripped his trigger. He'd gone to a predominantly Hispanic high school, and had even been briefly engaged to an Hispanic girl before she'd broken it off. What had gone so wrong in his life that he'd had to end up being the bag man for a white supremacist group?

She settled in as he slept, hoping he'd wake up so that she would definitely have to kill him. But he kept on sleeping like a little boy without a care in the world. When she became bored watching him sleep, she roamed his house, peeking into his life. She even pulled the blue blanket over his sleeping toddler son.

After she was satisfied she'd figured out every nuance of Randy Sorrenson's pathetic life, she returned to the master bedroom and sat on the chair across from his bed again and contemplated the fact that they were both assassins. The difference between them was that Odessa killed people who deserved the ultimate justice. Even though she'd used that as a justification many times, because bad people had to pay for their sins, she believed in what she did. The world was a safer place because of her. The world wasn't a better place because of him.

Sorenson was the same as the thugs she chased outside the borders of the country. He was a terrorist whose basic goal was to undermine the stability and well-being of the United States. He was just doing it from the inside. And she was sworn to protect her country against all enemies, foreign or domestic.

She stood and went to the bed, pulling her handgun out of the back holster and reaching for a pillow to muffle the shot. She leaned over and held the gun to the side of his head. Shoot, she told herself. Just shoot him. But something stopped her.

She couldn't pull the trigger. A thousand thoughts raced through her head. He was a pawn and she wanted the number one guy. Sorenson was like her, expendable, but he did have information she needed to know and she intended to get that information.

Dammit! She wasn't supposed to be a thinker. She was the action person, the problem solver and here she was hesitating. If she pulled the trigger now, Mr. Big would know the whole department was on to him and he'd find a hole so deep no one would ever flush him out.

Which meant she couldn't kill Sorenson just yet, not even to balance the score. For the moment, she'd walk away because this piece of crap was a detail, not the big picture. If she was going to hell, she'd do so with Mr. Big. Sorenson could rot in jail for the rest of his life for all she cared.

Deftly, she stepped out the casement window and pulled the screen back into position. Then she closed the window and put the gears back on the track. Sorenson would never know she'd been inside his house.

Silently, she left, heading toward her car, only to find Whitaker's truck parked behind her and Whitaker leaning against the fender of his truck.

"Are you here to arrest me?" she asked as she approached, not certain if she was angry or relieved to see him.

"You didn't kill him."

"You don't know that."

"Yes, I do." A distant street light cast a soft glow on the side of his face. His voice was so self-confident and self-assured, Odessa bristled.

"I wanted to." Damn, her finger still itched to pull the trigger. She slammed her hand down on the fender.

"Why are you so angry?"

"I don't get angry. I do my job and complete my mission, then go get a pedicure."

"This isn't a mission. It never has been, nor will it ever be."

She gave a dry, humorless laugh. "That's what I told myself to make it okay, but I can't stop thinking that the bastard in that house killed my father."

Wyatt reached out and touched her cheek. "I promise we'll get him. But we'll get him the right way."

She squeezed her eyes tight. "I don't know if that's going to be enough."

Wyatt ran a finger down her cheek to her neck. She had always gotten what she wanted through either her family connections or sheer determination. But she wasn't going to get what she wanted this time. He pulled her into his arms and hugged her. Her head rested against his chest and he felt a hot wetness scorch through his shirt. A sob caught in her throat. She was crying.

Of all the things he'd seen Odessa Ripley do, he'd never thought he'd ever see her cry so openly. Crying wasn't a part of who she was. And yet he liked the fact that she could cry.

"I've never failed to see a job though to the end before."

"You didn't fail, you made it possible for me to do my job the right way." He hugged her tighter and smoothed her hair back from her face. "Come home with me. I need to make love to you." And more love. He so wanted to protect her, but of any woman he'd ever known she was the least in need of protection. And that was one of the things he liked, no, dammit, loved about her.

She pushed herself out of his arms, wiping her eyes with the back of her hand. "I can't. I have to go home and talk to my mom."

He whipped out his cell phone. "Call her." He didn't want to let her go. He needed her to be with him.

"I can't tell her this on the phone." She dug into her pants pocket and pulled out the car keys. "I'll see you in the morning."

He watched her drive away, the red tail lights of her car sliding through the darkness. Bereft, he climbed into the cab of his truck, a hole the size of Texas in his heart. Dammit, why did he have to fall in love with her? She was not the kind of woman that a smart man loved. He liked to think he was a smart man.

He rubbed scratchy eyes. He was tired, frustrated and horny.A week ago, his life had been simple. Boring and lonely, but simple. And just one little five-foot-one woman had strutted into his life and everything had gone to shit. He didn't ask for this. Hell, he didn't want or need it. He wanted his simple, boring, lonely life back—now. He was in love and he was straight hating his life right now.

His cell phone rang. Odessa's number showed on the display. He answered. "Yeah?"

"Thank you."

"For what?"

"For having faith in me."

Before he could answer, she disconnected. He closed his phone and shoved it back into his pocket. He started the truck and put it in gear, did a U-turn and headed home.

CHAPTER TWELVE

Odessa sat in her car watching the diner where Randy Sorenson usually had breakfast. When he arrived in his Explorer, she gave him five minutes to get settled and then she walked across the busy street to the diner and entered. As cool as she was feeling, she could have had an ice cube stuck up her ass. But she had to force Randy out into the open, even if she had to drag him into Dawson's arms kicking and screaming. This was her one shot at doing something right. If Randy didn't cooperate, she thought she might pull out her gun and shoot off his toes one by one until she got the answer she wanted. She was going to do this for her mom and maybe a little bit for Wyatt. His ass was on the line too. She was here alone because one of her rules was to never take anyone with her if she had to travel the dark road.

The café was decorated in fifties kitsch with red vinyl booths and chrome edging the tables. The floor was a white and black check that made Odessa almost dizzy looking at it.

Sorenson sat in a back corner booth, dressed for work in his winter uniform. He smiled at a hovering waitress who held a coffee pot in her hand, and she poured the coffee, then walked back behind a screened area.

Odessa slid into the booth across from him. Randy looked surprised, then displeased, and finally blank.

"How you doin', Randy?"

"May I help you, ma'am?"

How formal, Odessa thought. She gave him a malevolent laugh. She stuck out her hand. "Ma'am, that's funny. You remember Phil Ripley, don't you? I'm Odessa, his daughter."

He stared at her outstretched hand as though it were covered in dirt and bugs. Then he glanced up at her, saying nothing, doing nothing.

Part of her wanted to reassure him that the color of her skin wouldn't rub off on him, but she didn't. "By the way," she said in a conversational tone, "I know you killed my daddy."

He went still and alert, his eyes darting around the café. "You have me confused with someone else."

Did this guy have a pulse? She kinda admired his coolness. "No, I don't. You're the one your compatriots call the Gunslinger. I saw you twirling your piece on the surveillance video. From one professional to another, you should never mark your kills in any way."

Hid hand reached under the table. "I don't know what you're talking about."

Odessa shook her head and he pulled his hand back. "Yeah, you do, Randy. Give me my props. Did you really think someone wouldn't eventually figure out that you killed another cop?"

The waitress came and Odessa ordered coffee.

Randy raised his coffee cup to his lips, watching her warily over the edge. "You're mistaken. I'm a cop. I don't kill people. I protect them."

Odessa put her elbow on the table and rested her chin on her fist. Now she was gonna pull out the past and rattle him a bit. "From what I can see, you protect a very select group and you're just an average cop. You aren't even good enough to go up the ranks and get off patrol. How many times have you taken the test to make sergeant? You barely made it through college. You barely managed to graduate from the academy. Your life seems to be 'barely' everything. What are you good at? Oh yeah, you're a cop-killer. You were pretty decent with that. The actual killing part, but not the getting away with it part, the most important part. I know this because I'm a professional."

"A professional what?"

"I'm a professional problem solver."

He started to slide out of the booth. Odessa reached over and grabbed his hand. "I'm not finished yet. I know you're not smart enough to plan my father's killing. I want your boss. I want names, dates, and every little piece of information that might have found its way into your head."

"Screw you, bitch. You can't make me talk about something I don't know about."

She leaned forward. Now he was gonna get the bitch slap. "Last night I was in your house. I watched you sleep. I went through your underwear drawer. I even petted your cat. I watched your wife sleep and was even tempted to change your son's diaper. Beautiful little boy, too bad he has a racist bastard father like you. What's his name? Michael?"

Sorenson went pale and he clutched the handle of his cup. He trembled slightly, the coffee sloshing up the sides and over the top.

"I realize," Odessa continued, "you probably pay a lot for that basic security system you have. For the most part it's adequate, and would stop some junkie too shaky to figure out what to do, but not a pro. I disabled your alarm in fifteen seconds. I didn't even have time to sweat."

Beads of perspiration popped out on his forehead.

She squeezed his wrist on a pressure point. "Randy, am I making you nervous? Aren't you glad we're having this conversation?" She let go and patted his hand. He wasn't going anywhere

He licked his lips and said, "I'll give you some credit. You have some balls coming into a cop's diner trying to shake me down. Your kind aren't known for being brave."

"My kind? What do you mean by that? Girl kind? Black kind? Short kind? What kind? And since I have a hundred fifty-three IQ, that makes me the genius kind, too. I'm Poindexter smart. But that's just a number, isn't it, Mr. One Hundred Ten Average Intelligence?"

He wiped the sweat off his upper lip. "What do you want?"

"Many things. A cure for sickle cell, the preservation of the rain forest, and the end of cellulite."

He laughed nervously. "What about world peace?"

"If we had world peace, I'd be out of a job."

His eyes went wide for a moment.

"But," she continued in a casual tone, "those are just pipe dreams. Let's deal with my immediate needs. What I need you to do is confess."

"Confess to what?"

Oh, he was giving her a good game, but she had his balls. She just needed to squeeze a tiny bit harder. Part of her couldn't believe she was doing this, but another part couldn't make herself stop. "You are going to make this hard on me, aren't you?"

"I don't know what you're talking about, bitch."

Her fingers itched with the need to smack him upside the head. "You are going to call me that one too many times and I'm going to have beat you up."

He laughed again, the tone a little too high and tense.

Odessa figured he wanted to sound like a tough guy, but his chuckle sounded more like a nervous twitter. With one more tiny nudge, she figured he'd crack. *Limp dick bastard had no heart.* "Okay, this is the deal. You're going to have a talk with Lieutenant Dawson at Cold Case and tell her all your sins, or I'm going to get up, go to your house and put a bullet in your pretty wife's head. Then I'm going to walk down the hall and do baby Mikey. If I still don't get no love from you, I'm gonna kill your cat. I've come face to face with some of the worst scum the world has to offer and I've walked away every time. If you think you can take me on or hide from me, you'd best reconsider because I have the resources and the patience to hunt you down no matter what hole you hide in." She stood up. "You have until I get to my car to make a choice." She reached in her pocket and threw down a twenty. "I insist you let me pay for breakfast."

She walked out of the diner, stood for a moment at the door watching Sorenson. She waited for traffic to clear and headed for her car. As she opened the car door and slid inside, Sorenson walked out of the diner and stood on the sidewalk settling his cap on his head. He looked around, saw her and started to cross the street. At that moment black Nissan Passport passed her. Odessa saw four people inside, and then heard the sound of two pops. By the time she was out of the car and running across the street, Sorenson lay spread-eagled on the sidewalk, blood pooling beneath his body, his eyes clouding over.

The Nissan slowed. Odessa drew out her handgun. As the car sped up, she ran after it, shooting. Someone in a ski mask leaned out the rear window and shot at her. She pointed her handgun at the man and saw him jerk as a bullet hit him. His body sagged and a hand reached out and dragged him back in.

The car turned a corner and with a squeal of tires was gone. Odessa halted and stared after it. *Damn! Damn! Damn!*

The interrogation room was painted a depressing institutional gray, and the table and chairs were battered and scratched. Odessa sat at the table watching the two cops who sat across from her as they tried to intimidate her. One of them, Detective Mendoza, she remembered from her troubled youth, but she wasn't going to remind him. She wanted to laugh. Were these two guys the best Phoenix could do?

They'd been at it for an hour now and she was ready to move on. But the two cops facing her weren't letting her go. The younger one she didn't know, but Mendoza hadn't been a threat before and he wasn't one now. She zoned them out. Not until Mendoza slapped the table and leaned over her did she realize they'd been firing questions at her. She didn't have to stay, but she wanted to know what these two cops knew. She wanted to know if Sorenson's philosophy had infected more than just him and his dirty friends.

Mendoza had a hard-edged face and looked as if he could get a confession out of a rock. "What were you doing with Sorenson before he was killed?"

"He gave me a buzz. I met him for breakfast and didn't care for his vibe, so I left."

"So why did he come after you?"

"Probably to give me my change. I left a twenty on the table. This is the same answer I've told you five times. And each time you ask the same question again and just rephrase it."

"Why would Sorenson invite someone like you to breakfast?"

Obviously Sorenson's political attitudes were well-known in the department. She really couldn't say anything because she didn't want to get Dawson and her people in trouble. After all, the whole Cold Case unit had gone out on a limb for her. "Maybe Sorenson found God and wanted to do a nice thing for a black person. Maybe he had some information, but we never got down to business." She'd had enough. "Look, dudes, you know I did not pop Sorenson. Why am I here?"

"All right, Miss Ripley," Mendoza growled, "you want to know why you're here? Because I feel like it."

I'm so scared, Odessa thought. "Right." These two men couldn't begin to compare with some of the characters Odessa had dealt with over the years.

"Second of all," he continued, "since you arrived in town there's been a lot of death and destruction sort of swirling around you."

She held her hands up in supplication. "My bad."

"Thirdly…"

"For crying out loud, shut up," she said. "Whip out the rubber hose and beat me. Put me in a coma because I'm bored out of my skull."

Mendoza's lips twitched. "Yeah, you're Phil Ripley's kid."

"Detective Mendoza, I was kind of worried you wouldn't remember me."

"I remember you. I busted you on your first shoplifting beef. You were twelve years old then." He looked at his fellow detective. "You know, Cranston, she wouldn't talk then and I know she isn't going to talk now. We're just not that good."

Got that right, she thought, as laughter bubbled. "Look, fellows. Cards on the table. This is how it's going to go. I'm not happy with the investigation of my dad's homicide. So I'm checking out a few leads. And all this crap is the result of my asking a couple of questions here and there. I've just been defending myself. And the last time I looked that was constitutionally allowed."

"Aren't you a fitness instructor?" Cranston asked.

"Personal trainer," she corrected.

The door opened and Derek Lange, the husband of Odessa's best friend, walked into the interrogation room. Seeing him in a suit, Odessa almost burst out laughing. She had never seen Derek in a suit before. He'd worn a tuxedo at his wedding and that was it.

"Gentlemen," he said, "I'd like some time alone with my client."

Cranston looked dubious, but Mendoza nodded seriously. "And you are?"

Derek held out a business card, "Derek Lange, Esquire, Attorney at Law."

Mendoza studied the card and then pushed back from the table. "She's all yours."

"Thanks." Derek glanced at the mirrored wall.

The two cops left and Derek pulled a pen from his pocket, twisted it and set it on the table.

"I see you're pulling out your secret, audio jamming pen. I like that. I'm so proud of you. You've turned into one great spy."

He pulled at his jacket lapel. "I would have been here sooner, but I had to go to get a suit. You know how hard it is to be fitted?"

"You look damn snacky."

"Every girl is crazy for a sharp-dressed man. But let's get down to business. Exactly what the hell are you doing?"

He already knew. She had to send love to Raven for sending her a secret weapon. "Since you're here, you already know."

"I want to hear it from you because I have to call Raven and tell her word for word what you said."

Odessa spread her hands. Silly man, she thought. "That's what you get for being married to my best friend."

"I had no idea your social life came with the deal."

She glanced at the one way mirror and was tempted to stick out her tongue, because she knew they were being watched. "How long have you been in Phoenix?"

"About five minutes after Raven picked up your brother and took him and his family to the safe house. Did you think she was going to just follow your instructions and not question anything. Oh no. Now I'm her errand boy and I'm supposed to keep an eye on you and make sure you don't do anything—like kill somebody—and here I am, too late for that."

Like this man should complain; he had the plush life. "You're a good looking errand boy with some terrific perks. Like being married to a supermodel."

"Look, I landed in town about five hours after you were attacked by those skinheads. I've been following you around. I put Stan on the bus. I called the fire department when your mom's house was torched. And I made sure no one came and got you after your little raid on the skinhead bar. And we aren't even gonna talk about your nocturnal activities."

She flashed back to her wild night with Wyatt. How had he been able to get the drop on her? Damn, this had never happened before. She was getting lousy in her old age or at least too preoccupied to care. "You didn't see me naked, did you?"

"I can still see, can't I?"

She shook her head in disbelief. "I must be getting old."

"What do you and the cop have going on?" Derek sat on the table. "He's just not the kind of guy I would have put you with."

Odessa couldn't believe that would be an issue with him. "Because he's white?"

"No, because he's a cowboy."

Now she really felt dumb. "We have nothing going on, besides the case and a little extra-curricular exercise on the side."

"Didn't look like a whole lot of nothing to me, midget."

"I'm a little uncomfortable that you know about my sex life."

"Me, too," he replied. "So what have you told Raven?"

"About what?"

"You know, your sex life. Do you really think I can keep that under wraps?"

She wasn't about to answer any of his questions. "You're supposed to be my lawyer. Get me the hell out of here. These guys don't have a clue what's going on."

"They really can't hold you. If you really want to, just get up and walk out. There are three witnesses that say you didn't pull your piece and start shooting until after Sorenson was down."

She stood up. "Okay, let's do it." She marched to the door and pulled it open.

Mendoza looked up from a report he was reading. "Going somewhere?"

"Home. You know where the house is. Come on by for some beer when you have a moment."

Mendoza nodded. "Give my regards to your mother."

The other cop grumbled as Odessa walked across the squad room and out into the hall. Derek followed her.

In the parking lot, Whitaker waited, leaning up against his truck, frowning. "What the hell were you doing talking to Sorenson?"

"Doing what I had to."

Derek stood back a few feet and grinned at Odessa. She glared at him as she approached Whitaker.

"Who the hell is this?" Whitaker demanded with a low growl, bristling with antagonism as he gestured at Derek.

"What does it matter to you?" she said.

"It just does," he replied with a frown.

He was jealous. She'd never had a man be jealous before. Most of the time they were trying to get away from her so she wouldn't kill them.

Derek held out a hand. "I'm Derek Lange." He slanted a glance at Odessa. "Don't let Ripley yank your chain. I'm just trying to keep her out of trouble."

Wyatt glared at her. "You haven't done a very good job."

"I've been seeing the job that you've been doing." Derek said with one raised eyebrow, "and I have to say, my man, that you are brave. Messing with her is like putting an angry badger in the box and expecting it to sit still and behave."

Odessa rolled her eyes. "You'll have to forgive Derek, he's country."

"Right," Whitaker replied. He opened the passenger door of the truck. "Get in the truck. Dawson wants to see you."

"Can I stop by your house," Odessa said to Whitaker, "and get a rocket launcher? Because things are going to get ugly."

"Is Dawson the pregnant cop?" Derek asked.

"Yeah," Odessa replied, "and compared to her, I'm just a baby badger. Come on, mouthpiece, I may need you to jump in front of me in case the bullets start flying."

Derek laughed. "Damn, we're gonna have some fun, aren't we?"

She leaned toward him. "Behave yourself and I might let you off your leash."

Derek just grinned. "I'm on it." He started toward a beige rental car.

Whitaker shoved Odessa into the cab and slammed the door. Odessa barely had time to get her seat belt buckled before he jumped in behind the wheel, started the truck and peeled out of the parking lot.

"What the hell were you doing talking to Sorenson?"

"I'm not talking to you." She stuck out her chin and crossed her arms over her chest. "Not until you calm down."

He gripped the steering wheel so tightly his knuckles turned white. "Fine."

The trip to Dawson's house was made in silence. Twice Odessa looked back to see that Derek followed in his rental. How was she going to explain him?

Wyatt parked the truck in the driveway. Dawson stood on the porch, one hand on her hip and her belly thrust forward. From the thunderous look on her face, Dawson was mad with a capital M.

Wyatt opened the door and stepped out. Ripley jumped down and came around the back of the truck as her friend pulled into the driveway and parked his rental.

Wyatt followed Ripley up the walk to the steps.

"Teacher's mad today," Wyatt said.

"Does this mean I'm gonna have to sit in a corner?" Ripley asked. She was acting childishly, but damned if she cared.

"You're probably going to wear the dunce cap, too."

Ripley put one foot on the step. Dawson opened her mouth to say something, but Wyatt forestalled her. "Hold on, boss, we have someone new joining the party."

Lange stepped out of his car. He'd loosened his tie and removed the suit jacket despite the coolness of the day. He walked up the sidewalk and stopped at the look on Dawson's face.

Dawson turned and entered the house, the door slamming behind her. Wyatt flinched. This was going to be bad. Dawson was not happy. Not happy at all.

Wyatt entered the living room. Dawson stood in the center of the room, hands on her hips. When Lange entered, she pointed a finger at him. "Who are you?"

He stuck out a hand. "Derek Lange. Nice to meet you."

She didn't even look at his hand. He slowly pulled his hand back, looking intimidated. Yeah, the fireworks were going to start now.

Dawson pointed to her office. When everyone had entered she slammed the door so hard that the glass panes on her display cabinet rattled.

Wyatt pictured himself in Arizona penitentiary pink. He didn't look good.

Dawson circled them like a hungry shark. "First of all, were they shooting at you and Sorenson got in the way, or were they just shooting at Sorenson?"

Ripley gave Dawson an I-don't-know shrug.

Dawson's lips tightened as she glanced at Whitaker. "What the hell were you doing letting her go out there on her own?"

He rocked back on his heels. "You didn't tell me I had to keep her out of trouble, too."

Odessa held up her hands. "Look, I just wanted to talk to Sorenson and bring him to see you."

Dawson turned her gaze on Ripley. "You threatened him, didn't you?"

Wyatt watched Lange lean over and whisper in Ripley's ear.

"No," Ripley responded, "he had a cat."

Wyatt wondered what that meant, but knew for sure he didn't want to know. Was it some secret code for 'I beat the shit out of him'?

"What about his cat?" Dawson demanded.

"Nothing," Ripley replied.

Dawson stepped toward Ripley to get in her face, but her belly got in the way. "Answer the question. What about his cat?"

Odessa huffed. "I told him if he didn't come talk to you, I'd kill his cat."

Wyatt couldn't help it. He burst out laughing. Even Lange's lips twitched.

Ripley shrugged. "It's very effective."

"Nothing like threatening a man's pussy," Lange said in a low voice.

Wyatt couldn't stop laughing. Even Dawson's lips quirked, but she maintained her war face. She couldn't laugh even though Wyatt could see she wanted to.

Dawson put her finger up in the air and Wyatt fell silent. "This is not party time. This is serious business. A cop who was a vital link to our case is dead. And you, Ripley, are right in the center of this storm, messing up my life and my career."

Ripley said, "I did what I do best. I didn't threaten a hair on his head. I motivated him to come talk to you. He was on his way."

"How did you motivate him besides threatening to kill his cat?"

Ripley rolled her eyes. "What I said isn't important."

Dawson stared at Odessa. "I let you tag along with Whitaker as a courtesy."

"Tag along, my ass," Ripley exploded. "You would have nothing if not for me."

Wyatt stepped back. It was either that or pull his piece. And he wasn't about to so that. The last time he'd stepped between two women about to get it on, he'd ended up with six stitches.

"I have nothing with you," Dawson jabbed her finger in the air. "The evidence you've developed so far is tainted beyond redemption. To get these people we need something that isn't tainted."

"That's low," Wyatt said, trying to defend Odessa.

"I tried to get you a confession."

Dawson pinched the bridge of her nose. "Okay, people, this is what we're gonna do. You have the rest of the day to bring me something relevant that I can use to close this case. I want you all back here at six with what you have and we'll start comparing information." She dismissed them.

As Wyatt walked down the front walkway, he felt as though his hair had been singed. Dawson was on a rampage and Ripley wasn't making things easier. He pointed his remote at the truck and unlocked it. "I'm going to call in some favors. You go home and stay there. And don't kill anybody." He strode toward his truck. "I'll meet you back here at six." He hadn't been angry before, but suddenly he was and didn't know why.

"Don't get snippy with me," she said.

"I'm way beyond snippy. This case is so compromised, I'm going to have to come up with some way to fix it." Rabbits out of a hat had always been his trademark, but he didn't know if he had enough rabbits to repair this situation when what he really wanted to do was shake this woman. She was like a blister on a foot with five miles of rough walking left and no Band-aids.

He climbed in his truck and waited a moment while Lange and Ripley drove away. Then he started the motor and headed back to the station.

CHAPTER THIRTEEN

Odessa leaned against the kitchen counter tapping her fingers on the counter top. Her mother poured coffee into a mug and handed it to Derek. "You will leave us now."

Derek turned to Odessa. She nodded. She'd be fine. What could her mother do to her? She wasn't five years old anymore and intimidated by the threat of a time-out.

She sat down at the table and studied her mother. Celeste had dark circles under her eyes and her lips were pinched. Her mother was tired and Odessa knew in part that she was to blame.

As soon as they were alone, her mother turned to her. "A half hour ago I received a phone call from Detective Louis Mendoza."

Odessa stopped drumming her fingers and smiled. "How's he doing?"

Celeste frowned. "Since you spent some time with him today, I assume you already know the answer."

"I wasn't lying. I just wanted to clarify that."

"He tells me you were involved in a shooting."

"Someone shot at me and I shot back."

"Is that the best answer you can come up with?"

For the moment. Odessa nodded. "It's the one I'm sticking to."

"And this man Sorenson?"

"He was either the target or in the way. I'm still not sure."

"He was a police officer."

"A bad one and in some way responsible for your husband's death." *Okay, Celeste, swirl that one around in your I-don't-want-revenge mind.* As soon as the words left her mouth, Odessa regretted them.

She almost apologized, but Celeste sighed, sat down at the table and covered her face with her hands. "I know. Your father was investigating something and this man Sorenson's name came up."

Odessa pushed herself away from the counter. "Did Dad tell you this?"

Celeste shook her head. "No, I read it."

Odessa frowned. "Were you reading Dad's case files?" She sat down next to her mother and touched the back of her mother's hand.

"Sometimes I'm desperate for something to read," Celeste said quietly.

Odessa hadn't even considered that her dad had anything else besides what he'd mailed to her. "Mom, do you have dad's notes now?"

Her mother nodded as tears tracked down her face. "In our bedroom. I know I should have given them to the police, but they were your father's, in his handwriting, in the leather notebooks I purchased for him. If I'd given them up, I would have been giving a part of him away."

Odessa squeezed her mom's hand. She'd been wrestling with her own demons long enough to understand her mother's. "No one's going to be mad at you. Can I see them?"

Her mother glanced up. "*May* I see them."

Odessa sighed. Her mother never changed and for the first time she was comforted by that knowledge. "May I see them, please?"

Her mother led the way down the back hall to the bedrooms. The smell of smoke was still strong in the hall, but the sound of hammering from the front told Odessa that the construction crew was hard at work.

Her mother opened the bottom drawer of her dresser and pulled out five small leather bound notebooks that would easily fit into the inside pocket of a man's jacket. She handed them to Odessa along with a large manilla file folder stuffed with paper. "I should have given these to you earlier."

Once her hand was wrapped around the leather, a warm feeling swirled through Odessa, as though her father were in the room with her. "Thanks, Mom."

"Odessa," her mother's voice was grave. "Don't use this information in a bad way."

That's a matter of opinion. "I don't know if this is information the police can use." That was a nice, non-committal answer.

"I'm worried about you, Odessa." Her mother gripped Odessa's arm tightly.

Odessa patted her mother's hand. "Don't be. I'm all grown up."

"That's not what I mean. When was the last time you went to church?"

She didn't have to think hard. "Dad's funeral."

"Otherwise?"

Odessa had to think about her answer. Church had never been a huge part of her belief system. She'd never found justice in church. The CIA gave her the power to carry out justice. She found her truth in the belief that she was doing what was right for the good of humanity. *Oh what a humanitarian I am*, she thought wryly.

"Answer my question," her mother said sternly.

"I don't remember." It was the best answer she could come up with unless she wanted to use her best friend's wedding. But she didn't think her mother would go for that since Raven and Derek had been married in a civil ceremony in Paris and then a second time in a Baptist church in Florida. The second ceremony had been to make Raven's father happy.

A tear rolled down her cheek. "God remembers."

Odessa reached up and wiped it away. "Don't worry about me. When I was little you always told me that God helps those who help themselves." Odessa had been helping herself since childhood. Odessa respected her mother's beliefs, because they worked for her mother. They just didn't happen to work for Odessa.

She hugged her mother. "Thanks, Mom." She gripped the folder and the notebooks tightly and headed toward her bedroom.

Odessa's bedroom was homage to her childhood with movie posters on the walls, closet still filled with her Catholic school uniforms and diaries hidden in a shoebox at the back of the closet. The walls were painted a bright yellow with splashes of color matching souvenirs she'd collected on her many trips to Martinique with her mother. Being back in her old bedroom was like being a part of another long-ago life. And yet she felt innocent here, clean, untainted by the evil of the world.

Odessa sat cross-legged in the middle of her bed and touched the leather notebooks with reverence. Then she opened the first one and started reading.

"You've been holed up in here for over an hour," Derek said as he entered the room and glanced around curiously.

She waved the notebook at him. "I'm gonna kill them. I'm gonna kill their families. I'm gonna kill their pets."

"Did you find the guy who ordered the hit on your dad?"

She held out a book. "I don't know, but a local businessman named Robert Chapman with a connection to Randy Sorenson has come up in my dad's notes. My dad Googled Sorenson and found out that on some fishing trip to Idaho he caught a huge Chinook, whatever the hell that is—"

"A salmon," Derek interrupted.

"Thank you, Forest Ranger Derek," she replied. "Sorenson went on this trip with Chapman and a half dozen other local Phoenix cops." She rustled through an open file folder and brought up a sheet of paper. "I have to wonder why Robert Chapman, multi-millionaire industrialist, appears to be playing with cops. And all of these names match people in my father's notebook. These cops are Chapman's goons."

"You don't know that."

She rolled her eyes. "Two plus two equals conspiracy. Even I can figure that out."

Derek shook his head. "Too slight."

Maybe for the police, but for her this was rock solid evidence. "Then let's call A.J. and see what she can find out. She has resources we can't even begin to develop." After reaching into her pocket for her cell phone, she called A.J. and gave her all the names from the notebook.

"If anything exists," A.J. said, "I'll find it."

"I know you will."

"Sit tight, I'll get back to you in a couple hours," A.J. responded.

Odessa disconnected and rustled through the pile of papers in the folder.

"I know what you're thinking." Derek flopped down in the only comfortable chair in the bedroom.

"Okay, I give up. What am I thinking?"

"You're thinking of putting this guy Chapman down."

She waved her dad's notebook. "I have enough info on him."

"You have squat."

"So what? You'd do the same thing."

"Not on such scanty intell. You can't kill this guy based on a news article," he glanced at the article, "that's almost five years old."

Hell, she'd killed for less. "I'll wait for A.J. to finalize everything."

"Killing this guy doesn't solve shit. If he's involved in all these murders, killing him won't stop any more murders from happening. You have to bring down his whole organization. If he's the only one out of the picture, someone else will just step into his shoes."

Odessa shrugged. "I don't care. I'll take them all down, too."

Derek looked sad. "Odessa, Chapman isn't an assignment; he's a vendetta."

She sighed. "Don't tell me you're worried about my soul just like my mother."

"I'm not worried about your soul. I'm worried that I'll have to kill you after this because you went rogue. And if it comes down to me and you—"

"We'd probably kill each other."

"And Raven would then exhume the bodies and kill us both again."

Odessa shuddered. The thought of Raven on a rampage chilled her. "Not if she broke a fingernail first."

"Don't underestimate my wife. You didn't spend a week with her in the desert with no toilet paper."

And Odessa never wanted to. Raven might be a supermodel undercover spy, but she was hard as nails. "If I promise not to do anything without talking to you first, will that be okay? That's the best you'll get out of me."

Derek didn't look totally convinced. "Don't do anything foolish, Odessa."

"I never do." But, Odessa thought, everything depended on what A.J. found. Odessa would rewrite the rules when Derek wasn't looking.

Wyatt stood on the front porch of Dawson's elegant Victorian and glanced at his watch for the fiftieth time. The street was ablaze with Christmas lights and a couple of kids played in an adjacent yard with a fake snowman. Odessa was late and Whitaker didn't like that. He should have stayed with her.

His cell phone rang and he flipped it open.

"Dude," Derek Lange said, "we have a problem."

Dread filled him. "What sort of problem?" he asked, hoping Odessa wasn't a part of it. For a small woman, she had gotten under his skin big time. She was like an itch that never stopped.

Lange sounded tired. "Odessa isn't showing up for your little powwow."

"Shit," Wyatt said.

"You ever hear of a Robert Chapman?" Lange asked.

"Yeah, I've heard about him. Big time businessman with his fingers in a thousand pies." Wyatt had long ago learned to distrust anyone who spent all his time grabbing headlines to make himself look better than he probably was and Chapman was a prime headline grabber. Photos of him with the mayor of Phoenix, the governor of the state and even the president of the United States decorated the newspapers and the TV on a regular basis.

"He's your money man."

Chapman couldn't possibly be a murderer. He was in bed with every politician in the state. Wait, maybe that did qualify him to be a murderer. "How do you know?" Wyatt's mouth went bone dry. Instinct told him there would be no stuffing this genie back in its bottle.

"I have a hacker who can find out every detail in your life right down to the brand of condom you use."

"What kind of information did your hacker find out about Chapman?"

"Wire transfers to six cops, including Sorenson. Each corresponded to the dates of all your homicides. These cops are your killers and Robert Chapman ordered all of these deaths. A.J. faxed all the information on his financials. With the information Phil Ripley had in his case journals, makes for a good case."

So close, Wyatt thought. "Damn, we can't use jack diddley. It's all tainted. No judge in the state will let the department use what you found."

"Let me take him out. I can make it look like a heart attack."

Wyatt rubbed his forehead. This guy definitely worked for the CIA. "You sound like Odessa."

There was a mirthless laugh on the other end of the phone. "Who do you think taught me that trick? The Company is all about being on the sly."

Shit, that's what he needed, something on the sly. Think, Wyatt, think. You can't let this bastard go or you'll be arresting the woman you love. Why did love have to complicate everything?

"This guy is international," Lange said. "Maybe my people can make a case."

Dawson might hate it, but if Wyatt could get this guy in jail safe where he belonged, it would forestall anything Odessa had in mind. "I have an idea. I need you to take the information you have and give it to someone. And then I need you out of Phoenix as clandestinely as possible."

"Clandestine is my style," Lange said with a small chuckle.

Wyatt started down the porch steps to his truck. "Just get out of town after you deliver the information."

"Got ya."

Wyatt gave him the name and address of Special Agent in Charge Giancarlo Jackson of the Phoenix FBI. "Don't talk to him, don't be drawn into answering any questions. Just hand him all the information you have on Chapman and get the hell away. No name, no personal information of any kind. Be a ghost. Giancarlo will take it from there."

"You got it. I'm in the wind. But what about Odessa?"

"I have that covered," Wyatt answered as he unlocked his truck with the remote. "Did your hacker give you an address for Chapman?" Derek rattled off the address.

Lange disconnected. Wyatt opened the truck door, but Dawson's voice from behind stopped him. "Where are you going, Whitaker? We have a meeting scheduled."

Wyatt didn't answer. He stepped up into his truck, started the motor and roared down the street without a backward look at his boss. All he could think of was that he was going to get fired.

Odessa sat at Robert Chapman's desk. She'd been in his office for almost an hour and had managed to find out a lot about him. Especially his decorating preferences. His office was large and airy and filled with a large collection of Nazi memorabilia, if such objects could be called collectibles.

People often considered their home offices private space and seldom put things away. Chapman was no exception. His desk had yielded a lot of information, even a file on her, though he didn't have much more than her name and social security number and her position as a personal trainer. She laughed. In her hand was a list of names with hers neatly penciled at the top. She'd made his hit parade. In a strange, twisted, sort of way she was flattered.

The door opened and Robert Chapman entered in a swirl of cigar smoke. Odessa glanced up and smiled. Chapman was tall and slender with short-cropped blonde hair and piercing blue eyes. The information A.J. had given her stated his age at forty-one, but he looked older. Chapman stopped on the threshold to stare at her. Then he entered and closed the door firmly.

This was the man who'd had her father killed and seeing her father's name on the list with a single slash through it had left her feeling numb.

He took a drag off his cigar and blew out the smoke. "Well, if it isn't the talented Miss Ripley. I've been expecting you."

Odessa tossed the file on the desk and reached for the Sig Saur in her waistband. "No, you haven't. If you'd known I was coming, you would have been a bit more prepared."

"You've caused me a lot of trouble." He walked over to the desk, smiling.

Containing the rage swirling inside her, she shrugged. "I'm a troublemaker from way back."

"I've read your file."

She concentrated on every breath, keeping each one even. "This paltry piece of intelligence?" She picked up the file and waved it. "For a man with your money I should think you'd have better intel."

Chapman studied her for a second. "What's so special about you?"

Her eyes met his. Behind his bravado she saw fear. She could use that. This guy was gonna talk all kinds of shit; he knew he'd come to the end of the road. "I guess since I'm going to kill you I can tell you the truth. I'm the best your tax money can buy."

"Taxes are for the little people."

She waited for elation to come but strangely enough it didn't. "Obviously, you don't realize you're speaking to an agent for the United States government."

His eyebrows rose. "You're a tax collector."

"Hardly. I'm a professional assassin." She glanced around the room.

"I don't believe you."

She was going to break it down for him, like in the movies. "Bob, you have the best security system money can buy. I broke into it in thirty seconds flat. I know the last book you ordered on Amazon. I know your greedy little tentacles reach from here to Stockholm, Amsterdam, Paris and Melbourne. I know you wired money to private accounts in the Caymans set up for Phoenix cops to do your dirty work. I have all the account numbers, the dates of the transfers which correspond to the deaths of all those people who you ordered murdered, including my father, and I have to tell you I have no respect for you. Dude, if you did your own killing, no one would have ever found out." She leaned forward. "Do you know what it's like to look into someone's eyes before you kill them?"

He shrugged. "I don't have to get my hands dirty. That's what the little people are for. Aren't you given orders?"

"Of course, by someone I respect. Someone who has been in the trenches. You're kinda smug for a guy who's about to die."

"Really?" He sat down in a overstuffed chair and crossed his legs at the knee. "Stanley told me that for a little woman you talk big."

"And here I thought Stan was on a bus to Alaska. Too bad for him. For a little woman, I kicked his ass. See what happens when you let a little fish go? They run to the management and tattle their little hearts out. When I'm done with you, I'll have to find him and do him in. What a waste of a good bullet."

He steepled his fingers together. "He is strong in his beliefs."

No, he wasn't, he was hedging his bets. She'd bet if she had the call traced, they'd find him far far away. She would have done the same. "I'll make sure that's carved on his headstone." She held up his hit list. "I noticed you put me on your hit list right above Luc Broussard and Cher Dawson. Don't like them much, do you?"

"Neither one of them knows their place."

Odessa simply shook her head. "And what would that be, Bob?"

His weak little chin went up as though he were trying to look tough. "On the bottom with all the rest of the trash."

"Bob, Bob, Bob. You just went from a single fast bullet in the head to slow, painful torture." A small spark of hatred opened inside her. She stood. "I'm tired of you. Let's do this."

She moved around the desk. Chapman stiffened, a look of surprise on his face. "You can't kill me."

"Sure I can. I won't even lose any sleep. And no one is going to catch me."

A voice sounded from the door. "I will."

Wyatt. She turned. Whitaker stood framed in the doorway looking grave and sad. "Whitaker, this doesn't involve you."

He folded his arms over his chest. "If it involves you, it involves me. I'm not going to let you kill this man."

She grabbed Chapman by the shirt collar and yanked him back in his chair. Wyatt was not going to talk her out this. She didn't care if he was right. Some things were more important than being right. "This stupid ass will wriggle his way out of trial. I'm going to save the government a whole shitload of money by killing him now."

"That's not your call." Wyatt walked into the office and didn't stop until he was right on her.

Odessa could see the pleading in his eyes. That wasn't fair. She held back the tears that threatened to fall. "Get out and let me do this. Put me in jail afterward, but this scum needs to die."

"You'd better listen to this race traitor, Ripley," Chapman said. "Whitaker is a lot smarter than you think."

"Would you shut up?" Whitaker said in an exasperated tone. "I'm trying to save your sorry ass."

"Don't do—"

Whitaker slapped the back of Chapman's head. Chapman fell over the arm of the chair he'd been sitting in and landed on the floor with a thump. "Let him be unconscious for awhile." Whitaker touched Odessa's face. "I'm not going to lose you because of this man."

"What are you trying to say?"

"I love you and I'm not going to let you throw it away. You're mine."

For a second, Odessa couldn't move. What the hell was he saying? This man with his too-big truck and arrogant manner couldn't possibly love her. He was too much a cowboy. Okay, he'd roused feelings in her that she'd never experienced before, but it wasn't love, was it? "You like country western music and watch wrestling."

"What do you like to do besides kill people?"

"I like the ballet." Her resolve hardened. Her father deserved to rest easy.

His mouth fell open for a second. "Now that surprises me."

She held up her hands. "It was the only thing I can share with my mom."

He reached out and pulled her to him, kissing her, and then tugging her toward the door. "Let's get out of here."

She pulled away. "No, I have a job to do." She pulled her gun out and walked around the chair. She pushed Chapman on his back and straddled him. His eyes were open and they widened as she put her gun against his lips. He stiffened as she glared at him. "I guess I don't have time for that special torture I promised you. Pity."

"He's not worth killing," Wyatt said. "Isn't a lifetime of watching him suffer in jail better than a moment of watching him die?"

Her finger caressed the trigger. But she paused and glanced up at Whitaker. "What did you do?"

"I made things right." Whitaker's voice was almost pleading.

Odessa froze with indecision. What should she do? She pressed the barrel of the gun down harder. She thought of her father dead because of this man, and she thought of all the other people who had died because of him.

She sat back and the fear on his face disappeared. "If I let this scum go who's to say he won't hop a plane for wherever and be gone forever."

Whitaker looked at his watch. "He's not going anywhere. He has about five minutes before his life takes a turn for the worse."

She stared into Chapman's frightened eyes. She'd seen the look more times then she cared to admit, but this time her guts were threatening to empty. Was she feeling guilty? And what about Wyatt? He confused her. She wanted to pull the trigger, but she wanted Wyatt to keep loving her. He wouldn't if she killed Chapman. "And what's that supposed to mean?"

Wyatt slipped his hand around her upper arm and tried to lift her up. "That means we have four minutes to get the hell out of here."

She held up her hand. "I'm not going anywhere. I came to kill this man. I want to kill this man. I messed up this case. Your boss has told me often enough. If I don't kill him, he gets off scot free."

"Odessa, you wouldn't believe how many cases I've broken on anonymous tips. I'm sure that's true of a lot of agencies." He held his hand out to her, his eyes pleading with her to come with him.

She didn't know how he could make everything right so she could walk away free and not hate herself for the rest of her life. "Who did you call?"

"I didn't call anyone." He crouched down level with her. "I had your friend Lange make a special delivery. To Special Agent Giancarlo Jackson." He gave her that wicked grin.

"Who the hell is he?"

"He's another Jackson."

"You mean with the Feds?"

"Exactly."

She didn't believe him. "I thought you didn't like working with them."

He pulled her to her feet. "What makes you think I'm going to stick around here to work with them?" He glanced at his watch again.

"But—."

"The Phoenix PD may not be able to use the evidence we found out, but that doesn't mean another agency can't. I don't care who arrests this guy. In a federal prison he'll get good health care and be around for a long, long time."

Part of her still couldn't believe him. He'd outsmarted her screw-up. "You worked with the FBI for me?"

"I did it for us."

Now he was talking crazy. "What *us*? There is no *us*."

"The sex is awesome, you make me laugh and you like me. That's love. What else do we need?"

Odessa frowned at him. "But…but—"

"No buts. We're getting married and having babies. We're going to make a life together and I'm not going to let you jeopardize that for this toad." He pointed at Chapman still lying on the floor, his face deathly pale. "Now let's get the hell out of here."

Wyatt had fixed everything. She could walk. With her freedom, her life and her soul. And the man she wanted for the rest of her life. There was no way she was turning down this deal. But she had one thing to do first. She held up a finger. "One second." She bent over Chapman, pulled him up by his shirt, then kneed him in the crotch. As he groaned and started to fall, she pulled her knee up again and knocked him flat. He sprawled back on the floor.

Odessa wiped her hands. "Okay, I'm good for the revenge part."

Whitaker grabbed her and dragged her down the hallway and out the front door. "Just run," he ordered as he sprinted down the walkway and out onto the street. "Don't look back."

Halfway down the block a line of unmarked black sedans turned the corner and sped toward the Chapman mansion. Whitaker grabbed her and pulled her behind some bushes. When the cars passed them, he grabbed her hand and sprinted across the street toward his truck.

Once inside the truck, Odessa leaned her head back against the headrest. "That was fun, although I'm a tad disappointed. I didn't get to kill anyone."

"You haven't said the most important thing of the evening."

"What's that?" she asked.

"That you love me."

She didn't say anything for a long moment as she examined her feelings. She'd often thought that falling in love was weak, even though Raven and Derek obviously loved each other and neither of them was weak. But Odessa was different. She'd never thought that love would ever be a part of her life. She'd had a vision of spending the rest of her life working for The Company, following orders and being the best little agent they ever had. But now she had a vision of spending the rest of her life with Wyatt and the babies they'd have. She wasn't certain about baby thing, because she had a hard time thinking of herself as a mother, but then again, Celeste was only a phone call away.

"Well," Wyatt demanded, "tell me you love me."

She slid next to him and snuggled against his side. The Company be damned. Wyatt's future was so much more enticing. "I love you." The second she said the words, she knew they were true. She did love him. She loved him more than she'd ever believed she could love anyone.

He kissed her and for a long moment just before their lips parted, Odessa felt an odd warmth spread through her. Damn, she thought, I guess I really do love him.

CHAPTER FOURTEEN

A Month Later

Odessa lay in the bed. “You got your tattoo fixed for me?”

Wyatt kissed her stomach and his light touches tickled. “Just for you.” He lifted himself up, hovering over her, love shining in his eyes.

Giggling, she said. “Let me see it.” She’d never been ticklish before. Wyatt must have brought it out in her. He’d brought out a lot of new and intriguing aspects in her. She reached for the large white bandage taped to his chest.

“Set a date,” he commanded in a low husky voice, his I’m-gonna-make-you-moan voice.

“For what?”

“A wedding, what do you think?”

She snatched the bandage off his chest. The broken black heart now had a red bandage over it. With her name written on it. “So I fixed your broken heart?”

He gave her a quick kiss. “You did.”

She lifted her head and kissed him just above the tattoo. “You fixed a couple of things broken in my life too.”

“Set a date.”

The whisper of a door sounded. “What’s that?”

“No way, you’re not getting away from me this easily.”

She reached into the nightstand for her gun just as the sound of breaking glass came from the living room. Someone cursed. Wyatt scrambled out of bed.

“Carlyle!” she yelled, recognizing the voice and his choice of curse. Wyatt tossed a shirt at her. “What’s this for?”

“I don’t want anyone seeing you naked.”

Carlyle appeared in the doorway before Odessa could put the shirt on. She pulled the sheet up to cover her breasts. She hadn't talked to Carlyle since she'd sent him a vague letter of resignation. "Are you here to kill me?" she asked. What else would he be doing here in the middle of the night.

Wyatt reached for his gun in the bedside table, but Odessa touched his arm and shook her head. Carlyle wanted only her.

Carlyle's face relaxed into a smile. "Ripley, relax, I'm not here to get rid of you. But I am gonna miss you more than I miss most of my agents. I gave you a lot of rope because you're good, but I'm not gonna miss the attitude."

Relaxing, she gave him a half smile. "You're sure you're not here to whack me?"

He sighed and shook his head. "You are safe for the moment, even though you really shook up the Phoenix PD and several international corporations. You never do anything small, do you?"

"No, sir."

"How's the family?"

"My brother is running for the district attorney's office next year with the backing of a very powerful senator. I have rediscovered my mother. We've made peace with each other and she's not a bad old girl. I spent a lot of my life being angry with her for no reason. And, I'm in love." She glanced at Wyatt who had pulled on his shirt and pants.

Wyatt looked pained. "Is this an episode of *Oprah*?"

She dug her elbow into his side. "Look, I'm trying to be kinder and gentler, okay? Stop ruining the picture."

Wyatt grinned at her.

Carlyle nodded. "If you get tired of playing footsie, you can always come back and freelance for me."

"I don't think so. I just got a cool gig working for a security firm. They pay me more than you for half the work. And this man here wants to make babies with me. My babies." Imagine that. Odessa Ripley, mother, PTA president and former government assassin. They probably wouldn't allow guns at the meetings. "So what the hell are you doing here?"

"I'm your alibi."

"My alibi for what? I'm out of the business."

Carlyle looked at his watch. "In about five minutes, Chapman's going to take a header in the prison shower."

"Wait a second," Wyatt interrupted. "Do you realize that I'm a cop and not only are you demonstrating previous knowledge of a crime, but you're making my woman an accessory?"

Carlyle's gaze flickered at Wyatt. "I have special orders to do this."

Odessa grinned, amused at the way they both bristled over her. "Who's doing Chapman?"

"You know I'm not at liberty to discuss an ongoing assignment. You're not working for me anymore and therefore no longer in the loop."

Odessa stood and wrapped the sheet around her, the gun still held at her side. Even though she didn't really have to worry, she was not one to let her guard down, even with Carlyle. "You never let me do anyone in prison. Come on, tell me."

"I have a new Nemesis."

Odessa frowned. "You didn't give Derek my job, did you?" No, Raven probably wouldn't allow that.

"No. I gave it to A.J."

Odessa sniffled. "A.J! My baby has grown up." She pretended to dab a tear from her eye.

"How can you be happy about this?" Wyatt asked curiously.

"Wait a minute," Odessa said. "You made me promise not to kill him and I fulfilled that part of our bargain. I frankly was looking forward to visiting him for the rest of his life in prison just to poke at him once in a while, but I can say with all honesty, I'm not unhappy with the turn of events."

"You set a date right now," Wyatt said, "or I'm going to the phone and calling the prison."

"That's blackmail," Odessa objected.

Carlyle caressed the gun in the holster at his belt. "I'll be happy to—"

"No way. Back off, Carlyle," Odessa said.

"A date," Wyatt insisted.

She groaned and frowned at him. She'd been beaten. "Okay, fine. June 12, next summer."

"That's almost six months away."

Carlyle sat in a chair to watch the byplay. Odessa wanted to toss him out on his ear, but the five minutes wasn't up yet. And if he needed to verify her whereabouts, she wasn't about to let him go.

"You said set a date," she said. "I did. I'm perfectly happy living in sin. Why do you want to marry me?"

"Other than the fact that I love you to distraction…"

"Thank you. I love you, too." And she did. Being with Wyatt had changed her. She wasn't certain the change was for the better, but he seemed to think so and so did her mother. Odessa had come to value her mother's opinion.

Carlyle groaned in the background.

"And we have to get started on making babies." He rubbed his hands together. "Little Odessas and Wyatts running around with my good looks and your attitude."

"I have a news flash for you, man. You're having chocolate babies."

Wyatt grabbed her by the hand and pulled her to him. He wrapped an arm around her waist and glanced at Carlyle. "Hit the road. I'm alibi enough for her."

Carlyle reached into his pocket and tossed a bullet with a red ribbon tied around it at Odessa. She grabbed at it, but missed. Wyatt caught the bullet. "What does this mean?"

"I'm off the radar." She smiled at Carlyle. "Thanks."

He pushed out of the chair. "If you ever want to freelance…"

"I'm done. I'm getting married and having babies." She grabbed Wyatt and kissed him. She broke the kiss and pointed at her former boss. "Will you get out? I don't need a witness for this." She let the sheet drop and Carlyle couldn't stop grinning.

"Have a good life, Ripley."

She touched Wyatt's face. Love shone in his eyes. "I will, Carlyle. I will."

ABOUT THE AUTHOR

The writing team of **J. M. Jeffries** is composed of **Miriam Pace** and **Jacqueline Hamilton**, who met in a critique group. Before the meetings, they would walk around the neighborhood brainstorming and eventually decided that they needed to collaborate. They sold their first suspense thriller, *A Dangerous Love*, to Genesis Press and since then have published six books with Genesis. Two more will be released in 2006. Recently their romantic comedies, featuring Cupid and Venus as matchmakers to modern day lovers, have been optioned by Tivoli Productions as a possible TV series. In 2004, they won the prestigious Emma Award for their book, *A Dangerous Obsession*, and recently won the 2005 Lories Award for *Code Name: Diva*. Their books consistently receive 4 ½ star reviews from *Romantic Times* and they were nominated for Best Multi-Cultural in 2001 for *A Dangerous Love*. The hero in *A Dangerous Love* won a coveted spot on the Bad to the Bone hero list from *Romantic Times.*

2006 Publication Schedule

January

A Lover's Legacy Veronica Parker 1-58571-167-5 $9.95	Love Lasts Forever Dominiqua Douglas 1-58571-187-X $9.95	Under the Cherry Moon Christal Jordan-Mims 1-58571-169-1 $12.95

February

Second Chances at Love Cheris Hodges 1-58571-188-8 $9.95	Enchanted Desire Wanda Y. Thomas 1-58571-176-4 $9.95	Caught Up Deatri King Bey 1-58571-178-0 $12.95

March

I'm Gonna Make You Love Me Gwyneth Bolton 1-58571-181-0 $9.95	Through the Fire Seressia Glass 1-58571-173-X $9.95	Notes When Summer Ends Beverly Lauderdale 1-58571-180-2 $12.95

April

Sin and Surrender J.M. Jeffries 1-58571-189-6 $9.95	Unearthing Passions Elaine Sims 1-58571-184-5 $9.95	Between Tears Pamela Ridley 1-58571-179-9 $12.95

May

Misty Blue Dyanne Davis 1-58571-186-1 $9.95	Ironic Pamela Leigh Starr 1-58571-168-3 $9.95	Cricket's Serenade Carolita Blythe 1-58571-183-7 $12.95

June

Cupid Barbara Keaton 1-58571-174-8 $9.95	Havana Sunrise Kymberly Hunt 1-58571-182-9 $9.95

2006 Publication Schedule (continued)

July

Love Me Carefully	No Ordinary Love	Rehoboth Road
A.C. Arthur	Angela Weaver	Anita Ballard-Jones
1-58571-177-2	1-58571-198-5	1-58571-196-9
$9.95	$9.95	$12.95

August

Scent of Rain	Love in High Gear	Rise of the Phoenix
Annetta P. Lee	Charlotte Roy	Kenneth Whetstone
158571-199-3	158571-185-3	1-58571-197-7
$9.95	$9.95	$12.95

September

The Business of Love	Rock Star	A Dead Man Speaks
Cheris Hodges	Rosyln Hardy Holcomb	Lisa Jones Johnson
1-58571-193-4	1-58571-200-0	1-58571-203-5
$9.95	$9.95	$12.95

October

Rivers of the Soul-Part 1	A Dangerous Woman	Sinful Intentions
Leslie Esdaile	J.M. Jeffries	Crystal Rhodes
1-58571-223-X	1-58571-195-0	1-58571-201-9
$9.95	$9.95	$12.95

November

Only You	Ebony Eyes	Still Waters Run Deep – Part 2
Crystal Hubbard	Kei Swanson	Leslie Esdaile
1-58571-208-6	1-58571-194-2	1-58571-224-8
$9.95	$9.95	$9.95

December

Let's Get It On	Nights Over Egypt	A Pefect Place to Pray
Dyanne Davis	Barbara Keaton	I.L. Goodwin
1-58571-210-8	1-58571-192-6	1-58571-202-7
$9.95	$9.95	$12.95

Other Genesis Press, Inc. Titles

A Dangerous Deception	J.M. Jeffries	$8.95
A Dangerous Love	J.M. Jeffries	$8.95
A Dangerous Obsession	J.M. Jeffries	$8.95
A Drummer's Beat to Mend	Kei Swanson	$9.95
A Happy Life	Charlotte Harris	$9.95
A Heart's Awakening	Veronica Parker	$9.95
A Lark on the Wing	Phyliss Hamilton	$9.95
A Love of Her Own	Cheris F. Hodges	$9.95
A Love to Cherish	Beverly Clark	$8.95
A Risk of Rain	Dar Tomlinson	$8.95
A Twist of Fate	Beverly Clark	$8.95
A Will to Love	Angie Daniels	$9.95
Acquisitions	Kimberley White	$8.95
Across	Carol Payne	$12.95
After the Vows	Leslie Esdaile	$10.95
(Summer Anthology)	T.T. Henderson	
	Jacqueline Thomas	
Again My Love	Kayla Perrin	$10.95
Against the Wind	Gwynne Forster	$8.95
All I Ask	Barbara Keaton	$8.95
Ambrosia	T.T. Henderson	$8.95
An Unfinished Love Affair	Barbara Keaton	$8.95
And Then Came You	Dorothy Elizabeth Love	$8.95
Angel's Paradise	Janice Angelique	$9.95
At Last	Lisa G. Riley	$8.95
Best of Friends	Natalie Dunbar	$8.95
Beyond the Rapture	Beverly Clark	$9.95
Blaze	Barbara Keaton	$9.95
Blood Lust	J. M. Jeffries	$9.95
Bodyguard	Andrea Jackson	$9.95
Boss of Me	Diana Nyad	$8.95
Bound by Love	Beverly Clark	$8.95
Breeze	Robin Hampton Allen	$10.95

Other Genesis Press, Inc. Titles (continued)

Broken	Dar Tomlinson	$24.95
By Design	Barbara Keaton	$8.95
Cajun Heat	Charlene Berry	$8.95
Careless Whispers	Rochelle Alers	$8.95
Cats & Other Tales	Marilyn Wagner	$8.95
Caught in a Trap	Andre Michelle	$8.95
Caught Up In the Rapture	Lisa G. Riley	$9.95
Cautious Heart	Cheris F Hodges	$8.95
Chances	Pamela Leigh Starr	$8.95
Cherish the Flame	Beverly Clark	$8.95
Class Reunion	Irma Jenkins/John Brown	$12.95
Code Name: Diva	J.M. Jeffries	$9.95
Conquering Dr. Wexler's Heart	Kimberley White	$9.95
Crossing Paths, Tempting Memories	Dorothy Elizabeth Love	$9.95
Cypress Whisperings	Phyllis Hamilton	$8.95
Dark Embrace	Crystal Wilson Harris	$8.95
Dark Storm Rising	Chinelu Moore	$10.95
Daughter of the Wind	Joan Xian	$8.95
Deadly Sacrifice	Jack Kean	$22.95
Designer Passion	Dar Tomlinson	$8.95
Dreamtective	Liz Swados	$5.95
Ebony Butterfly II	Delilah Dawson	$14.95
Echoes of Yesterday	Beverly Clark	$9.95
Eden's Garden	Elizabeth Rose	$8.95
Everlastin' Love	Gay G. Gunn	$8.95
Everlasting Moments	Dorothy Elizabeth Love	$8.95
Everything and More	Sinclair Lebeau	$8.95
Everything but Love	Natalie Dunbar	$8.95
Eve's Prescription	Edwina Martin Arnold	$8.95
Falling	Natalie Dunbar	$9.95
Fate	Pamela Leigh Starr	$8.95
Finding Isabella	A.J. Garrotto	$8.95

Other Genesis Press, Inc. Titles (continued)

Forbidden Quest	Dar Tomlinson	$10.95
Forever Love	Wanda Thomas	$8.95
From the Ashes	Kathleen Suzanne Jeanne Sumerix	$8.95
Gentle Yearning	Rochelle Alers	$10.95
Glory of Love	Sinclair LeBeau	$10.95
Go Gentle into that Good Night	Malcom Boyd	$12.95
Goldengroove	Mary Beth Craft	$16.95
Groove, Bang, and Jive	Steve Cannon	$8.99
Hand in Glove	Andrea Jackson	$9.95
Hard to Love	Kimberley White	$9.95
Hart & Soul	Angie Daniels	$8.95
Heartbeat	Stephanie Bedwell-Grime	$8.95
Hearts Remember	M. Loui Quezada	$8.95
Hidden Memories	Robin Allen	$10.95
Higher Ground	Leah Latimer	$19.95
Hitler, the War, and the Pope	Ronald Rychiak	$26.95
How to Write a Romance	Kathryn Falk	$18.95
I Married a Reclining Chair	Lisa M. Fuhs	$8.95
Indigo After Dark Vol. I	Nia Dixon/Angelique	$10.95
Indigo After Dark Vol. II	Dolores Bundy/Cole Riley	$10.95
Indigo After Dark Vol. III	Montana Blue/Coco Morena	$10.95
Indigo After Dark Vol. IV	Cassandra Colt/ Diana Richeaux	$14.95
Indigo After Dark Vol. V	Delilah Dawson	$14.95
Icie	Pamela Leigh Starr	$8.95
I'll Be Your Shelter	Giselle Carmichael	$8.95
I'll Paint a Sun	A.J. Garrotto	$9.95
Illusions	Pamela Leigh Starr	$8.95
Indiscretions	Donna Hill	$8.95
Intentional Mistakes	Michele Sudler	$9.95
Interlude	Donna Hill	$8.95
Intimate Intentions	Angie Daniels	$8.95

Other Genesis Press, Inc. Titles (continued)

Jolie's Surrender	Edwina Martin-Arnold	$8.95
Kiss or Keep	Debra Phillips	$8.95
Lace	Giselle Carmichael	$9.95
Last Train to Memphis	Elsa Cook	$12.95
Lasting Valor	Ken Olsen	$24.95
Let Us Prey	Hunter Lundy	$25.95
Life Is Never As It Seems	J.J. Michael	$12.95
Lighter Shade of Brown	Vicki Andrews	$8.95
Love Always	Mildred E. Riley	$10.95
Love Doesn't Come Easy	Charlyne Dickerson	$8.95
Love Unveiled	Gloria Greene	$10.95
Love's Deception	Charlene Berry	$10.95
Love's Destiny	M. Loui Quezada	$8.95
Mae's Promise	Melody Walcott	$8.95
Magnolia Sunset	Giselle Carmichael	$8.95
Matters of Life and Death	Lesego Malepe, Ph.D.	$15.95
Meant to Be	Jeanne Sumerix	$8.95
Midnight Clear	Leslie Esdaile	$10.95
(Anthology)	Gwynne Forster	
	Carmen Green	
	Monica Jackson	
Midnight Magic	Gwynne Forster	$8.95
Midnight Peril	Vicki Andrews	$10.95
Misconceptions	Pamela Leigh Starr	$9.95
Montgomery's Children	Richard Perry	$14.95
My Buffalo Soldier	Barbara B. K. Reeves	$8.95
Naked Soul	Gwynne Forster	$8.95
Next to Last Chance	Louisa Dixon	$24.95
No Apologies	Seressia Glass	$8.95
No Commitment Required	Seressia Glass	$8.95
No Regrets	Mildred E. Riley	$8.95
Nowhere to Run	Gay G. Gunn	$10.95
O Bed! O Breakfast!	Rob Kuehnle	$14.95

Other Genesis Press, Inc. Titles (continued)

Object of His Desire	A. C. Arthur	$8.95
Office Policy	A. C. Arthur	$9.95
Once in a Blue Moon	Dorianne Cole	$9.95
One Day at a Time	Bella McFarland	$8.95
Outside Chance	Louisa Dixon	$24.95
Passion	T.T. Henderson	$10.95
Passion's Blood	Cherif Fortin	$22.95
Passion's Journey	Wanda Thomas	$8.95
Past Promises	Jahmel West	$8.95
Path of Fire	T.T. Henderson	$8.95
Path of Thorns	Annetta P. Lee	$9.95
Peace Be Still	Colette Haywood	$12.95
Picture Perfect	Reon Carter	$8.95
Playing for Keeps	Stephanie Salinas	$8.95
Pride & Joi	Gay G. Gunn	$15.95
Pride & Joi	Gay G. Gunn	$8.95
Promises to Keep	Alicia Wiggins	$8.95
Quiet Storm	Donna Hill	$10.95
Reckless Surrender	Rochelle Alers	$6.95
Red Polka Dot in a World of Plaid	Varian Johnson	$12.95
Reluctant Captive	Joyce Jackson	$8.95
Rendezvous with Fate	Jeanne Sumerix	$8.95
Revelations	Cheris F. Hodges	$8.95
Rivers of the Soul	Leslie Esdaile	$8.95
Rocky Mountain Romance	Kathleen Suzanne	$8.95
Rooms of the Heart	Donna Hill	$8.95
Rough on Rats and Tough on Cats	Chris Parker	$12.95
Secret Library Vol. 1	Nina Sheridan	$18.95
Secret Library Vol. 2	Cassandra Colt	$8.95
Shades of Brown	Denise Becker	$8.95
Shades of Desire	Monica White	$8.95

Other Genesis Press, Inc. Titles (continued)

Shadows in the Moonlight	Jeanne Sumerix	$8.95
Sin	Crystal Rhodes	$8.95
So Amazing	Sinclair LeBeau	$8.95
Somebody's Someone	Sinclair LeBeau	$8.95
Someone to Love	Alicia Wiggins	$8.95
Song in the Park	Martin Brant	$15.95
Soul Eyes	Wayne L. Wilson	$12.95
Soul to Soul	Donna Hill	$8.95
Southern Comfort	J.M. Jeffries	$8.95
Still the Storm	Sharon Robinson	$8.95
Still Waters Run Deep	Leslie Esdaile	$8.95
Stories to Excite You	Anna Forrest/Divine	$14.95
Subtle Secrets	Wanda Y. Thomas	$8.95
Suddenly You	Crystal Hubbard	$9.95
Sweet Repercussions	Kimberley White	$9.95
Sweet Tomorrows	Kimberly White	$8.95
Taken by You	Dorothy Elizabeth Love	$9.95
Tattooed Tears	T. T. Henderson	$8.95
The Color Line	Lizzette Grayson Carter	$9.95
The Color of Trouble	Dyanne Davis	$8.95
The Disappearance of Allison Jones	Kayla Perrin	$5.95
The Honey Dipper's Legacy	Pannell-Allen	$14.95
The Joker's Love Tune	Sidney Rickman	$15.95
The Little Pretender	Barbara Cartland	$10.95
The Love We Had	Natalie Dunbar	$8.95
The Man Who Could Fly	Bob & Milana Beamon	$18.95
The Missing Link	Charlyne Dickerson	$8.95
The Price of Love	Sinclair LeBeau	$8.95
The Smoking Life	Ilene Barth	$29.95
The Words of the Pitcher	Kei Swanson	$8.95
Three Wishes	Seressia Glass	$8.95
Ties That Bind	Kathleen Suzanne	$8.95
Tiger Woods	Libby Hughes	$5.95

Other Genesis Press, Inc. Titles (continued)

Time is of the Essence	Angie Daniels	$9.95
Timeless Devotion	Bella McFarland	$9.95
Tomorrow's Promise	Leslie Esdaile	$8.95
Truly Inseparable	Wanda Y. Thomas	$8.95
Unbreak My Heart	Dar Tomlinson	$8.95
Uncommon Prayer	Kenneth Swanson	$9.95
Unconditional	A.C. Arthur	$9.95
Unconditional Love	Alicia Wiggins	$8.95
Until Death Do Us Part	Susan Paul	$8.95
Vows of Passion	Bella McFarland	$9.95
Wedding Gown	Dyanne Davis	$8.95
What's Under Benjamin's Bed	Sandra Schaffer	$8.95
When Dreams Float	Dorothy Elizabeth Love	$8.95
Whispers in the Night	Dorothy Elizabeth Love	$8.95
Whispers in the Sand	LaFlorya Gauthier	$10.95
Wild Ravens	Altonya Washington	$9.95
Yesterday Is Gone	Beverly Clark	$10.95
Yesterday's Dreams, Tomorrow's Promises	Reon Laudat	$8.95
Your Precious Love	Sinclair LeBeau	$8.95

Order Form

Mail to: Genesis Press, Inc.
P.O. Box 101
Columbus, MS 39703

Name ______________________________
Address ______________________________
City/State ____________________ Zip ____________
Telephone ____________________

Ship to (if different from above)
Name ______________________________
Address ______________________________
City/State ____________________ Zip ____________
Telephone ____________________

Credit Card Information
Credit Card # ____________________ ☐ Visa ☐ Mastercard
Expiration Date (mm/yy) ____________ ☐ AmEx ☐ Discover

Qty.	Author	Title	Price	Total

Use this order form, or call 1-888-INDIGO-1

Total for books ____________
Shipping and handling:
$5 first two books,
$1 each additional book ____________
Total S & H ____________
Total amount enclosed ____________

Mississippi residents add 7% sales tax

Visit www.genesis-press.com for latest releases and excerpts.